A MATCH
AGAINST A MASTER

"Stop there, Lord Warrick," Gwen said as the magnificent marquess moved too close for comfortable coolness. "You press me too much. You scarce know me."

"Not know you?" Warrick echoed, smiling suddenly. Gwen blinked at the strength of that smile. Though she had reason to be armed against him, still she felt her pulse leap.

And his words were no less dangerous than his smile. "But I know a great deal about you, Mrs. Tarrant," Warrick insisted, his voice so soft it seemed to curl around her ear. "I know you are beautiful and intelligent, compassionate and humorous, quick-witted and spirited enough to take my breath away. I know, too, that your husband taught you little of the pleasures men and women can give one another. I would, Gwen. I would delight you."

Gwen no longer had any doubt she was playing a game of wits and will against a master. The only doubt now was whether she wanted to win. . . .

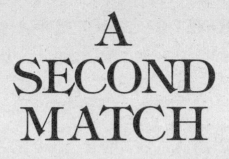

A SECOND MATCH

by

Emma Lange

A SIGNET BOOK

SIGNET
Published by the Penguin Group
Penguin Books USA Inc., 375 Hudson Street,
New York, New York 10014, U.S.A.
Penguin Books Ltd, 27 Wrights Lane,
London W8 5TZ, England
Penguin Books Australia Ltd, Ringwood,
Victoria, Australia
Penguin Books Canada Ltd, 10 Alcorn Avenue,
Toronto, Ontario, Canada M4V 3B2
Penguin Books (N.Z.) Ltd, 182–190 Wairau Road,
Auckland 10, New Zealand

Penguin Books Ltd, Registered Offices:
Harmondsworth, Middlesex, England

First published by Signet,
an imprint of Dutton Signet,
a division of Penguin Books USA Inc.

First Printing, November, 1993
10 9 8 7 6 5 4 3 2 1

Ⓡ REGISTERED TRADEMARK—MARCA REGISTRADA

Printed in the United States of America

Chapter 1

Gwendolyn Tarrant found the old shepherd's hut easily, despite the tangled thicket that had all but overtaken it. A gleaming bay horse stood before it. Gwendolyn's mouth tightened. The horse was a costly thoroughbred.

As she swung down from her mount, a dapper, portly, middle-aged man with hair nearly as black as hers, ducked through the shelter's dilapidated doorway.

"Well now, daughter!" he called out, an affable smile creasing a face that was striking, despite the lines etched by drink and late nights. "I am pleased you could follow my directions. And come upon such a mount! 'Tis the very sort of animal you were born to ride."

"Was I born to ride an Arabian, Papa?'' Gwen gave her father a smile that was cool in contrast to his. "How fortunate, then, that my employer has given me permission to exercise her late husband's cattle, else I'd have arrived on foot."

Lord Llanover allowed his gaze to slide to the sleeve of his coat, where he found an unsightly wrinkle and the courage to chide her, albeit carefully.

" 'Tis a sharp tongue you've got, Gwen, lass. I can't think where you came by it. Your mother, now, was sweet as honey."

"Aye, that she was, Papa," Gwen shot back, pushing a gleaming strand of black hair off her brow. "Yet I never saw that sweetness bring her much but the love of her children. Surely it did not—"

"Enough, daughter! I'll not allow you to tax me with my sins. They're between me and my Maker, not me and a girl thirty years my junior."

Unmoved by either her father's belligerent glare or his blustery volume, Gwen retorted flatly. "They are between me and you when your sins affect me! And you cannot deny your wastrel ways have affected me my life long."

From years of experience, the baron knew when to fold his cards. "Perhaps I've not been the best of parents," he allowed. "Nay, I know I have not, but I cannot be faulted for not loving you and your brothers and sisters or your mother. You know that, Gwen."

"I know that we saw you seldom in Cornwall, Papa," Gwen snapped, made impervious to his cajoling by long acquaintance with him. " 'Twas Grandfather Trevelyan served as our father, while you enjoyed yourself at the gaming tables from Plymouth to London. And I know too well that when he and mother died of the fever, you were nowhere to be found."

At that the baron winced. He had known the accounting would come, but unpleasantness anticipated is no easier to bear when it comes. And he was so grossly at fault in this particular matter.

"For that I am truly sorry, lass. Your letter never reached me—"

"How could it?" Gwen interrupted curtly. "You'd hied off from your rooms in London without leaving a forwarding address. What was it that sent you scurrying, Papa? Debts or an irate husband?"

"Blast it!" Righteousness reinvigorated the baron, lifting his head and amplifying his voice. "I was never unfaithful to your mother! I loved her!" At his daughter's response, a sharp, dismissive snort, he fixed her with a scowl. "You've no idea at all what love is, missy, so I'll not hear your thoughts on the matter. When you married, you married for pounds and pennies. I don't fault you for it!" he added quickly, when Gwen's eyes, eyes as light and gleaming a blue as his own, flashed with anger. " 'Twas the only thing you could do at the time. You're strong, Gwen, and that's to the good, but you must learn to admit you've a fault or two, along with the rest of us, or you're likely to remain a widow the rest of your days."

"That is precisely what I intend to do!"

Her father stared, nonplussed for once. "Don't be daft, Gwen. You're not made to be a lonely widow! You're . . ."

But Gwen shook her head impatiently. She knew how she

was made. She had only to look at the baron. They'd the same striking, fine-boned features, thick black hair, and milky white skin. He had once been slender as she was, too, and still possessed eyes as clear a blue as hers, though he did sport pouches beneath his now. Still, pouches or no, the baron was a handsome man.

"Oh, I am comely enough, but whether I could attract a husband again is not the point. I've seen little in the institution of marriage to make me eager for a second match."

Her own marriage had lasted only a short while, but she had been a close student of her parents'. As the oldest child she knew too well how little her father had kept to his wedding vow to cherish and protect her mother. Perhaps he had loved Lady Llanover as he said, but he had done little to show it, beyond giving her a new babe in her belly every time he'd come home to cadge money for one of his perpetual new starts from his father-in-law. Rested, money in his pocket, he soon left her again, a promise to make everything good "this time" on his lips but the gaming tables in his heart.

As for love . . . Gwen scowled. She'd learned how little to trust in that emotion.

The baron eyed his daughter closely. She could mask her expression when she wished, but he fancied he saw something like hurt cloud her clear blue eyes. "Tarrant did not beat you, did he?" he demanded, but she shook her head.

"Nay, Papa. John Tarrant never beat me. He was kind as . . ." Gwen nearly laughed for she had been about to say Mr. Tarrant had been kind as a father to her. "He was a good enough man, but he provided too temporary a port to convince me that my salvation lies in casting about for another man to provide for me and the children. I am determined to rely upon myself alone. At least I know precisely what my intentions are."

The baron took that last rather bitterly said remark as a reference to John Tarrant's failure during the few months of his marriage to Gwen to change his will. "I cannot say I blame you for your bitterness toward Tarrant, Gwen. It was a cursed, unconscionable oversight that he should neglect to name you, rather than that ingrate nephew of his, as his heir."

Gwen had not been referring to John Tarrant at all, but to a

London rake who had pledged his undying love only to laugh in her face when she mentioned marriage.

Her father knew nothing of Mr. Miles Dacre, however, and nothing would be gained by telling him. To clear her mind of the ugly memory, Gwen studied the glimmer of light she could see through the thicket behind the hut. She could not tell if it was the sky or the sea she saw, for they stood near Prawle Point, where the Saltcombe River empties into the Channel.

Remembering her father's anger toward John Tarrant, Gwen shrugged her shoulders. " 'Tis over and done now, Papa, and little can be gained from regret. Mr. Tarrant never imagined he would be killed within a year of marrying me. He was only forty. That runaway cart was the purest chance. But enough of this unpleasantness. Let us speak of you, instead." She swung her gaze back from the dark trees and the hint of light shimmering beyond them. "To what do I owe the honor of this meeting? Did you wish merely to show off your new mount, or are you in need of something?"

"Hermes is a mount to show off, isn't he?" her father exclaimed proudly, but Gwen thought it significant that at her mention of need the baron had looked off into the middle distance. "And he rides as well as he looks. Yes, it was a lucky day for me, when I came by Hermes."

"A lucky day or a lucky card game?" Gwen inquired ironically.

The baron gave a short laugh. "Are they not synonymous?" Another shorter laugh followed. To Gwen it sounded hollow, and then her father began tugging at his collar, as if, of a sudden, it were too tight for him.

She bit her lip against a rush of emotion. Blast, but she did not wish to feel the least pity toward him! He didn't deserve it. He had lost everything he'd inherited, his home, his estates, his bank accounts, almost every heirloom; and then he'd bled her grandfather of every penny old Mr. Trevelyan had. And now—she knew it—he expected to leech from her! Bitterness welled up in her, hardening her. Damn him! He did not mean to contribute one cent to the support of his own children. He did not even ask after them, or Esther Trevelyan, her mother's cousin and the woman Gwen had persuaded to take them.

"I take it you've had more unlucky than lucky days lately?" Gwen heard the caustic sharpness of her tone, could almost see it lance her father between his shoulder blades, but she could not restrain herself.

The baron scuffed the dirt with his toe a minute before he could bring himself to look at Gwen, and even then he wore a wan smile. "Aye, as usual," he admitted, flushing. "Gaming's a sickness with me. I know it! And the worse has happened now. They're after me, Gwen. If they catch me, they'll clap me in debtor's prison. It has come to that at last."

He looked old suddenly and even afraid. Gwen could not be certain that he was not acting, but she thought not. The white lines about his mouth would not be easy to counterfeit.

You are as weak as your mother! the harder portion of her mind shouted at her, urging her to coldness. But the baron was her father, and studying him, Gwen not only believed him, but realized she did not want him to be forced into one of England's overflowing, fetid debtor's prisons.

"How much do you need?"

"Five thousand pounds," her father replied hoarsely.

"Five thousand pounds?" Gwen gaped, stunned at the amount. "And then how much more? But why do I ask? I've not got ten pounds lying about idle."

The baron flushed uncomfortably. "Of course not, my dear. I never imagined you did. From you I only need a small, insignificant amount, a stake, if you will. At the moment, I fear, my pockets are to let, and I've nothing with which to earn the blunt I need to satisfy my creditors. With a stake, however— and the proceeds I realize when I sell Hermes—I'll come around quickly enough."

"Will you?" Gwen asked caustically, beyond caring if she hurt him. "Or will you lose it and be back again in a week?"

"I deserve that, I suppose." Llanover looked the picture of wretchedness, and if Gwen distrusted the look, she could also see he was genuinely pale. "But, Gwen, I assure you, this once, I do not intend to wager my stake. I've met a gentleman in Dartmouth who is in trade. He's invited me to help finance one of his enterprises."

"Is he a smuggler?" Gwen asked shrewdly. "Are you putting up the blunt for an illegal cask or two?"

"You refer to criminal activities, Gwen," the baron reproved with offended dignity. He did not, however, deny the gentleman's occupation.

"You'll have the magistrates after you for two reasons now." Gwen flung her father an exasperated look, but when he said no more, she shrugged. "I suppose you will do as you wish regardless of what I say, but you will be obliged to finance your gentleman's activities without my help. I've nothing to give you. It is I who support your children, do recall."

"You've the diamond brooch."

She did have the brooch. Of heavy silver and studded with diamonds, it was the last piece of jewelry left from all her father had inherited. How her mother had managed to save it from his profligate hands, Gwen did not know, but she'd not relinquish it easily.

"That brooch is the only inheritance Arthur will receive. Do you mean to rob him of it, too?"

Something hard flickered in the baron's blue eyes. "That brooch is mine. And I'll have it without accounting to my daughter for the taking of it." Gwen did not flinch, though she had never seen such a cold look in her father's eyes before. Then suddenly, like a chameleon, he changed, smiling and lifting his shoulders. "Come, come, Gwen, sweeting. You will either give the brooch to me or to the magistrates when they come to collect all that's left of my estate. At least, if you give it to me, you've a chance of getting it back for young Arthur."

He had a point. Though she did not expect she would ever see the brooch again if she gave it to the baron, Gwen could be certain she would not see it again if the magistrates took it. "I only want it for a stake," the baron wheedled, seeing her hesitate. "You would not wish to see me in prison for the lack of one brooch, surely?"

Gwen realized then that she had long judged her mother unfairly. Though she had thought her mother the dearest, kindest woman, she had also thought her weak-willed for giving in to the baron time and again. Now she saw she had not understood how adept the baron was at wheedling.

And the brooch was his, really.

"Very well, Papa, I shall relinquish the brooch to you, because it is yours, but do not make the mistake of thinking I will give you anything more, for anything else I have is mine. I shall bring it here tomorrow. You can't come to the Hall to collect it. Lady Chumleigh is having guests, and you might be seen by someone who knows you."

"Lady Chumleigh is having visitors?" Lord Llanover inquired but distractedly, for he was mentally counting the sum he would get for the brooch.

"Hmmm," Gwen replied as offhandedly. "It seems her nephew comes every summer with guests. There will not be so many as usual this year, though, due to her health."

"Lady Chumleigh's health is failing?"

"Not failing, but she is nearly seventy and does not feel so strong as she did. Still, she will entertain her nephew and his friends and even give a ball in their honor."

"Who's the nevvy?" the baron inquired. "Anyone I know?"

"I don't know who you know," Gwen observed more dryly than bitterly. "He is the Marquess of Warrick, the Duke of Grafton's son."

. She hadn't needed to add that last, Gwen realized when her father let out a long, low whistle. "Warrick, eh? He's the devil of a reputation, particularly where the ladies are concerned."

"You needn't worry for me, Papa," Gwen said, catching the sidelong look her father gave her. "I've no intention of being taken in by a London rake."

Again, Gwen added silently, her jaw tightening at the memory of the hurt and anger she'd felt when Miles Dacre had unraveled the romantic dreams she'd been gullible enough to weave around him.

Her determined look stirred a memory in her father's mind, and he half smiled. On the surface she was his image in feminine form. Perhaps she was more beautiful than he was handsome, but the extent of the difference between them was no more than that, a degree or so. Beneath the skin, though, it was not him she resembled at all, but her great-grandmother. He remembered the old dowager well, holding court in the moldy pile that had been the ancestral home of the Prideaux family until he lost it on an unlucky roll of the dice. Grandmama had sat upright in a chair so large he'd thought it a throne, her hair so gray, he had not realized it had once been black as his own, and her blue eyes piercing him through as Gwen's could do, when she was of a mind. Yes, she was a throwback to a . . . better, he admitted it . . . generation. Perhaps she would be the salvation of the Prideauxs as he'd dreamed when she was still young enough to smile at him with unreserved devotion.

"Why are you looking at me so, Papa?" Gwen's words sliced through the baron's unfocused musing. "You look as if you are making plans." She had no need to add that she did not trust his look. Her tone said that for her.

The baron laughed, for a sudden brilliant thought had, in fact, come to him. "I was only thinking that I do believe your determination to remain a widow will shortly be tested. You are a very beautiful lady, if I do say so myself, and Warrick has an eye for beauty, ergo . . ."

"Ergo, he would have no position higher than mistress in mind for me. I am not a lady, I must remind you, but a lady's companion."

"You are a Prideaux!" the baron riposted with a superb disregard for unpleasant facts. "And a Prideaux you remain, regardless of your current position."

"Actually, I am a Tarrant now, and as far as I know all of Mr. Tarrant's forebears were as undistinguished and steady as he. But were I to name my own relatives, should I mention that my father must skulk about the hedgerows for fear he will be recognized and carted off to debtor's prison? I am certain the marquess and all of his friends would be much impressed."

"I was not skulking about the hedgerows when I stopped you!" the baron protested indignantly. "I had merely gotten down to rest a moment. I intended to call upon you in the ordinary way, but meeting you as I did, there was no need. That is beside the point, however. My activities have naught to do with you. You are Grandmama's great-granddaughter, which counts for something."

But Gwen would not give an inch. She had learned the hard way that her threadbare pockets counted for little with those in the higher circles of English society. "The Prideaux may be a respected family in the far west of Cornwall, Papa, but I assure you they are unknown beyond the Tamar. I doubt the marquess will notice his aunt's companion at all, but if he does, he will not be thinking to marry me, and I've no desire at all to become the man's mistress of the month. I advise you to curb your daydreams on the subject of the Marquess of Warrick, or you will be doomed to disappointment. But I must go now,

Papa. Lady Chumleigh will need me soon. If you cannot be here tomorrow, do not worry. I'll hide the brooch behind that boulder where the horses are."

She even walked like his grandmama, the baron thought as he bid his daughter good-bye. She held her chin at the same regal angle and her back with the same unconscious pride.

As she wheeled her mount about and kicked the gelding to a gallop, he smiled faintly to himself. He did not question whether she would catch the marquess's eye. Even were her face not so striking, her figure would catch the man's attention. She'd a waist no thicker than a man's handspan that served to emphasize the womanly fullness of her breasts and hips.

Nor did Llanover much question Gwen's prediction that Warrick would offer her nothing more permanent than a position of his mistress. She would refuse, of course. She'd too much pride to accept so little. What would happen then?

The baron's eyes narrowed slightly. Warrick had all the experience on his side. Gwen knew not the first thing about flirtation. John Tarrant had not wooed her. The stolid farmer had not had a romantic turn of mind, nor at his age, the ability to acquire one. No, compared to Warrick, Gwen was a green girl.

Yet . . . the baron's mouth quirked slightly. Damn, if he didn't think she could do it! Warrick might well have gone through women like a drunkard goes through wine, but he'd not have encountered Gwen's like before. Llanover knew whereof he spoke, for he'd been to London, gamed with the gentlemen and, more to the point, the ladies of the *ton*. They might be beautiful in their way; they might be willful, too, but they weren't made of Gwen's mettle. She was fiercely proud, was his Gwen, like the woman for whom she'd been named. And she possessed the spirit, and more, truth be known, to hold off the marquess. She'd tantalize Warrick! And he would marry her.

The baron laughed aloud. Damn, but it seemed a certain wager! Perhaps . . . no, even he could not wager on whether his daughter would become Warrick's wife or mistress. No, he would simply have to trust in her to manage properly, God bless her, if she did!

And bless him with one of the wealthiest sons-in-law in the land.

Chapter 2

"I can scarce believe my eyes!" Richard Beecham, the Viscount Sheffield, gaped delightedly at the heavily laden platter a serving maid had slipped before him. "This portion is twice the one I was served last year. I swear it, Suddy!" he protested when his companion upon his left chuckled.

"Oh, I don't doubt you at all, Dickon," Major Robert Sudbury assured his old friend. "I do have one question for you though. Did you come down to Wensley with Lucian last August or did you come alone?"

"Why, I came alone." The viscount frowned. "Luc came down early last year." His puzzled gaze strayed across the table to the man in question, but Lucian Montfort, the Marquess of Warrick, and the final member of the trio that had stopped for luncheon at the White Hart in Kingsbridge, could provide Sheffield no enlightenment.

He was otherwise occupied. The obliging young maid who had served them lingered beside him, giggling and stammering and all the while drinking him in with her eyes.

Sheffield looked to Major Sudbury, shaking his head even as he laughed. "I take your point now, Suddy. Lud, but he does seem to have an invariable effect upon women."

Major Sudbury, too, shook his head. Neither had to elaborate upon their friend's effect—they were familiar enough with it—nor did they need to debate the cause.

And neither man thought the cause to be the wealth to which the marquess's expensive clothes attested nor even the air of unthinking assurance he possessed. Had the attraction Warrick exerted over women stemmed from either cause, the young maid would have been glued to Sheffield and Sudbury as well. Both men wore clothes as impeccably tailored as the marquess's, and they both possessed something of his aristocratic assurance.

And both of them were sitting up, looking respectable and at least relatively energetic. Warrick lounged indolently in his seat, his long legs stretched before him and crossed negligently at the ankles, for all the world as if he sat before his own fire.

Yet, Sheffield acknowledged, chuckling to himself, he and Suddy were no more than insubstantial shadows to the girl, if she remembered them at all. Warrick simply looked too good. He had features as beautiful as any archangel's—a very male archangel, of course. Warrick's nose was too straight and aristocratic, his jaw too firm for anyone to fault him for prettiness. And the whole of him, including a mouth that might have been drawn by some besotted cupid and waving, thick, dark tawny hair had fascinated women ever since Warrick had traded in his short pants for long ones.

Satisfied with his reasoning, the viscount turned his attention to more important matters; to whit, his stuffed capon. Had he, however, asked the buxom little maid why she could not seem to tear her eyes from Warrick, she'd have surprised him by saying it was not, really, the marquess's exceedingly handsome face that had her heart racing with excitement. She had seen handsome faces before. Nor was it even his eyes, though they were so deep a forest green she thought she could not look away from them. What made her giddier than she'd been in her life was the gleam in those eyes. Lord, but it was such a lazily wicked gleam, it made her think of all manner of delights and none of them what the vicar of her parish would approve.

She giggled at the thought of her vicar meeting this man. Poor spindly, virtuous vicar. He'd not even reach the man's shoulders. She sent her eyes skimming over the man. He had a proper set of shoulders on his loose-knit body. She thought he would be strong. Thinking she would like to feel just how strong, she giggled again.

Warrick lifted his tankard of ale to her and smiled a slow smile to match the lazy light in his eyes. "Here's to the ale you poured up, Rosie. It was Rosie, was it not?"

At that the girl was lost. When Warrick murmured her

name, her cheeks went so painfully hot, Sheffield winced for her. "Aye, m'lord! 'Tis Rosie," she allowed breathlessly, "Ye've only to call, if ye've a need."

"Well, thank you then, Rosie. You are very attentive. We'll not forget to call, I assure you."

It was, though charmingly said, undoubtedly a dismissal. The girl did not resent being dismissed however. She could scarcely think straight enough to wish for anything more than the opportunity to serve him further. Of course he wished to eat his meal, a fit man like him, she thought as she did the only thing she could think to do: bob an awkward curtsy.

She had no sooner taken her leave than Warrick lifted his still twinkling green eyes to his friends. "What was that I heard about taking Suddy's point, Dickon? If I am not mistaken the point had to do with me."

Sheffield laughed. "I am surprised you heard anything, given the attention that young thing was giving you. But if you must know, Suddy was pointing out that I've a heaping portion upon my platter, quite unlike last year, because you've the world's most astounding way with women. Lud, I thought that child might faint with pleasure when you recalled her name!"

"Everyone likes to be remembered," Warrick replied reasonably. "And I always remember the name of an appealing chit. You never know when the recollection may be of use."

"I vow, that is your secret!" Sheffield exclaimed with unusual vigor.

"What pray?" asked the marquess, smiling with amused affection at his friend of twenty or more years.

"Why, that you treat 'em all alike, women, that is, from the highest duchess to the lowest scullery maid. I can't think of another man would have remembered that chit's name."

"Of course I treat 'em all the same, Dickon." Warrick shrugged. "In my experience the lowest scullery maid can be every bit as pleasurable as the highest-born duchess."

Major Sudbury threw back his head with a laugh. "Undoubtedly true, you rogue! Do you intend to discover just how pleasurable that chit might be? Lud, but if she blushes as brightly below that sagging neckline as above, she'd be something to behold."

"But Warrick cannot take up her invitation, however taking

she is!" Sheffield protested. "Lady Chum expects us for tea. And I do not mention either your wife, Suddy, or Frances. I did not think either lady seemed particularly happy, when we deserted them to hare off across the country on horseback."

"I can speak for your wife, Sudbury," Warrick said, lazily. "She is my cousin and I know Tony as well as you. She did not resent our riding hell for leather across the country at all. She pouted only because she could not join us. And for that, she's only herself to blame. 'Twas she who chose to invite Frances to join us, and therefore, she who must bear the responsibility of entertaining the lady."

"Lucian, I hope you do not mind that Tony took it upon herself to invite Frances?" Major Sudbury glanced inquiringly over the rim of his tankard at his friend. "Though our party must be small this year on account of Lady Chum's uncertain energies, Tony did want to have some female company, and Frances was at hand."

"I would imagine Frances threw herself into Tony's hand." It was Sheffield who made the wry observation. "You would not know, Suddy, you've been in Vienna so long, but the Langdale is determined to have a grand passion for Warrick."

Major Sudbury looked distinctly unimpressed. "Every woman is determined to be in love with Lucian, and Frances has always proclaimed she had a *tendre* for him. As I recall, she even said so on the day of her wedding."

"On her wedding day?" the viscount repeated, looking to Warrick, who was occupied with his capon.

Warrick waited until he had disposed of his bite before answering offhandedly, "You know Frances as well as I, Dickon. She cannot hold a drop of champagne, and as I remember her father served a great deal of the stuff. Not bad stuff, either. But as to her appearance at Wensley this year, Suddy," he went on, turning to the major, "I am not the least put out. Tony may invite whom she pleases, as she well knows."

Major Sudbury smiled. "And you may decide to enjoy what Frances would seem to be offering as determinedly as ever?"

Warrick shrugged his broad shoulders, even as he grinned. "Perhaps. Who knows the future? It doesn't do to speculate prematurely."

"Which is your way of saying you've no intention of saying," Sheffield observed. "You've never been one to trumpet your successes, Lucian." He shook his head wryly. " 'Tis the lady, not you, who will boast to the world that you've had her. But my guess is you'll resist the Langdale. Married women are losing their appeal for you."

Major Sudbury's eyebrows shot nearly to his forehead. "Are you speaking of our mutual friend, Lucian Montfort, Dickon? This gentleman, just across from us?"

"I am," Sheffield replied unmoved by Sudbury's only partly sham astonishment. "I have observed a change in him this last year or so, as you've not been on hand to do. He avoided Marianna Longford's lures altogether, though they are lush and tempting, and if he tasted the pleasures Sally Arminster offered, he did it so briefly; Sally pouted for weeks. I could go on, if you wish, but to come to the point, I will simply say that Lucian has lost his taste for jaded married women like Frances, who crave distraction from their equally jaded and unfaithful husbands. Note that I did not say love, heaven forbid. They are too world weary for such trying emotions, and I believe it is that very ennui that is beginning to bore our good friend, Lucian, though, of course, bored or not, he still fascinates them. Perhaps even fascinates the more, as he is all the more elusive."

Warrick, entirely unmoved by his friend's speech, only remarked after a long swallow of ale, "You're coming it too strong on my ability to appeal to the fair sex, Dickon. Nay," he chuckled mildly when the viscount opened his mouth to protest. "I'll not argue the point. It is too wearisome a conversation. Tell me instead whether you enjoyed your capon?"

Eyes twinkling, Warrick looked pointedly at his friend's strikingly empty plate. The viscount, however, was not the least embarrassed and patted his comfortable paunch gently. "I enjoyed it immensely, dear fellow. Immensely. Which is why I shall stick to your side like a leech whenever we dine out in Devon, for I not only enjoyed the taste of my capon, but the abundance of it as well."

As if on cue, Rosie came to serve the three gentlemen more ale, though they had not quite emptied the tankards they had, but they did not linger as long over their ale as she'd have liked. After the Viscount Sheffield was done with the tart he alone ordered, they departed the inn.

"And now it is on to Aunt Vi," Warrick remarked with a full smile as they strode into the inn yard. "I wonder how the tough old hen will greet us this year?"

"With something caustic I don't doubt," Sheffield answered, though he, too, smiled.

"She's up to being caustic, Lucian, after her illness in June?" Major Sudbury asked.

"I imagine she'll be tart on her deathbed," Warrick said frankly, "but it is on account of that illness that I reduced the size of our party. Though her doctor says she is entirely recovered, and she insists upon having her ball while we are here as usual, I wanted to take every precaution I could against tiring her."

"At least we can be assured Lady Chum's not one to allow us to tax her unduly," Sheffield remarked as they mounted their horses. "I remember once that she actually ordered me to my bed, saying she could not go before I did."

"And if Lady Chum does not guard her energies," Major Sudbury said, chuckling, "we can be certain that her faithful Benny will intervene."

"But she's not got old Benny," Sheffield put in. "You really have been away being diplomatic, Suddy. Poor, faithful, unflagging Benny went to her reward almost two years ago."

"Good heavens! I'd have sent a note had I known. I cannot imagine Lady Chum without her."

"Losing Benny was, indeed, a blow to Aunt Vi," the marquess agreed. "She's dismissed four different companions since. I haven't met the fifth and latest one, but I've not got high hopes for her. She's a local farmer's widow with no experience at all as a companion. Smeddley, the vicar, you've met him, persuaded Aunt Vi to give the woman a try, because she'd dire need of a position after her husband died unexpectedly."

"And Lady Chum does have that surprising charitable streak in her," the major remarked. "Well, what does she report of the woman?"

Frowning, Warrick shrugged. "It's odd, that. She has said little about her at all. Normally she complains in excruciating detail, but of Mrs. Tarrant she has said only that the woman's a soothing voice."

"Well, that is to the good," reasoned Major Sudbury. "As for the rest, you'll see when you get to the Hall."

"Very true, Suddy, and now who's for a race to Prawle Point?"

"Not I!" declared Lord Sheffield firmly. "I'm too stuffed with stuffed capon to race anywhere."

"Nor I," chimed in Major Sudbury. "Racing you—futilely—to Salisbury yesterday proved my age to me. Like Lady Chum, I've not been growing younger, and while you have spent the last two years training at Gentleman Jim's, I have been sitting at diplomatic tables."

"Good heavens, I had not thought I traveled with old women!" Warrick laughed. "Well, I cannot come this way without a gallop to the Point. I am a slave to the tradition. I shall see you both when you are safely ensconced in your padded chairs at the Hall. Until then."

He saluted his friends, and wheeling his mount around, galloped away down a smaller track that led due south.

Chapter 3

While the baron indulged in wishful thinking about the future, Gwen proved herself more hardheaded. As she cantered away from the shepherd's hut, she didn't waste time dreaming about miracles concerning the Marquess of Warrick. She didn't dream at all. A hard look in her eye, she calculated how long it would be before her father came to her again, armed with another desperate reason he must be given another stake.

As if she sought to outrun her father's outstretched hand, Gwen spurred her horse to a faster pace. Doubts plagued her like angry flies. Perhaps she should have told him she had sold the brooch. She'd have consigned him to debtor's prison, but perhaps he had lied about that threat, having guessed where she would be vulnerable.

She shook her head abruptly. His fear had been too real. He was not so excellent an actor he could feign that pallor or the lines by his mouth. And he was her father, heaven help her. She'd not have felt easy with herself, had she not given him what was his.

But he'd get no more from her. Her mouth tightened. Let him try as he would, but every cent she possessed, she had earned by her own devices, and all of them would go to her brothers and sisters and herself.

Luckily, Lady Chumleigh was generous. Gwen earned enough to send her mother's cousin, Esther, not only enough to buy the children the necessities of life but an occasional treat as well. And even then, she had a bit left over to add to the secret hoard she had managed to set aside during her marriage to Mr. Tarrant.

She had plans for that growing pile. She intended to buy a small hat shop in Plymouth. The sharp frown Gwen had worn as she contemplated her father eased a little. She knew the shop she hoped to have. Esther Trevelyan had introduced her to the proprietress, who had confided she wished to retire in two years or so. It was just the amount of time Gwen needed to save enough to make a respectable offer. Mrs. Childress would not ask an exorbitant amount. She had taken a liking to Gwen, had even wanted Gwen to work for her as an assistant, but Gwen had had to refuse when Lady Chumleigh had made her more generous offer.

Gwen had the vicar of the parish, Mr. Smeddley, to thank for Lady Chumleigh's offer. The mild little man had a surprisingly astute eye for human character and had offered to speak to Lady Chumleigh of Gwen's desperate need of a position, for though most in the parish believed it was her husband who had started the Chumleigh Orphanage for Boys in Knightsbridge, Mr. Smeddley had long since guessed correctly that it had been at Lady Chumleigh's instigation that Lord Chumleigh had acted.

But he had had to convince Gwen of more than Lady Chumleigh's charitable instincts. Gwen's neighbors had been quick to warn her of the numerous companions Lady Chumleigh had driven from the Hall.

"Lady Chumleigh is, indeed, something of a tartar, my dear," Mr. Smeddley had admitted. "She is a great lady, after all, and cannot easily abide people of weak and indecisive character." Mr. Smeddley had permitted himself a small smile then. "Perhaps you can understand now why I believe you've no need for worry, Mrs. Tarrant? You've more than enough starch for Lady Chumleigh, my dear. I assure you."

Now, six months after moving to Wensley Hall, Gwen could smile herself. Mr. Smeddley had been correct on all counts. Charitable instincts had moved Lady Chumleigh to try Gwen as her companion, or caretaker, really. And Gwen did, indeed, have the starch to manage the old lady well enough.

Actually that was describing her relations with her employer too coolly. Lady Chumleigh's imperious and crusty exterior covered a generous core, and though there were difficult moments, as there would be with any elderly woman of autocratic disposition, for the most part Gwen actually enjoyed her employer.

Gwen's smile widened. She could not object, either, to the circumstances in which her employment placed her. Perhaps she had been born to such ease as that which prevailed at Wensley Hall, but she had not experienced it since she was a young girl, nor was she likely to in future.

She patted the sleek neck of her horse. One of her greatest pleasures was riding Sir Adolphus through Wensley's park. The south of Devon was not half so wild and dramatic as the far west of Cornwall, but it was still beautiful with its rich, rolling land bordered by wooded slopes that eased down by gentle degrees to one or another of the picturesque creeks that made up the Saltcombe River estuary. And for drama, if she needed it, she could ride out to the high, white chalk cliffs overlooking the Channel.

No, being companion to Lady Chumleigh was not a bad position, Gwen allowed, but still, she did not want to live out her life in other people's homes, caring for one older woman after another. Nor could she live forever separated from her brothers and sisters. Their letters were no replacement for them. And if she owned the hat shop, not only would she be reunited with them, but she would be, for once, mistress of her own fate.

In two years she could have enough money to leave Lady Chumleigh and go to Plymouth. It seemed an impossibly long time, but it was not really. Two years and she would be independent for life, if all went well; if her father did not cause some disaster. . . .

Deliberately Gwen spurred her mount to a gallop. She was Cornish, after all, and not immune to the superstition held by many of her people that merely naming calamities could actually precipitate them. Anyway it was too pretty a day to worry, and Sir Adolphus too fine a mount not to ride like the wind.

She could feel the horse stretch out as the soft summer air rushed by her ears. Her spirits quickened as the gelding's hooves pounded harder and harder.

Gwen never heard the stallion gaining on her. Her world consisted of the horse beneath her and the excitement of galloping headlong, nothing more. She knew only that something jolted her out of her absorption with her ride. And then, on the wind, she heard someone shout something indistinguishable. It could have been anything from "Hold on!" to "Get her!" And could have come from anywhere. When she did not see anyone of ahead of her, she flung a glance over her shoulder.

Gwen started with surprise. A man, riding as hard as she,

was just behind her. She blinked the wind from her eyes, scarcely able to believe she had not heard him at all. But he was definitely there, and now he was actually edging along-side her, for Sir Adolphus had slackened his pace fractionally while she had been distracted.

Immediately Gwen gave the horse an urgent kick. She did not know the man, could not begin to guess his intentions, and she was alone. She was too late as well. The stranger's stallion was stronger than her gelding. Before Gwen had the least inkling of the man's intentions, he leaned toward her and suddenly swept her from her horse.

Her hat went flying, the pins holding it no match for the jolt she took when he thrust her down before him. But the last thing of which Gwen was aware was her black hair tumbling down her back. Terrified now of falling beneath the stallion's hooves, she grabbed at the man's coat to steady herself, but the minute she felt his horse slowing, it was fury she felt.

"Blackguard!" She screamed. "Stop! Let me down!"

"Quiet!" he commanded sharply. "What the deuce is wrong with you? Haven't you any sense at all! You'll make *my* horse bolt now!"

"Idiot! My horse did not bolt! Let me down!"

With the stallion protesting the new and active load it carried, the man was too preoccupied controlling his plunging animal to reply. Gwen could feel the muscles in his thighs working beneath her bottom, and when he pulled back hard on his reins, he pulled her back, too, so that he held her as close as a lover.

She jerked in reaction.

He swore sharply. "Devil it! Stop that! Ares doesn't take to squirming females. He'll dump us both."

"It would be no more than you deserve." Gwen shouted the retort, but with her face buried in the man's chest, her protest emerged too muffled to be effective.

He smelled good. The thought came from nowhere. Nor did it displace Gwen's anger in the least. It only hung a moment in her mind, along with the realization that the shirt rubbing against her cheek was of the finest lawn.

He was a wealthy man. He did not mean to capture her for ransom or some other criminal purpose. No, but he might still mean her harm of the worst sort. Wealthy men were as capable of base behavior as poor men. At the thought Gwen began to struggle again, registering now above the smell and feel of him, his strength. His chest felt solid as a wall, and his arm seemed an iron shackle about her waist.

"Stop wiggling, for the love of God!"

Gwen felt the horse beneath her come to a skittering halt, and the man pull back from her. She flung up her head, eyes flashing to tell him what he could do with his commands. And she did tell him, but a half second later, for when she first looked up at the face of the man who held her, she tripped, mentally speaking, for that split second.

He was unbelievably handsome. She thought fleetingly, fancifully, of Apollo, and Gwen wasn't given to flights of fancy. But good Lord, she had never seen quite such strong, flawlessly cut masculine features, all set off by waving dark gold hair Apollo would have envied. The Greek god's eyes would have been blue, though, she thought distractedly. Poor Apollo. He'd have gnashed his teeth, had he seen this man's eyes. Gwen could not remember if she'd even seen green eyes before, but certainly she had never seen eyes of such a deep, fathomless forest green as his.

A new dismay, one springing from a quite different source than that which she had felt before, assailed Gwen. The man's very attractiveness rattled her.

"Well now, who can it be I've plucked from the back of that bolting animal?"

Of a sudden, the man's eyes lightened perceptibly. Gwen might even have admired the golden lights dancing in them, but the lazily appreciative look with which he raked her only made her the more uncomfortable. She did not care for the feeling at all and became all the more furious with the cause of it. Cuffing his chest, she spat irately, "You have plucked no one from the back of a bolting animal, you fool, because that animal was not bolting!"

Warrick stiffened fractionally at the unflattering address. He was not accustomed to being called a fool, and most certainly not by a woman, but the appreciative sparkle in his eyes did not dim.

He had known from the first she was a female. Her gender

was what had given him alarm when he saw her horse racing hell-for-leather toward the woods. When he had flung her down before him, he had noted further that she was a woman, not a girl. Though he had been fighting to control Ares, a part of his mind had not been so distracted it could not register the soft lushness of the breasts clapped against his chest.

Now, however, that he'd the leisure he could not only remark the slenderness of the waist his arm encircled and the gentle flare of the hips resting on his thighs, but that she was, in two quite inadequate words, a stunning beauty.

Her hair alone, a shining cloud of ebony that fell in a waving mass to her waist, would have caught his interest, but her hair set off skin that was pale as milk except for her cheeks, where exercise and temper had turned her smooth skin a rose pink. Those cheeks were, as well as delightfully tinted, high and well defined in her triangular face, and like her stubborn chin, fine boned. So, too, her slim nose, but not her mouth. Though it was as well defined as her other features, her mouth was unexpectedly full. It looked to be a giving mouth.

Warrick grinned to himself. Whatever her mouth might be tempted to give, her eyes would take back. Wide, the color of the sky on a clear day and fringed by thick, black lashes, they were beautiful, but, at that moment at least, they snapped with more angry life than Warrick had ever even thought to see.

He'd never excited such a response in a woman, and his reaction to the ire flashing in those blue eyes was entirely unexpected. Interest quickened the gleam in his eyes. Indeed, had the little maid at the White Hart seen Warrick then, she'd have been surprised to see how far from lazy the gleam in his eyes could be.

He wanted to know who she was.

"Put me down at once!" Gwen demanded, interrupting Warrick's perusal of her. If she did not know how rare was the intensity of the gleam in Warrick's eyes, she nonetheless could read his interest. Curiously, however, she was no longer afraid he meant to do her harm. "Do as I say!" she snapped furiously. "Put me down. I do not care to be manhandled."

A grin began to tease the corners of Warrick's mouth. "I do not think you can say I am manhandling you, Miss . . . ?"

"I wish to be put down this instant," Gwen ground out, ignoring both the grin curving the man's mouth and his question as to her identity.

"But I cannot allow you to be put to the discomfort of walking home, Miss Mysterious Fair." He chuckled at his own nonsense. It was a rich, infectious sound, and almost had the power to throw Gwen off her stride. "If, indeed, I did mistake what you were about on your mount, then I feel obliged, at the least, to see you home."

Ride in his lap the mile or more to Wensley Hall? Appear before Dabney, the butler, and whoever else was watching, in the embrace of a stranger? Gwen thought not. "You did entirely mistake what I was about upon my mount," she informed him tensely. "I have never had a horse run off with me. But you have no obligation to me now, unless I wish you to be obliged, and I most certainly do not. For the last time, put me down!"

"And where is that—home I mean?" Warrick asked, grinning just a little, as if he wished to tempt Gwen to laugh with him at the way he had utterly ignored her request.

Gwen's flashing blue eyes registered her answer to that notion. "My residence is none of your affair, sir! I shall make my own way quite well, thank you. Doubtless I shall find my mount in those woods yonder."

"Doubtless you will not," Warrick countered with a lazy ease that threatened to drive Gwen to madness. "Your mount is in his own stable by now, or I am much mistaken, and, Miss Mysterious Fair, you may as well understand, I've no intention of leaving you to make your own way home alone and on foot. If it is your wish to be set down, then you would be advised to tell me where it is I am to take you, that I may get on with delivering you safely . . . although I must say"—he gave a slow, unholy grin—"I am delighted to linger here with you in my arms. I don't think I have had so pleasant, or intriguing, an armful in many a day."

"Oh!" It was a furious explosion of sound. Gwen could have slapped his grinning face. It was obvious that, like the other well-to-do Englishman she'd known, he thought of suiting no one but himself. She could rail and demand all she liked, but she was the weaker and could not force him to her will. He would not only hold her until she told him what he wished to know, but in the process he would enjoy himself hugely at her expense.

"Very well then," Gwen conceded tightly. "You may take me to Wensley Hall, sir."

Instantly, and somehow gratifyingly, she saw she had taken the entirely too self-assured gentleman holding her by surprise. "Wensley Hall?" he echoed, a single tawny eyebrow lifting abruptly.

"Wensley Hall," she repeated very slowly as if he were a half-wit, though she thought he was anything but that. "It is just beyond those trees there." She turned to point the way, a little to her right.

He ignored her again, however. "Just who are you?" he demanded, his eyes narrowing speculatively.

Gwen cared little for his curiosity. He had not made knowing her identity part of his bargain, and she was not about to tell him more than he needed to know.

She lifted her chin crisply. "Who I am, sir, is none of your affair, only my transportation to Wensley Hall. Now, either you get on with taking me there, or I shall scream furiously enough to bring someone to my aid."

She made the threat seriously and suffered the most acute frustration when he threw back his head and laughed aloud. "By the gods, you are a spitfire. But you are right. It's at Wensley we'll settle the matter."

Gwen did not like the sound of that, but she had no opportunity to demand he clarify what he meant, for no sooner had he done speaking, than the man spurred his mount. Caught off guard, she fell back against him, and he took instant advantage, tightening the hold he had around her waist.

"Easy, don't wiggle," he whispered low in her ear, when she sought to put some room between them. "You'll spook Ares, and we will both be on the ground without a mount to ride."

Given how she felt in the circle of his arms, the heat of his body surrounding her and his voice a husky thread in her ear, Gwen wondered if it would not be wise to risk a fall. But it seemed her companion read her mind, for abruptly he urged the stallion to a canter, a pace at which Gwen knew she would suffer more than she would gain by chancing a fall.

Chapter 4

Gwen kept her body stiff and turned away from her unwanted companion, though her side ached abominably before they had traveled even a quarter of the distance to Wensley Hall. She never considered relaxing her posture, though. Had she, she'd have ended by nestling against him as if she had no quarrel with where she was.

And she most emphatically did not care for where she was. She was too, too aware of him. With his arm wrapped tightly about her, they were all but joined at the waist, and with every stride of the horse, Gwen literally felt the length of him from his warm, solid chest to his hard stomach.

She fought to clear her mind. It unnerved her to be so aware of him, or of any man, for that matter. She counted flowers, trees, hoof beats, anything, but midcount her thoughts would stray suddenly and she would find herself thinking, for example, that he must be quite strong, for he had lifted her from the back of a galloping horse as easily if she were a feather, which she was not, though she was no Amazon either.

She thought, too, that he must spend a great deal of time out of doors. Not only was his skin lightly bronzed, but he rode a horse like no one she had ever known, effortlessly controlling a mettlesome stallion even with the hindrance of a body in his lap.

Devil it! Gwen swore beneath her breath when she realized where and for how long her thoughts had drifted.

"Relax, cherie. Your tenseness only makes us both the more uncomfortable."

The lazy whisper brought Gwen's head around, a rebuke on her lips. She was not his "dear." She did give him an angry glare, but she whipped her head back again before she said a word. She could not imagine what she had been thinking to look up at him then, when they were only a hand's breadth apart.

His closeness had made the breath catch in her throat. No, that was not quite honest. Had he been old and grizzled, her breathing would not have been affected by him, regardless of how close he was. His tawny good looks had affected her, and with such force, she might have never seen him before, nor looked directly into green eyes that danced with golden lights, laughing and tempting all at once. For some reason she found herself thinking of a highwayman, though she had never been inclined to read the penny novels about gentlemen of the road who enticed highborn ladies to ride away with them into the night.

She was doing it again. And so absurdly! Gwen bit her lip hard and stared angrily ahead. They must come to Wensley soon! Surely the trees seemed to be thinning.

The trees were thinning. Before Gwen's thoughts wandered again, Wensley Hall burst into view. Across a quarter of a mile or so of rolling parkland, the house looked as lovely as it had when it was built over a century before, only now ivy covered much of the building, and where the ivy did not grow, the old stone of the walls had mellowed to a warm, tawny gold.

"It would seem you are highly prized."

Gwen jumped, startled not by his voice, but by the feel of his warm breath on her ear. Thrown off stride again, she did not mark the surprise in his voice, though when she looked ahead, she found herself surprised by what he'd seen.

Two riders were galloping away from the Hall, one toward the cliffs overlooking the Channel and the other directly for them.

She could not really credit the riders were galloping out on her account until the one coming toward them, evidently realizing there were two people on the black stallion making for him, took up a horn and blew a long blast. Immediately the other rider pulled up and turned back to the Hall.

Clearly someone had taken alarm when Sir Adolphus returned home riderless. Gwen guessed, reluctantly, who it was had displayed such concern for her—or prized her so highly as the devil behind her had said. And it was not Lady Chumleigh, who was almost certainly still napping.

Gwen's guess was confirmed when the rider who had taken their direction came close enough to recognize. Tim O'Rourke, the head groom at Wensley Hall, and a bachelor, waved his arm and called out, "Hello! We were worried for you, Mrs. Tarrant."

"Mrs. Tarrant?"

This time Gwen did remark the surprise, even astonishment, in her companion's voice, but even so she was not prepared when he threw back his head and laughed as if he'd unexpectedly been given the greatest pleasure.

"You are squeezing me in two!" Gwen protested, though she was more annoyed by his mysterious reaction to her name than by the inadverent tensing of the arm that held her in place.

His answer, however, did anger her fully, for he laughed again, and said, holding her even closer, "All the better for O'Rourke to see, my dear Mrs. Tarrant."

Gwen did register surprise that he should know O'Rourke, but she was far too infuriated by his utter disregard for her wishes to think further than that everyone in the area knew Wensley's head groom.

She did not want to arrive at the Hall seeming to all but recline in the arms of a handsome, virile stranger. "Loosen your grip!" she demanded again, rapping his arm with her fist for good measure. Her fist might have been made of rubber, or his arm of iron, for all the impression she made on it or on him, however.

"Temper, temper," he chided low in her ear, laughter still coloring his voice. "You'll only succeed at breaking both our legs."

"I would like to break yours," she muttered, forgetting that the wind would carry her voice to his ears. Actually, she did not give a fig that he had heard her ill-tempered remark, but that he laughed again.

They breezed by O'Rourke with her companion yelling out, "She's fine."

O'Rourke returned a response, Gwen could not make out what, and circled to gallop after them. Gwen closed her eyes and prayed for patience. O'Rourke had meant well when he set out to look for her, yet now she would arrive at Wensley not only in the arms of a stranger but under full escort. The tiny hope she'd harbored that Lady Chumleigh might hear nothing of the episode died completely.

Before they reached the drive, O'Rourke overtook them. To Gwen's surprise he did not pull up beside them but rode on to dismount and await them. She heard the man behind her grunt softly, as if he were not entirely pleased. She didn't understand his reaction, nor did she think much on it, after she noted movement in the terraced gardens on the west side of the Hall.

The marquess had arrived! No one else would have adjourned with guests to the gardens. He must have wished to take refreshments in the open-air pavilion there, Gwen guessed and felt the fiercest wave of anger she had experienced yet toward the gentleman holding her.

Were the marquess to see them and investigate . . . she could not bear to think what impression he would form, were she, his aunt's companion, to be presented to him from the vantage point of a gentleman's lap. The marquess would not think the worse of her companion. No, the arrogant devil would not receive so much as a lifted eyebrow. She, the woman and the paid employee, would be the one to bear the censure.

And Lord Warrick was influential with Lady Chumleigh. Everyone said so from Mrs. Ames, the housekeeper at the Hall, to Lady Chumleigh herself.

As Gwen flung up another prayer to heaven, this one more fervent than any before it, her companion began to slow his mount, and O'Rourke to stride toward them. Oddly the head groom was not looking at her, Gwen realized. He was looking behind her to her companion, and then he was lifting the cap he wore from his head.

O'Rourke was an independent fellow with an eye for her. He'd have come to help her down before he lifted his cap to any man, unless . . . unless the man behind her was as good as master of the Hall.

At that moment Gwen felt so many things, she squeezed her eyes shut to escape them all, particularly the feeling of mortification. She had been inspired to call Lady Chumleigh's favorite relative and heir an idiot, a fool, and a blackguard. And only moments before, she had told him she would like to break his leg.

Lord Warrick! Somehow she had gotten it into her mind that the marquess was middle aged. Lady Chumleigh had not said so, but Lady Chumleigh was so old. . . . All Gwen wanted to do was to disappear into a large hole. Later, when she was composed and her cheeks were no longer hot with embarrassment, she would look at him, and in her meekest manner, beg his forgiveness.

"Lord Warrick." It was O'Rourke, in a voice as toneless as the look in his eyes was carefully banked, who confirmed for Gwen who held her. "It's glad we all are to see ye back at the Hall, and glad, too, to see that ye found Mrs. Tarrant unhurt. Y'are unhurt, ma'am?"

There was a change, a softening, in O'Rourke's expression when he looked to Gwen. She saw it and wanted to sigh.

"Yes, Mr. O'Rourke, I am fine. It was all," she added, her voice sharpening noticeably despite herself, "a great misunderstanding."

She held out her arms, and Warrick released her to O'Rourke, who did not catch her hands but caught her by the waist. She had not expected the Irishman to hold her so, and stumbled a little, when her toes touched the ground.

"Ye are hurt!" He frowned down at her, tightening his grip.

The burden of O'Rourke's interest was a complication Gwen devoutly did not wish to have, and therefore she assured him of her well-being a trifle more sharply than she would have otherwise. "I am fine, Mr. O'Rourke." She stepped away from him to stand on her own. "Thank you."

Because she was facing in any direction but his, Gwen did not see the gleam of satisfaction that flared in Warrick's eyes when she responded to O'Rourke. She did, however, hear him say from behind her in a cool, clipped voice, "Thank you, O'Rourke. That will be all."

The Irishman nodded, but he looked to Gwen before he accepted Warrick's dismissal and left Gwen all alone with the "devil."

Abruptly, before the moment could draw out too long, Gwen turned about to face him. He was watching her, and he was smiling broadly. "I am pleased to meet you at last, Mrs. Tarrant."

It was the moment to be meek and mild, to beg forgiveness, to vow she did not know what had come over her. But her sense of self-preservation had evaporated. That smile had restoked her sense of ill-usage. Looking directly into the too familiar dancing green eyes, she said, "You might have told me."

If Warrick thought it odd that his aunt's companion, a farmer's widow, should address him as if she were his equal, he did not show it. "I might have," he said, mastering the smile on his lips, if not the one in his eyes. "However, my name so often produces an odd effect upon people that I use it sparingly. Still, even were I in the habit of making quite free with it, I did receive the impression, Mrs. Tarrant, that you did not care to exchange names."

Gwen didn't spare a moment's pity for the odd effect his name had upon the world. Of course people immediately toadied to him. It was a small price to pay for being unbelievably wealthy and completely in charge of one's fate. And she wished she had known to behave like a pattern card!

There was, though, his final point, that she had refused to exchange her name for his.

With a shrug for the whims of fate, Gwen conceded the point. But she did not apologize for being a vixen. The words lodged in her throat as she remembered how he had scared her half to death. And besides, it seemed to her high time he realized he could not go about the countryside hauling any female off her horse without taking care to be certain said female wished to be so rudely used.

Gwen did, however, accept that it was time to change her footing with Lady Chumleigh's nephew and said courteously enough, if a trifle stiffly, "Well, my lord, though we've gotten off to an . . . odd start, I do wish you welcome to Wensley." She made her best curtsy and was not well pleased to find, when she rose, that Warrick was grinning outright. Perhaps he had expected an apology. He would be disappointed, if so. "And now," Gwen said as coolly as if they had just met, "I must go to your aunt, my lord. She will be waking."

"Warrick!"

"Lucian!"

"Luc, we are here in the gardens."

Warrick had caught Gwen's arm even before the first voice called out hailing him. "Aunt Vi won't mind if you take the time to meet the remainder of the party, Mrs. Tarrant," he said, when Gwen stiffened at his touch.

She could hardly balk, given his position in the house.

Glancing to the gardens, she saw a stout but dapper gentleman escorting a blond woman of distinct and sophisticated beauty down to greet them. Above in the gardens, another man and woman leaned over the stone balustrade. Taking in the group as a whole, Gwen had an impression of gay colors, expensive, immaculate toilettes, and sinkingly, four pairs of eyes upon her.

The woman in the gardens, a vivacious-looking brunette, called out, "We've been waiting for you an age, Lucian! We feared you might have come to harm."

"But instead, it would seem you were playing the knight-errant, Warrick."

That was drawled by the beauty on the steps in such an idle, bored tone, Gwen could not tell if she were being testy. Whatever the woman's mood, though, she was certainly beautiful and sumptuously dressed as well in a cream-colored, silk afternoon creation trimmed with what looked to be miles of the finest lace. Cunningly, the same lace had been used across the décolletage of the dress. Through the tracery, Gwen could easily see the swell of heavy, glistening breasts.

"I always try to be of service, Frances," was Warrick's distinctly bland reply to the lady. Perhaps he had read reproach in her remark, Gwen thought, but even had she cared, she didn't have time to decide.

The woman's escort was saying, "I vow we were foolish indeed to worry where you had got to, Lucian. We should have known that you, of all men, would have the luck to go to the Point and return with a Ravishing Fair."

To Gwen's sensitive ears the man might as well have said, "Ravished Fair." Her chin went up a notch, and she fixed the pair before her with an unflinching look.

Warrick, feeling her stiffen, looked down and then smiled to himself. The sudden worry he'd entertained that Frances would make mincemeat of the farmer's widow died a happy death. Even Frances would not readily take on a woman, whatever her status, who looked haughty as any queen.

Lady Langdale did give Gwen an opaque look from over the top of her fan when Warrick presented her, but she refrained from saying anything, cutting or otherwise. Lord Sheffield, in contrast, bowed courteously over Gwen's hand and remarked something to the effect that he had never thought to be envious of Lady Chumleigh.

Gwen took it as a polite nothing and murmured an equally polite and meaningless response. She also thought she might be able to excuse herself, but Warrick kept his hold on her and urged her up the stairs to the pair that turned out to be his cousin, Mrs. Antonia Sudbury, and her husband, Major Sudbury.

There were questions as to how they had met, of course, and when Warrick related the story, Mrs. Sudbury, a pretty woman if not the beauty Lady Langdale was, teased him for his mistake. The men did as well, and there was a great deal made, too, of the danger of his feat, and the strength it must have required. Gwen scarcely heard a word. She felt very uncomfortable in the *ton*nish, fashionable group and not only because Warrick stood exceedingly close by her. With her hair hanging loose and her only serviceable clothes, she felt a crow among canaries. But then it occurred to her that at least crows were larger than canaries, and more self-sufficient besides. Likely they even enjoyed canaries for lunch.

The thought so amused Gwen, she missed that Major Sudbury was addressing her until their eyes chanced to meet.

". . . half the women in England must have plotted how they might fool Warrick into making just such a mistake! They'll all be green with envy when the story makes its rounds, Mrs. Tarrant."

He smiled in a knowing way, obviously certain she was delighted to have been wrested from her horse and thrust without a by-your-leave before his so marvelous lordship.

And was he equally certain she wished to be the marquess's paramour of the month?

Gwen's look was cool, indeed, when she replied to Major Sudbury. "I cannot speak for half the women in England,

Major, only myself, but when I am enjoying a gallop, I like to enjoy it unhindered."

She had spoken softly and without emphasis, but Major Sudbury's eyebrows lifted almost comically, and from the marquess's far side Gwen heard a throaty, "Well!" that could only have come from Lady Langdale. Mrs. Sudbury's response and Lord Sheffield's she did not pause to gauge. She looked to Warrick.

And he was smiling. No, worse, he was grinning. She had an urge to slap him. That should get through to him, as it seemed nothing else did, but she had to content herself with letting her eyes flash up at him. Then she took her leave. "Excuse me, my lord," she said firmly. "I wish to see to Lady Chumleigh."

Not, "I must see to Lady Chumleigh," or "Lady Chumleigh will miss me." Oh no, Mrs. Tarrant whisked herself off to do as she wished. Warrick caught Sudbury's stunned eye, and suddenly they both grinned.

"My heavens," Sudbury remarked drolly. "And we were afraid a mere farmer's widow would be too dull for Lady Chum."

Sheffield, having followed Gwen's militantly rigid back until it disappeared from sight through the French windows opening into the library, shook his head. "She could not have been wed to a farmer. There must be some mistake."

Chapter 5

Major Sudbury's theme, that there were women who would do almost anything to bring themselves to the attention of the Marquess of Warrick, even pretend to have their horses run off with them, was sounded again later in the day by Lady Chumleigh.

Gwen was assisting her employer to dress for dinner, a duty she assumed whenever Lady Chumleigh's aged dresser, Finch, was abed with aching joints, which was often of late, when Lady Chumleigh remarked with seeming idleness, "I do fear there will be those who, when they hear the curious story of your encounter with Lucian today, will leap to the conclusion that your meeting was no coincidence. Even Hermione," she went on, referring to the Viscountess Dent, one of her oldest friends, "remarked rather archly, when she came to greet Lucian, that you not only knew the day he was expected, but must have heard from me that he is an excellent horseman who keeps an annual tradition of galloping to Prawle Point to look over the sea before he rides on to Wensley."

Even were Lady Chumleigh only toying with her as Gwen half suspected, she did not care for being the subject of unfounded speculation.

Lifting her head to look into the pier glass, she met the old woman's shrewd, hooded eyes. "If you did mention to me his lordship's horsemanship or his fondness for Prawle Point, my lady, I fear I must admit that I did not attend you. I knew not who rode after me today and even feared the stranger meant me harm. As to the suggestion that I schemed to put myself in Lord Warrick's path, that is . . . with all due respect to Lady Dent, laughable. I had no need. I was to meet him anyway, with, I might add, considerably less danger to myself. He hauled me off a galloping horse, destroyed my ride, and scared me half to death."

Lady Chumleigh snorted. "From the kindling look in your eye, Gwendolyn, I should say he infuriated you more like."

"I was not pleased, no."

Lady Chumleigh hmmphed again, but she seemed satisfied both by Gwen's response and by her own careful study of her companion's expression. She'd another point of interest to probe, however, and did so, saying with calculated idleness, "I've been given to understand that O'Rourke went half out of his mind with worry when Adolphus galloped into the stable yard riderless."

This line of questioning did not affront Gwen as the other had done, and she shrugged lightly as she smoothed her mistress's dress across the shoulders. "I cannot say, my lady. I was not there. However, if Mr. O'Rourke was concerned for me, I am grateful, of course. That is all I am, though." She lifted her gaze, again meeting Lady Chumleigh's in the glass. "I've no desire for more than concern from O'Rourke or any man when it comes to it."

"Silly chit!" Lady Chumleigh chided with unexpected vigor. "A man would support you. You'd not be obliged to earn your living humoring old tartars."

Gwen might not have found cause to smile often, but perhaps for that reason, when she did, a rare warmth lit her beauty. "It is not such bad work when the old tartar is amusing."

"Impertinent chit!" Lady Chumleigh scolded, without a trace of heat. "You need a man to take you in hand."

"I do not think I would much care for being taken in hand," Gwen quipped lightly enough, but she'd enough conviction on the matter. She didn't care to argue further with her employer and took herself off to find the elder lady a suitable fan. "You've a purple fan, my lady, but there is more red in it than in your dress. I think this black one very pretty. Which do you prefer?"

"Heaven forbid that I should suit myself and offend your taste!" Lady Chumleigh retorted, nodding toward the black fan. "Finch is forever extolling your sense of style."

"Finch is a dear."

"An old, sick dear," Lady Chumleigh grumped. "It is fast approaching time I turn her out to pasture. She is growing more humped and useless by the day."

Gwen said nothing. She had learned since she'd been at Wensley Hall that though Lady Chumleigh enjoyed grumbling and grumbling sharply, she did not mean half of what she said. Gwen guessed Finch would not be turned out to pasture for years, if she lived so long.

"You could do worse than learn from my old Finch," Lady Chumleigh said abruptly. Puzzled, Gwen looked a question at her. "I mean, slow wit, that she's in the devil of a situation being old and infirm and dependent entirely upon the charity of others. A husband would support you in your old age."

Gwen's expression cooled. She had thought the subject settled. "I have not met many dependable men in my life, and as it is difficult to know who is likely to prove dependable over the years and who is not, I shall depend upon the one person I know is dependable, myself."

"Get me my cane!" Lady Chumleigh often became surly when she was crossed, and so Gwen was not surprised to have an order cracked out at her as if she were no better than a serf.

"The cane topped with the lion's head or the turtle's?" she asked with every evidence of meekness.

Lady Chumleigh, however, was not fooled. "The lion's head!" she snapped. "And though you may convince me that you mean to turn up your dainty nose at O'Rourke, you will not persuade me that you are immune to Lucian. Half the women in England are panting after the boy."

Gwen had heard enough about the marquess's admirers. "Then you may count me among the other half, my lady."

"Well, you had best remain indifferent, though I doubt you'll have the strength," Lady Chumleigh shot back. "Lucian would not think to support you in any legitimate way, Mrs. Tarrant. While O'Rourke would offer you marriage, you'll get no more than a slip on the shoulder from a marquess."

"Precisely."

Gwen held out the cane with the lion's head on top that had belonged to Lady Chumleigh's husband. The old woman's eyes met hers, and it was, remarkably enough, Lady Chumleigh's expression that softened first.

"Lud, just look at you! You look as proud as a queen. I fear I shall soon be in danger of forgetting who is the servant here." She took the cane, but held Gwen's eyes. "I often speak in haste, child, as you know, I don't doubt. If I offended a moment ago, I repent now. At least I repent the manner in which I spoke. The substance is the truth as I see it. I would not have you come to harm while you are under my wing, and Lucian is not only a charmer. He's a highborn rogue. It is the plain truth."

"It is the truth as well that I've no interest in him, my lady," Gwen replied, her tone, too, a great deal more moderate. "I am no gullible girl easily swayed by a practiced rake. You may wipe that furrowed brow quite clear. Yes, that's better. So much better, indeed, I vow you'll be the belle of the evening."

"The belle of the evening, indeed! I was not that even in my salad days. I . . ."

Lady Chumleigh successfully distracted from the subject of Gwen's future and the men in it, or lack thereof, Gwen stepped around to adjust her shawl, and was herself distracted.

She only happened to glance to the door, but when she did, she looked directly into the green eyes of the man who had so recently been the subject of discussion.

And he had heard enough to have heard her proclaim herself immune to him. His lazy posture, one shoulder propped against the doorway, arms crossed over his chest, suggested he had been listening for some time. But even had he been standing straight, Gwen would have known he heard her. His mouth was only faintly curved, but his eyes were alive with laughter, and challenge, too.

She could not look away. She was caught only for a moment, granted, but too long for Gwen. She stood riveted by green eyes that somehow all at once teased her, caressed her, and promised . . .

Danger. Oh, aye. She felt as breathless as if she'd run a race. Jerking her gaze from Warrick's, she announced his arrival to Lady Chumleigh, then took herself off to the shadows of the room where her blush could not be seen.

She deeply resented that heat in her cheeks. She did not care to have any reaction at all to the man. Yet even then, his image danced before her eyes, almost taunting her.

There was reason. She was still not accustomed to his looks. And, as if he needed it, he'd a fresh advantage. The understated elegance of his evening dress, a chocolate brown coat, white, starched cravat, and dark kerseymere trousers was the perfect foil for his extravagant good looks.

And none of that was to mention the faint curve of his sensuous mouth, or the golden light in his green eyes.

As if she hoped to blot out the sight of those green eyes, Gwen closed her own eyes briefly. Undistracted, she heard Warrick say indulgently, "Now who is turning whom up sweet, Aunt Vi? From what I heard, Mrs. Tarrant entertains you admirably."

Gwen kept her attention upon the toilette articles that had long since been put in order. She would not turn and acknowledge not only that he had referred to her but that he had looked to her. And she knew he had. The back of her neck had grown warm, as if he had caressed it with his hand.

"Gwen does amuse me, Lucian," Lady Chumleigh agreed, but with a slight edge to her voice. "Indeed, she amuses me so well I would say, even at the risk of spoiling her, that I dote on her so, I am quite determined, as I am certain you will understand, to keep her with me."

In the shadows Gwen's cheeks went hot again and Warrick's amused chuckle did little to cool them. "Do you mean to play the dragon that guards the priceless treasure, Aunt Vi? If so," he went on smoothly before his aunt could remark that he'd given her no assurance what role he intended to play vis-à-vis that treasure, "I am curious as to why you mean to starve your treasure. Does not Mrs. Tarrant come to dinner with us?"

"She does not."

Gwen did not care for being spoken of and for as if she were a stick of furniture. She took such offense; indeed, she consigned her strategy of discreet retreat to the dust bin. Turning, she stepped into the light and directed a winsome smile at Lady Chumleigh. "I do, however, wish you a pleasant evening, my lady. May I get you anything else?"

"Do you see?" Lady Chumleigh shot Warrick a smug look. "She is delighted to be delivered from dinner with us. Gwen likes to be alone, and even if she did not, I'd not have her join us tonight. She would upset my numbers."

Warrick's tawny brow drifted upward. "Is that the best reason you have for not treating your companion as a respected member of the household, Aunt Vi?"

"I feel quite sufficiently respected, my lord!" Gwen intervened rather sharply before Lady Chumleigh could speak. The devil did not care how she was treated, she was quite certain. He wanted her at dinner only for his own amusement, though Gwen could not understand why Lady Langdale would not provide him sufficient entertainment. Perhaps he operated on the principle of the more the merrier, she thought, and added a trifle more tartly. "But if, hypothetically, I did not believe myself to be adequately respected, the issue would lie between Lady Chumleigh and myself alone."

Warrick's response was a broad smile, as if he thoroughly enjoyed being put in his place. Gwen glared at him, exasperated nothing seemed to prick his thick skin, but Lady Chumleigh was delighted by her show of spirit.

"Aha! Gwen has put you in your place, Lucian! And she's right to boot. My companion and where she eats is my affair. You'll have to make do with La Langdale and the Godolphin chits. Now help me heave up my bulk that I may make the grand entrance you have both promised me."

Finally something caused Warrick's good humor to fade. "The Godolphin chits?" he repeated, looking away from Gwen at last. "Who the devil are they?"

"Sir James Godolphin's girls, of course. I know of no other Godolphins living nearby. They are just beginning to go about in society."

"Of eligible age, are they?" Warrick inquired dryly.

"Jane is eighteen and Amy seventeen, as a matter of fact."

"I see. Well, Mrs. Tarrant, it would seem that you may indeed, be best out of this evening." Looking across his aunt's turbaned head, Warrick gave Gwen such a sincerely rueful smile that, had she not been steeled against him, she might have been persuaded to smile back. "Just eligible girls and their doting parents are not the liveliest of dinner companions."

"Tut, tut! I'll hear no such thing!" Lady Chumleigh commanded. "They are charming girls!"

"Exactly." Lucian inclined his head at Gwen. "Enjoy your solitary state, Mrs. Tarrant, for now."

Gwen did enjoy the solitary meal she took on a tray in her room. She might have eaten with Mrs. Ames, the housekeeper, but she had not lied when she excused herself on the grounds that she was tired.

She was weary but of worrying. It seemed an age since that morning when she had been congratulating herself on the seeming security of her future. In the interim two very different men had, each in his own way, come along to unsteady her.

Her father was no small source of anxiety, but it was the Marquess of Warrick who concerned Gwen most that evening. She had heard the warning in that "enjoy your solitary state for now." He meant to pursue her. Why continued to mystify her. Surely it was not by chance that Lady Langdale had come to Wensley without her husband. And the elder Godolphin girl, Jane, was a flirtatious thing. With such willing women about, he'd no reason to fasten on a widowed servant.

Gwen's mouth quirked suddenly in a bitter smile. If it was challenge he wanted, Warrick did not know how well armored she was. She'd the experience to know lovemaking was for the man's benefit not the woman's. Mr. Tarrant had been a good, kind man, and yet she had found little pleasure in fulfilling her marriage duties, though her husband had often enough professed himself well pleased with her.

Nor would she fall so in love with the marquess that she would give all merely to please him. Gwen smiled thinly again. Mr. Miles Dacre had taught her too well not to trust that emotion.

She had been seventeen when Miles came to St. Ives to visit for the summer. His friends must have been dull, though, for he soon came into the village and spying her, returned almost every day. An attractive young man with more sophistication and polish than all the young men Gwen knew put together, he'd dazzled her.

Soon they were meeting almost every day. At first they had only talked, or rather Miles had held forth. Having been only as far as Plymouth once, all Miles had seen fascinated her. For his part Miles must have been pleased to have such an attentive audience.

He had admired her looks, too. He'd told her that often enough and soon begged a kiss from her. After a little Gwen had allowed herself to be persuaded and then she had granted him another, then longer embraces. In time Miles was holding her and telling her how imcomparable she was; how she would take the town by storm when he took her to London; and, of course, how he loved her.

Their embraces became more heated and might have led to Gwen's undoing, but tragedy intervened, when within a few days of each other, her mother and grandfather fell ill with fever after they returned from a trip to Plymouth. Gwen and Marta, their housekeeper, had taken turns with the nursing. Miles had not come to call, but Gwen had not faulted him in the least. No one knew what caused the fever, and Gwen had even taken the precaution of sending her brothers and sisters to a neighbor. The old doctor in St. Ives had wanted her to go, too, but that had been out of the question.

Miles did come again to see her, after her mother and grandfather had died, and after her grandfather's solicitor had given her the news there was nothing left in her grandfather's modest estate. Not even the house was theirs. Along with everything else, it had been put up as surety to fund one or another of her father's new starts.

Stunned, with no one to turn to, for her father had not answered any of her frantic letters, Gwen had sat in her mother's favorite rocking chair in the parlor, staring into the fire until the answer had finally come. She was only seventeen, but she would have to marry.

No sooner had she the thought, than Marta had padded in to tell her she'd a visitor. "'Tis the fine 'un, Mr. Dacre," Marta had said, lifting her brow meaningfully.

Miles! Surely it was not coincidence that at the very moment of her greatest need, the young man who had sworn he loved her so often she believed him, should come.

When he asked her to go for walk, Gwen had gladly escaped the mournful stillness of the house. When he had taken her hand, she'd held tightly to him, relieved beyond measure to find she was not alone in the world. When he had whispered he loved her and kissed her, she'd yielded her lips gladly, too grateful to be held in strong, healthy arms to protest even when he pulled her down to the grass with him. He loved her. He had said so.

When he slid his hand under her skirts, though, he startled her. "What are you doing, Miles?" she'd whispered softly. "We cannot do more until we are married."

Miles had had a white smile he could flash to effect. "Don't be a tease, Gwen," he'd cajoled. "You've gotten me ready to explode. We cannot stop now."

Cannot stop? Even not knowing precisely what he meant, Gwen had not liked the sound of that. She was not so lost in sadness she wanted to be ruined. Stiffening, she had asked, "You do mean to marry me, Miles? You do love me?"

"Of course I love you!" he'd sworn with a charming smile. "I love everything about you. Just looking at you makes me throb with need. Now come, Gwen, sweeting, let me touch you."

He'd started to slide his hand up her thigh again, but Gwen had pushed him back, holding him at arm's length. "Miles, do you mean to marry me as you said you wished to do?" she had asked, her voice neither soft nor indulgent any longer.

"Marry?" he had parried, his eyes dropping from hers in the way she'd seen her father's do innumerable times when he had been about to dissemble. "Of course, we'll marry." He'd looked at her then, fixing her with another affecting smile. "I couldn't let a beauty like you get away from me."

She would not have known he lied but for that one telltale dropping of his eyes. Later she would think that at least she had one thing for which to be grateful to her father. Just then she was not so dispassionate.

She leaped to her feet and realizing she looked the veriest trollop with her bodice gaping open and her hair tumbling wildly around her face, screamed in a voice shrill with anger at his betrayal, and perhaps, too, with all the loss and pain of the previous weeks, "You are lying, Miles Dacre! You do not mean to marry me at all. You mean to seduce me today, when I am aching with loss! You are a despicable cad! I spit on you!"

Miles Dacre, thwarted and spat upon, was not a pretty sight.

A cruel, derisive smile on his face, he jumped to his feet, looking almost a stranger. "Did I have any intention of marrying you?" he sneered. "Of course not. I'll have better than a penniless baron's wild and unkempt daughter! You were entertainment only, sweet Gwen!"

At that, Gwen had gone a little mad and shown how wild she could be. She dove for a rock and threw it at him, hitting him hard on the shoulder. When he staggered backward, she found a whole handful of sharp rocks and then another and another. Why Miles had not come after her, Gwen would never know. Perhaps he'd been frightened by the wild light in her eye. Perhaps he'd been afraid she would scar his handsome face. Whatever he thought, yelling imprecations at her, he'd made for his horse and ridden away.

Two weeks later Mr. Tarrant, who had visited a sister in St. Ives regularly over the years, came to the Trevelyan house to convey his condolences. A month later, though she was in mourning, Gwen had married him after he agreed she could bring her brothers and sisters to Devon with her.

Gwen had had the last word with Miles Dacre, sending him running as she had, but her experience with him had left its mark. She had learned to doubt love, and she'd also learned not to trust a word a highborn rake might say.

Chapter 6

"Who can remember the names of the characters in the play
we've been reading?" When a half dozen small hands shot into
the air, Gwen pensively studied the boys before her. "Timothy,
you've not had a turn yet."

"D-dunstan, and L-l-lady Macbeth, m-ma'am," the boy
piped, reddening unmercifully when Gwen smiled her ap-
proval.

Other boys were eager to add names to the list of characters
in the tragedy they were reading, and Gwen readily spared
Timothy more attention than he could bear.

She knew the idiosyncracies of the twenty odd boys before
her. She had been working with them for almost five months.
Lady Chumleigh had requested her to take on the duty early in
the spring. Lady Chumleigh's principal charity, the Chumleigh
Home for Boys, had found itself in difficulty. Due to an extremely poor harvest the fall before, a tragic number of fami-
lies in the south of Devon had had to send sons to the
orphanage. Lady Chumleigh had insisted the additional boys
be accommodated, but she was no spendthrift. She thought
many of the boys would be reclaimed as soon as the next harvest, and she saw no need to hire a new tutor for them. Instead
she had said she would lend the director of the orphanage, Mr.
Middleworth, the services of her companion, who had nothing
to do in the mornings as Lady Chumleigh did not require her
before eleven. Gwen had a good hand. She could teach the
boys penmanship and whatever else was necessary three
mornings a week.

Poor Mr. Middlesworth had been shocked to the tips of his
staid toes by the suggestion that a female could teach boys.
They would take the grossest advantage of her soft nature, he

protested. They would never respect her! And surely Lady Chumleigh must see that it simply was not done for a female to teach a male.

"Stuff" had been Lady Chumleigh's pithily barked reply. Mrs. Tarrant was accustomed to dealing with boys. She had two brothers of her own. Nor was she weak-willed, as Lady Chumleigh could, herself, testify. As to a woman teaching a man, Mr. Middlesworth's patroness snorted, it happened every day, only men were too blind to see it.

Gwen had proven Lady Chumleigh right. Though some of the boys had tried, as boys will do, to take advantage of their unusual tutor, Gwen had hardly wilted. She'd given the troublemakers a look that had made them flinch and had kept them after class to scrub the floor on their hands and knees. In the perverse way of students, her stock had risen instantly, not only with the other boys but with the troublemakers as well, and she'd had a most enjoyable time since at the Chumleigh orphanage.

Gwen's own education had been unconventional. Because she'd a bright mind, her grandfather had taken it upon himself to tutor her in subjects not normally taught to young women, such as literature and history, but his good friend, the doctor in St. Ives, Dr. Penrwyn, had also indulged her curiosity. Tagging along with the doctor, she had gained some understanding of anatomy and healing, but it being too easy to imagine Mr. Middlesworth's response were she to propose teaching anatomy to young boys, Gwen had decided to begin by discussing the subject to which she had most looked forward with her grandfather, the plays of Shakespeare.

That day she planned to recite the beginning to the fourth act of *Macbeth*, the famous "double, double toil and trouble" witches' scene, and then to have the boys copy it to practice their penmanship.

Seating herself upon her desk, Gwen hunched her shoulders forward. "Thrice the brinded cat had mew'd," she intoned in a witch's scratchy, cackling voice, her mouth drawn in a convincing grimace and her hands pulled into talons. "Thrice and once the hedgepig whined. / Harpier cries, 'Tis time, 'tis time. / Round about the cauldron go," she continued on from memory, holding the boys spellbound. Then, when she was nearly done, she cocked her ear. "By the pricking of my thumbs, something wicked this way comes!"

Sweeping the class with slitted eyes, Gwen opened her mouth to speak the final lines, "Open, locks, whoever knocks!", and almost had them die on her tongue. As if she had conjured him, "something wicked" had come. He stood at the door. It was open, as always, for Mr. Middlesworth, though he had yielded on the matter of Gwen's teaching at the orphanage, had insisted she, alone of all the teachers, leave open the door to her classroom. She hadn't objected. If he learned something listening from the hallway, all the better. But it was not Mr. Middlesworth who stood in the open door that day. Or rather it was not Mr. Middlesworth alone who stood there.

Gwen lifted her chin the moment she saw who it was eclipsed Mr. Middleworth. As Lady Chumleigh had not warned her Warrick would visit the school, she could not think why else he had come but to object to her presence there.

Gwen was not the only one to notice the visitor. When she finished her recitation, a general stir broke out in the class as the boys craned their necks to study Warrick. Gwen soon returned their attention where it belonged, however. "We've twenty minutes yet, gentlemen. I wish you to copy the lines I have just read, and I wish your efforts to be particularly careful."

With varying degrees of alacrity, the boys tore their eyes from the object of their interest. That they did so at all spoke to the respect they had for Gwen, for practicing their writing held not half the appeal studying the bang-up lord did.

That he was a nobleman, they did not question, though they'd seen few of the breed in their lives. He simply looked as assured as they imagined a nobleman would look. Mr. Middlesworth, at his side and several inches the shorter, looked, by contrast, inconsequential, and of course, not half so well turned out.

The boys could not imagine, though they tried, how much the visitor's coat must have set him back. Impeccably cut, it fit him like a glove, but, nonetheless, they did not mistake their visitor for a dandy. They'd an eye for sham and could tell the difference between natural muscle and padding. However elegant he was, they understood the gent would be able take care of himself, if need be.

The boys also saw who it was had caught the nobleman's attention. Not a one was surprised. If two or three had tested Gwen the first day, they had done so as much to gain her attention as to be difficult, for they were not blind. The half of the boys not in love with her were in awe of her, and they all thought it only natural the man in the doorway would also be interested in Mrs. Tarrant. Any real man would be.

Surreptitiously the more knowing boys glanced to Mrs. Tarrant. Only half to their surprise, they found she did not seem flustered by the man's interest. Perhaps there was some color in her cheeks, but there always was a dusting of rose to tint the smooth paleness of her complexion. Cor, but she was as striking as he, even if not half so finely turned out.

"That will be all for today, gentlemen. If you have not finished, you may do so this evening. I shall collect your papers on Friday. Thank you."

Gwen had purposely kept her back to the door, as she walked around working with each boy individually. Now she shot a sidelong glance toward it. Seeing the doorway stood empty, she bit back a sigh of relief, not wanting to betray to the boys how tense Warrick's presence had made her. For that matter, she didn't want to acknowledge it to herself.

She thought she could guess where the marquess and director had gone, however. It was Wednesday, the day Gwen normally went to Mr. Middlesworth's office to give her weekly report, and she did not doubt the two men were waiting for her there to reargue the propriety of a woman teaching boys. When she left her room, Gwen turned away from Mr. Middlesworth's office. If she were going to argue the subject with Warrick, she would do it in Lady Chumleigh's company, when the numbers, and authority, would be on her side.

Feeling rather smug at having eluded Warrick and a difficult encounter, Gwen breezed out the front door of the orphanage only to pull up short. Mr. Middlesworth was indeed still occupied with his patroness's nephew, but not within the building as she had assumed. The two men stood on the front steps and turned in unison when she stepped outside. Behind them Gwen saw not only that her trap had been brought around, but that Warrick had ordered his mount—she recognized Ares—be tied to the back of the trap.

Warrick grinned when he saw her, as if he thought to charm her out of being provoked by his presumption.

Gwen returned him a furious glare. She did not have to guess what Mr. Middlesworth would make of Warrick's attention to her. Middlesworth would not be ignorant of Warrick's reputation with women. The director was shrewd enough, and gossip enough, to inform himself fully on his patroness and her family, and he would assume Gwen was the marquess's latest conquest.

"Ah, here you are Mrs. Tarrant!" Mr. Middlesworth beamed in a way he had never done before. Gwen could not tell whether his giddiness stemmed from his being in company with a marquess, or from his imagining what said marquess might soon be doing with her. "Lord Warrick has waited for you! I know you must be delighted by the honor he does you. And not only will you have his escort all the way to the Hall, but you will save your lovely hands being chafed by the reins."

Middlesworth might have babbled that she had lobster claws for hands for the look Gwen gave him. "Good day, sir," she said, ice dripping from her voice, and ignoring Warrick completely, she proceeded down the steps.

He followed her, though. She heard him behind her, but when one of the boys who served as a groom came running up, she gave the lad the honor of handing her up onto the seat of the trap. For him she had a smile.

It was no good protesting Warrick's summary commandeering of the trap. It was more his than hers, for one thing, and for another she did not care to stage an argument for Mr. Middlesworth's delectation.

Gwen did not even look at Warrick as he joined her, however. She was too angry. Her back rigid, and her eyes fixed straight ahead, she settled herself on the seat and waited in thundering silence for him to pull away.

He did so, flicking the reins and waving briefly to Mr. Middlesworth before he guided the stolid horse used for the trap out the semicircular drive, down Kingsbridge's principal street, and finally out of the town.

When the traffic had thinned to an occasional farmer's cart, Lucian glanced over at Gwen. And grinned again. She might have been an ice figure or the figurehead on a ship. Yes, the latter, for she was beautiful enough to entice men over the sea, and she resembled his idea of a sea witch, with her dark-as-midnight hair and those sky blue eyes.

"I take it you are less than pleased to have been denied your customary conversation with steady, earnest, and I must say, admiring, Mr. Middlingsworth."

Gwen wavered a moment before deciding silence would provoke him more than a cursory reply. "Mr. Middlesworth"—she pronounced the director's correct name without emphasis—"is married, my lord. He is a professional colleague, nothing more, and I find speaking with him to be, generally, an exercise in tedium."

The minute she said that last, Gwen wanted to gnash her teeth. The very last thing she wished to do was amuse Warrick.

And she had. She could hear the smile in his voice. "Well, it would seem we do agree on one thing, at least, Mrs. Tarrant. But I cannot be overjoyed, I fear, because I must now deduce that you are looking like an icicle because I came to the orphanage."

"I wish you would not play the innocent with me!" Gwen flared, unable to control herself. "I can scarcely be pleased that you have undermined my position with Mr. Middlesworth!"

"Middlesworth does not accord you respect?"

It was not at all the answer Gwen had expected nor the tone. Warrick suddenly sounded and even looked a hard man.

"Mr. Middlesworth has been respectful enough," she clarified, if a little grudgingly. "However, as a woman I am on trial with him even after five months of, at the least, adequate work, and I would not like to lose my position at the school because he mistakenly believes me to be your latest conquest."

Warrick's expression eased markedly. "I see. And you enjoy your teaching?"

"Yes." A cart rumbled toward them, and Warrick turned his attention to the narrow road ahead. Without his green eyes upon her, Gwen felt easier, and before she quite realized it, she was elaborating. "The boys remind me of my brothers and sisters. I used to read to them a great deal."

"Shakespeare?"

Gwen thought the look Warrick slanted her was doubting. Her hackles lifted instantly. "Are you surprised, my lord?"

"Very," he provoked her deliberately, his eyes lighting. "I've never known a beautiful woman who could recite Shakespeare. You were an excellent witch."

He'd deftly pulled the ground out from beneath her, and he knew it. Quickly, before she could become lost in it, she looked away from his highwayman's gleaming grin.

"Thank you."

Gwen was conscious of him watching her for a moment, then he said entirely unexpectedly, "I did not visit the orphanage to object to your presence there, Mrs. Tarrant. I visit every year to see that matters are running smoothly. From what I observed, I should say your presence is entirely beneficial to Aunt Vi's boys, and that is what I said to Mr. Middlesbody."

"Middlesworth," Gwen said automatically, before repeating, a little stiffly, for the second time in as many minutes, "thank you."

Her grudging tone made Warrick smile wryly down at her. "Could this meeting of our minds not herald a new beginning in our relations, Mrs. Tarrant?"

She found it so exceedingly difficult to resist the appeal in his voice, she had to summon the specter of Miles Dacre to harden herself. "I am sure our relations are as they should be, my lord."

"Ah," he replied, nodding sagely, but she could hear the irony lacing his voice. "You mean that we should have no relations. That is why you have been avoiding me, I take it?"

"You much mistake the matter, my lord. I have not avoided you at all," Gwen returned loftily, and lying through her teeth.

"Have you not? Then I must admit, I am most surprised to see you out and about today, when only yesterday, according to Aunt Vi, you were too indisposed to join us not only for our picnic by the sea, but dinner as well. Actually, now I think on it, you have been otherwise, ah, occupied for every meal including tea since I arrived two days ago."

"It is not my habit to join Lady Chumleigh's guests at table."

"Lady Dent made a great deal of missing you last night," Lucian provoked in a too innocent drawl.

"Lady Dent is Lady Chumleigh's closest friend. She is a different matter."

"Her nephew, Mr. Edmundson, also asked after you."

"Did he? I cannot imagine why."

"Can you not, Mrs. Tarrant? You have not looked into a pier glass lately then."

Abruptly Gwen decided to change tactics, evasion having gotten her nowhere. "Lord Warrick," she said in a voice that suggested she'd little patience left. "It may astound you to learn this, but I am not at Wensley for your amusement."

Warrick shot her a dancing look. "If not quite astounded, I am chagrined to learn it, Mrs. Tarrant."

In another place and time, in another life, she'd have been caught. His dancing green eyes and strong, amused smile were almost irresistible. But in that place and time, Gwen was too aware what was at stake, and she lost her temper.

"Is it that you do not understand or that you will not?" she burst out. "If it is the latter, allow me to explain. A flirtation with you could well cost me my livelihood, my lord. I am not a peer of the realm, able to do as I please without the least fear of consequences. I must support myself and my four brothers and sisters. Currently I keep bread in all our mouths by working for your aunt. In return for the generous salary she pays me, I must fulfill certain duties and obligations, and they do not, by her express edict, include entertaining you. You may understand that, if you try, I believe."

Frustratingly Warrick studied Gwen with an expression she could not read, then said carefully, "Do you not understand that I would make good any loss you suffered by entertaining me, my dear Mrs. Tarrant—were it to come to that?"

It took Gwen a moment to understand what he meant. And then an angry flush burned her cheeks. It was one thing to know that he would offer nothing more than carte blanche, and quite another to hear the offending offer actually, if oh so discreetly, made.

Gwen looked Warrick full in the eyes. "I wonder what is

proper to say here, my lord? You would know better than I. I've never been asked to—how did you put it?—entertain a man before. Lacking the requisite experience, I suppose I shall simply have to say baldly that entertaining you holds no appeal whatsoever for me, whatever the recompense. And, furthermore, I should be greatly pleased if you never again insult me by proposing that I compromise my self-respect for your pleasure."

Gwen had thought to anger Warrick, to offend him so he would lose all interest in her. Instead, to her considerable frustration, she thought she detected a twinkle in his eye. If she had, though, he banished it before she completely lost the very thin control she had on her temper and resorted to pelting him with rocks.

"I see, Mrs. Tarrant. I had not meant to offend you. Indeed it was the very last thing I wished to do. And I promise I shall keep your position firmly in mind, but I must add one thing." He took his attention from the road to look down at Gwen. He was not smiling outright, but she'd the galling suspicion that he was to himself. "I do not believe, my dear Mrs. Tarrant, that anything in the world could compromise your self-respect."

What could she say to that? Not well pleased to have been denied the last word, Gwen jerked her gaze from Warrick's green and now faintly gleaming eyes and stared straight ahead, not deigning to speak to him again until they reached the Hall, where she bid him a decidedly curt farewell.

Chapter 7

Confident Lady Chumleigh would expose her to Warrick as little as possible, Gwen failed to school her expression when her employer announced imperiously the next afternoon that Gwen would dine *en famille* that evening.

"It is the third Thursday of the month," Lady Chumleigh replied to Gwen's look of less than pleased surprise, "Smeddley's day to dine at Wensley, and he is invariably lost with Lucian's party."

Gwen could readily comprehend that Mr. Smeddley would have little in common with the marquess and his sophisticated friends. For the Anglican church, the vicar of Kingsbridge was a most devout, unworldly man whose interests ranged little beyond the concerns of the plain country folk who were his parishioners.

"You've the blue silk to wear," Lady Chumleigh continued, meeting the only possible objection Gwen could make and referring to a dress she, herself, had given Gwen when an investigation of her companion's wardrobe had yielded not one dress Lady Chumleigh considered appropriate for dinner at Wensley. "It won't be up to what Tony and the Langdale wear, of course, but it will do well enough. Whether fortunately or not, you've the luck of looking very well, regardless what you wear."

The more grudging-than-not tone in which Lady Chumleigh uttered the compliment caused Gwen to smile. "You are too kind, my lady," she murmured only to receive a darkling glare.

"Your looks are not an unalloyed blessing, Mrs. Pert. Warrick's done nothing but harp each night on the most unsingular fact of your absence from the dinner table."

The mention of Warrick, and the proof that his unwanted interest did not please Lady Chumleigh, effectively doused Gwen's good humor. "I cannot believe that the marquess truly languishes for want of my company, my lady. I suspect he harps only because he is accustomed to having his way in all things."

Lady Chumleigh waved her hand dismissively, not the least mollified by the observation. "He is a Montfort. Of course he's accustomed to having his own way."

Bitterness rose to sour the taste in Gwen's mouth. Accustomed to ease and privilege, the man had never suffered so much as a pin prick in his life. Little wonder he had not even a scrap of understanding for the difficulties of others. "He will not have his way in regards to me, I assure you, ma'am."

Lady Chumleigh caught the fierceness in Gwen's tone, and after giving her a considering look, decided it would be the better part of discretion to find a new subject.

Gwen was somewhat late for the predinner gathering of Lady Chumleigh's guests in the West Saloon, a gracious, airy room named for the direction in which it faced. She had not had to assist Lady Chumleigh to dress. Finch had been able to perform her duties that evening, but Gwen had not found dressing herself to be easy.

Just the positioning of a single camellia in her hair had taken her almost a quarter of an hour. Gwen had thought to make up for her lack of jewelry with a flower, and in truth the effect was everything she wanted. Her black hair gleamed strikingly against the soft white of the camellia, yet she had pinned and repinned the flower until she wanted to tear her hair from the smooth coronet she'd pinned atop her head and send a note down to Lady Chumleigh, saying she had suddenly taken terribly ill.

She told herself that it was for the sake of her pride she fretted so. Granted she could not turn herself out half so elegantly as Lady Langdale and Mrs. Sudbury, but she did not want to look pitiful beside them, either. However, when she stood before her pier glass, Gwen caught herself using not the ladies of the party as a measure for her looks, but the host of it.

The minute she realized she was attempting to look at herself through Warrick's eyes, she spun from the glass, and taking up the Norwich shawl her father had brought her mother when he had once been temporarily flush, went down to face the evening.

To Gwen's pleasant **surprise**, after all the fretting she'd done, her entrance was **anti**climatic. Lady Chumleigh had mentioned that the Godolphins were to come again, but she'd not added that the Godolphins had guests staying with them. The result was that there were enough people milling about that Gwen could slip in to the room very nearly unnoticed.

Briefly she caught Lady Chumleigh's eye, signaling to her employer that she was present, if needed, then she dutifully joined the group of which Mr. Smeddley was part. As he was speaking to Thomas Godolphin, Sir James's eldest son, and the young man's wife, conversation was easy. The couple were young parents eager to relate every feat, good or bad, their two sons had accomplished since birth.

While she spoke with Mr. and Mrs. Godolphin, and later Mr. Godolphin's parents and sisters, Gwen successfully battled a desire to scan the room for Warrick. Though she wanted like the devil to avoid him, she wanted far more to avoid conveying the impression that she'd the least interest in him.

The result was that when Gwen agreed to Lord Sheffield's request to settle a wager he'd made with Major Sudbury about her, and she allowed the viscount to lead her across the room, she was not prepared to see Warrick straight ahead of her. Her heart skipped oddly. She told herself it was surprise made her heart behave so oddly, and that may have been true. Gwen did not care to examine her reaction any closer. What she did desire above all was to seem not to notice Warrick at all, and she sent her gaze careening to Lord Sheffield and Major Sudbury at once.

But she was aware of Warrick. His elegant broad-shouldered figure loomed out of all proportion to actual size in her peripheral vision. As usual he lounged casually against something, in this case the chimneypiece. She'd have liked to deride him as hopelessly indolent-looking, but she could not. He gave too clearly the impression of loose-limbed strength resting gracefully.

His eyes weren't resting, though. She felt their gaze gliding along her neck, and had the guilty sense she had bared her neck for his pleasure when she put up her hair.

Almost immediately, she upbraided herself for being completely foolish. Every woman in the room wore her hair up. It was the fashion, and Warrick probably wasn't even looking at her at all, while Lord Sheffield was not only looking at her but speaking to her.

". . . at any rate, Suddy and I wish to know from whence you hail. I do not believe you come from Devon, Mrs. Tarrant. Am I right?"

"Yes." She looked to Sheffield, rather mystified. "My husband was from Devon, but I am Cornish."

Oddly, though Lord Sheffield and Major Sudbury each exclaimed aloud, the response Gwen heard the most clearly was the single "Ah" that came from the far side of the group. Warrick sounded as if he had been somehow enlightened.

Lord Sheffield reclaimed her attention by lifting her hand to his lips and saying, "Yes, indeed! I knew you were Cornish, Mrs. Tarrant!" Gwen reacted with such surprise to his enthusiasm, he laughed unself-consciously. "It is so seldom I win a wager with Suddy or Luc that I must celebrate extravagantly when I do. But I knew you must be Celtic, you see. It is all that magnificent black hair and those blue eyes. You've the look of a Celtic princess."

"My, my, Richard." The wry drawl came from Lady Langdale, seated, Gwen saw belatedly, just to the left of where Warrick stood. "I did not realize you'd acquaintance with Celtic royalty."

Not the least deflated, Sheffield replied readily, "Can't say there is any Celtic royalty left to be acquainted with, Frances, m'dear. However, if there were, and if there were a princess of the house, she would, were anything fair in the world, look precisely like Mrs. Tarrant."

The fanciful compliment and quixotic explanation of it made Gwen laugh, and she smiled at Lord Sheffield the rare smile that lit her beauty.

She also told Lord Sheffield she thought him very gallant. He turned a pleased pink, and seemed lost for a moment, staring at her, but Gwen never noticed. Warrick had shifted his position, straightening away from the chimneypiece, and before she could stop herself, she was looking at him.

She did not easily look away, nor could she read his expression. For once he was not smiling. Instead there was an intensity in the look he gave her that made her feel for just a moment they were the only two people in the room.

The exchange did not last over a second. Dabney interrupted it with the quavering announcement that dinner was served, but the length of time mattered not at all to Gwen.

It was the second time he had held her with nothing but his eyes. After the first experience she had thought herself better armed, but the last time it had been the highwayman's gleam that held her. Now it had been a look of such intensity, it had taken her breath away.

Recalling that look too, too keenly as she went into dinner on Mr. Smeddley's arm, she forgot to think about the cause of it, or even, just then, her reaction. She found herself too angry with Warrick for looking at her like that in the first place. Anyone could have noted the way he had singled her out, though due to Dabney's fortuitous appearance, she did not think anyone had. Still, did Warrick mean to look at her so anytime, at dinner, say, with Lady Chumleigh to see?

To her great relief Gwen found herself seated in the middle of the table between Mr. Smeddley and the Viscount Sheffield. If she leaned back a little, she could not even see Warrick, who sat at the end of the table opposite Lady Chumleigh.

The meal was pleasant in fact, and Gwen was particularly delighted when Lord Sheffield told her his father had been an amateur astronomer. She had been thinking of reading some of the Greek myths to her students, and the two subjects dovetailed very nicely indeed. Responding to her enthusiasm, Lord Sheffield promptly offered to take her out to the gardens after dinner and share with her the benefit of what he'd learned from his father. Gwen accepted as promptly, delighted not only to learn what she could, but to have a reason to avoid the drawing room and Warrick after dinner.

But Gwen was relieved too soon. She had not known that Lady Chumleigh had invited Lady Godolphin's daughters to entertain the company with their musical abilities after dinner. All was not lost, however. She knew that by sitting beside

Lady Chumleigh she would evade Warrick almost as neatly, for he would be obliged to attend to his aunt's guests.

Her plan would have worked as smoothly as she hoped but for two things. First Lady Chumleigh sent her to open a window at the back of the drawing room, and second, Warrick entered the room later than the other men and by another door.

The consequence of Gwen's ill luck was that she was standing quite alone and only a foot or so from Warrick, when he stepped through the doorway. Fastening on her, his eyes lit with surprise and something else. She noted the something else and took a step sideways, toward the group assembling before the piano. He slid his hand under her elbow before she could slip away.

Gwen flung up her chin, her eyes flashing, and Warrick gave her a decidedly lopsided smile. "It is the gentlemanly thing to escort you to your seat."

She had to fight the effect of that self-aware, even self-deprecating smile. It crept like a sure-footed cat under her defenses—as did his voice. Its soft timbre unsettled her almost as much as his smile. "I do not care to be appropriated at your convenience, my lord," she said, jaw clenched.

"But escorted with all due respect?"

He sounded the essence of innocence, but Gwen saw the deviltry dancing just at the back of his green eyes. "Very well, my lord," she said tightly, deciding that if her opposition served only to amuse him, she would deny him his laughter at her expense. "You may escort me to the chair by Lady Chumleigh."

"A most uncomfortable seat," Warrick murmured indistinctly as, transferring his hand to the small of her back, he propelled Gwen forward and smoothly deposited her upon a small couch well back of the small audience. Nor could she do much but stiffen when he dropped down by her. The Godolphin girls were just beginning their recital.

When something brushed against her bare neck, Gwen realized Warrick had not only stretched his legs out comfortably before him, but had extended his arm behind her along the back of the couch. From the corner of her eye she could see his hand dangling just above her shoulder. Were he to extend his fingers even a little, he would brush her bare skin.

The couch was for two, really. They almost touched. His arm, half encircling her still, did brush her neck again, and there were his fingers more felt than seen, but exceedingly prominent in her awareness nonetheless. She did not know why she had not worn a thick piece of cloth over her décolletage. His fingers could not be a threat to her then. Nor his eyes. Even looking straight ahead, Gwen became more aware of what her décolletage exposed. It seemed to her sensitive eyes that the swell of her breasts was to all intents and purposes served up for his pleasure. And he was looking down. She knew he was.

She was as stiff as a board by the time Jane and Amy Godolphin made their first curtsy, and then she felt Warrick's long fingers drift casually along her exposed shoulder. He might as well have stuck her with a needle, Gwen turned so sharply, her blue eyes snapping with indignation and not a little frustration.

He did not allow her the time to reprimand him, however. "Dabney is here, Mrs. Tarrant." He smiled oh, so blandly. "Would you care for a cup of tea?"

Gwen allowed herself a fierce glare to warn him off her shoulder, before she turned to Lady Chumleigh's venerable butler to say for herself that she would enjoy a cup of tea, while the music continued. Dabney had a glass of something more substantial than tea for Warrick. When he was served, Warrick lifted his glass to Gwen.

It threw her off stride that she could find little trace of his smile even in his eyes.

"You are as distinctive and rare as the brandy in this glass, Mrs. Tarrant," he said softly enough that no one else heard. "And that is saying a great deal, because brandy as fine as this comes along perhaps once in a century."

She blushed hotly—and wanted to sink through the floor, or better, fling her tea in his face, to hide her embarrassment. How could she be undone, she wondered a little desperately, when she knew he was the greatest rake and must say such things to half the women he met?

"You embarrass me," she bit out, taking refuge in the bottom of her tea cup.

"I spoke no more than the truth, and any man would tell you so."

"Please!" Gwen glanced about to see if anyone heard them and sent up a prayer of thanks that they seemed almost forgotten in their secluded seat. "You know precisely why I am uncomfortable."

"Discomfort, yes, I do understand that, but not embarrassment."

He was being willfully obtuse, and she flung up her head to tell him so, only to find him now grinning his teasing grin. Before she could find the epithet on the tip of her tongue, however, he lifted his glass again. "I might as well be damned for a devil as a lamb. You've the most glorious eyes I've ever seen, Mrs. Tarrant. They crackle with more life than the eyes of half a dozen other women put together."

It was fortunate for Gwen's composure that the Godolphin girls began their final piece then. Their performance muzzled Warrick.

He did not stay silent long after they were done, though. The moment the company began to applaud, he leaned down to whisper in Gwen's ear. "Come to the gardens with me. I promise not to do anything of which you do not approve."

She'd have died before she admitted even to herself that she had a flashing image of something she would not approve. Happily her slight hesitation was not noticed. Lord Sheffield strolled up.

"A fine performance, indeed," he remarked genially. "Sir James and Lady Godolphin must be very proud of their girls. But I cannot say I am sorry they have ended their performance, as I get you to myself, Mrs. Tarrant. You do still wish to see what stars are out?" Lord Sheffield asked, looking with sudden uncertainty from Gwen to Warrick.

Gwen shot to her feet and smiled more brightly than she had ever done in her life. "Yes, yes, my lord. It is not often I've a chance to scan the skies with the son of an amateur astronomer."

At dinner, under the influence of his claret and Gwen's interest, Lord Sheffield had, forgivably, exaggerated. Now, conscious of Warrick listening and not showing signs of the greatest pleasure, the viscount flushed. "Actually, my father wasn't quite an astronomer, you know. He knew a few stars. That's all, really."

"If he knew a few, he knew more than I, Lord Sheffield. I shall learn a great deal, I'm sure." Then, a smile just teasing her mouth, she looked down to give Warrick one of his own, oh-so-innocent looks. "Good night, my lord. Will you commend the Godolphin girls for me? I fear I may not have the opportunity before they leave. . . ."

She had to give the devil his due then. He smiled back at her, albeit dryly. She also had to give him that even so little as a dry smile won him at least a partial victory. She may not have gone into the gardens with him, but he and his smile remained in her mind all the while she was there with Lord Sheffield.

Chapter 8

Lady Chumleigh did not sleep well that night, and, as was her habit, she awakened Gwen to read to her. Clad in her robe and slippers, her long hair in a thick braid, Gwen found Milton among several books on a table near the elder lady's bed, and chose him as being most likely to put anyone to sleep. Eventually Milton did have his way with Lady Chumleigh, soothing her into a sound sleep she continued to enjoy when Gwen tiptoed into her room the next morning to check upon her. After alerting Finch that her mistress should not be disturbed, Gwen sent a message to Dr. Hobson, Lady Chumleigh's physician, asking that he stop by in the afternoon to look in upon his patient. In all probability, Lady Chumleigh had been restless because her nephew and his guests had excited her, but Gwen thought it wise to be certain.

Desiring as well to be near at hand should Lady Chumleigh have need of her, Gwen spent most of the morning in her room, writing a letter to her brothers and sisters. She missed them sorely and looked forward to Christmas, when she had been promised a week's leave from her duties at the Hall. As it was only early August, however, she had nearly four months to wait. Arthur would be nearly fourteen by then; Meg, impossibly, thirteen; Tristan an energetic eleven, and little Anne, all of nine. She'd have missed almost a year of their lives. Six years older than Arthur, Gwen had always felt herself, and acted, as much a second mother to her siblings as their sister. She was satisfied her mother's cousin, Esther Trevelyan, would care for them as if they were her own, but knowing they were in a good hands was not enough. When she felt at a low ebb, Gwen fretted whether Annie was being read to enough, and whether Meg was being encouraged gently out of her shyness. Tristan could be so exuberant. Was he too much for Esther? And what of Arthur? He had been so subdued when she had explained she must take employment away from them. Was he reconciled now?

Gwen had been wise to occupy herself close to Lady Chumleigh. When the older woman awakened, her temper was as uncertain as the night she'd spent. Just sealing her letter, Gwen heard Finch cry out from the dressing room beside Gwen's room.

When Gwen hurried in, she found Lady Chumleigh brandishing a fan with which, evidently, she had rapped poor Finch's knuckles, and screaming at Finch to get out of her sight. "Ah!" Lady Chumleigh rounded malevolently upon Gwen. "I see you are not so occupied with snaring a protector that you cannot come to defend this pitiful drudge. Get her out!"

"I do believe a little sunshine is in order, my lady," Gwen replied as Finch faded into the background, nursing her sore knuckles.

Lady Chumleigh's brow drew down even more sharply. "What's that! You taunting me, chit?"

"Not at all," Gwen said smoothly, and taking Lady Chumleigh's arm in a firm hold, half lifted the old woman from her dressing table chair before Lady Chumleigh could balk entirely. She was still able to complain, however.

"Where are you hauling me like a sack of meal! Heartless chit! I'll sack you, see if I don't! I've not done with my toilette. Ah, at last." She sank into the depths of the comfortable chaise to which Gwen had walked her with a sigh worthy of a mile's walk across uneven ground. Slitting her eye, she saw Gwen turning to go and demanded with a return to touchiness, "Where the devil do you think you are going now?"

"I am going to ring for a cup of chamomile tea. When my grandfather did not sleep well, he said a cup of it refreshed him."

"Chamomile tea?" Lady Chumleigh snorted derisively. "Sounds like some witch's remedy. Where will you find such a thing? We don't receive weeds with our Chinese tea from town."

"No," Gwen agreed, half smiling. " 'Tis too simple a tea to

come from town, but I found a little shop in Kingsbridge sells such things as chamomile and bought some for just such an occasion as this."

With a glance Gwen signaled Finch to go for the chamomile she'd given to Mrs. Ames. Lady Chumleigh snorted as Finch escaped the room. "I don't trust her to get it. Lackbrain that Finch is, she'll mistake foxglove for chamomile."

Gwen bit her tongue against the tart observation that Finch had reason to substitute a deadly herb for a healing one. Taking up a brush, she seated herself behind Lady Chumleigh and began slowly to brush out the older woman's thinning, gray hair.

Though the brushing and the chamomile tea did have some soothing effect, and Lady Chumleigh was in a better temper soon enough, she took luncheon in her room and decided to cry off a dinner engagement at the Godolphins'. She wished, she said grandly, to conserve her energies for her annual summer's ball. Less grandly, she added she'd seen enough of the Godolphins in the past week to last her a lifetime.

With the care Lady Chumleigh demanded, Gwen saw nothing of Warrick and his guests that morning, but Finch reported after luncheon on their activities. While the ladies were making an excursion into Kingsbridge to see what the shops there offered, the gentlemen intended to ride down to Goodshelter creek, which marked the eastern boundary of Lady Chumleigh's property. Gwen did not have to ask what they intended to do there. A part of the Salcombe River estuary, Goodshelter creek was renowned for its good fishing.

After Dr. Hobson looked in and rather importantly proclaimed he could find nothing amiss with his patient that a good sleep would not cure, Lady Chumleigh had Gwen read more of Milton, partly in penance for having summoned the doctor without permission, but also because Milton had put her to sleep so effectively the night before. He exerted the same effect now.

Hearing a soft snore, Gwen looked up in relief, but still she thought it wise to remain within easy call. Lady Chumleigh had been unusually irritable, and there was no guarantee her mood would improve with sleep.

Desiring something slightly more entertaining than MIlton

to get her through the afternoon, and happily certain the Hall was free of the marquess and his guests, Gwen left word with Finch to look for her in the library, if she was needed. Meeting Dabney in the front hall, she stopped to give him the same message, but they were both distracted when a lackey threw open the front door, and Lord Sheffield stepped into the house, dripping muddy water everywhere.

"Dabney!" he cried, obviously much upset. "Get me linen, man, to soak up this mess I'm making. Mrs. Tarrant!" Gwen had not thought it possible the usually natty viscount could blush any brighter, but at the sight of her, he became an alarming lobster color. "Deuce! but it just took this to have you see me in such a state! I hate to fish. I detest the sport, and I cannot think why I invariably allow Luc to persuade me into an expedition. I never catch anything but mud and water."

Gwen bit the inside of her cheek to keep even the suggestion of a smile from her face. The poor man had caught mud and water aplenty. His buckskins and much of his coat were sopping with muddy water. His boots his valet likely would not reclaim. They were caked with mud almost to their tops and made an unpleasant squelching sound with every step he took.

"You needn't worry about my opinion, Lord Sheffield," Gwen said equably as several footmen rushed into the hall with every sort of linen and cloth imaginable. "I have known many men to fish, and all of them to come home wet and muddy at some time or other. I was just going to the library. Would you care to join me there when you are dry? Dabney could bring you some brandy. That should help to restore you, I believe."

Lord Sheffield's color had righted somewhat during Gwen's soothing speech, and he even began to smile. "You are a capital lady, Mrs. Tarrant! I don't feel half the nitwit I should feel. I'll be right along to the library, you may be sure. You'll restore me as quickly as the brandy."

Gwen did not know quite what had prompted her to sacrifice her privacy on Lord Sheffield's behalf. She had not had to do it, certainly, but he had served her well the night before, giving her the means to thumb her nose at Warrick. He'd done something else, too, or rather hadn't done it. For the hour they'd been together, Lord Sheffield had not once attempted to take advantage of either the dark or her inferior status, but had treated her with every respect, as if she were the young woman of good family she in fact was. For that, she would gladly help restore his equanimity.

In the event, Gwen did not regret her altruism. Lord Sheffield was a most comfortable companion, and in gratitude for her aplomb in the face of his pitiable state, he set out to entertain her with the story of his fall.

She was entertained, but she was enlightened by it, too, for the story involved an interesting digression.

"I simply lost my footing," the viscount began. "Would that I could claim something more heroic—that the French navy had attacked me, perhaps, or even pirates. But alas, it was only a pile of slick leaves caused me to slip, and with my hands full of all the dratted equipment required to snare a simple fish, rods and bait baskets and so on, I could not catch myself. I did slip fairly hard, I suppose, and before I knew it I was fairly skating down the hill through all of last autumn's leaves and this summer's mud, my arms milling helplessly, for there was nothing I could catch hold of, and then I was flying off the hillside into the air to land upon my . . . well to land sitting in a waist-deep puddle of extremely unappetizing water. All, you will understand, to the accompaniment of the hilarious laughter of my supposed friends."

Gwen laughed, too, seeing beyond the viscount's lugubrious expression to the wry twinkle in his eye. "I believe that in retaliation, sir, you ought to leave off calling them friends for at least a day. Imagine laughing at you in such a predicament."

"Yes, imagine! And imagine laughing when my contretemps was, really, the fault of one of them. Yes, Mrs. Tarrant. I lay the entire responsibility for my fall from grace at Luc's door."

"I suspected the marquess would be at fault," Gwen muttered under her breath and without much irony.

"Luc and his women," the viscount sighed, adding a new element to the story. Despite herself, Gwen lifted her eyebrows in question. Sheffield nodded. "I think I am being fair to distribute the blame evenly. Surely it would not be the gentlemanly thing to say that the Misses Godolphin were the only reason I fell, though it was to avoid them that Luc proposed we descend a particularly steep section of hill leading down to Goodshelter Creek. You see, originally, we were to clamber down the easiest of inclines, but somehow last night the elder Miss Godolphin got wind of our precise plans, and lo and behold, whom should we espy riding toward that low and inviting section of the hillside? I see from your expression, Mrs. Tarrant, that you have divined the answer. Women are forever throwing themselves at Luc, sometimes with little ill effect, but not always."

"At least the ill effect in this case was not permanent," Gwen murmured.

Sheffield agreed with a chuckle, but his amusement was short-lived. After only a moment he began to frown seriously. "Lud, were it always so! There is a story unfolding now that may not end so well. I am reluctant to say, poor Luc, for the obvious reason that he's so many advantages, but in this case it is all I can think to say. This Season past he honored one of the girls making her come out with an invitation to dance once or twice, though he rarely bothers with young misses. Why he did with this chit, I can't say. Luc's not in the habit of explaining himself, but at any rate, the girl quite mistook the depth of his interest, and got it into her foolish head that he'd fallen head over heels for her and only needed some encouragement from her to declare himself to her father. To encourage Lucian, she'd the inventive notion she would visit him in the evening. In the late evening, if you take my meaning, Mrs. Tarrant. Luckily for all involved, Lucian was not at home that night. He was, er, well, he was otherwise engaged, but his mother was at his house. You can imagine her surprise when a young woman in cloak and mask came knocking at Luc's door some time after midnight, though I think the girl must have been the one truly stunned when she met Lady Grafton, not her son, just returning from some entertainment. Lady Grafton bundled her back home with no one the wiser, whereupon her mama and papa, stunned by their child's outrageous behavior, immediately whisked her back to the tamer atmosphere of the country.

"Alas, she would be prospering very happily there with no harm done, but for the unfortunate coincidence that the young man to whom she was all but betrothed was discharged from the army earlier than expected. Had he come at Christmas, when he was supposed to, he'd have expected to find her in the country, but in July he thought she would be in town and not surprisingly inquired why she was not. Now it is my belief that the real villain in the story is the lad's elder brother. He's a wretch, Mrs. Tarrant, who's never been able to mask his envy of Luc. I believe he accused Luc to his brother, hoping either to discredit Luc in society's eyes or even cause him serious injury, were the matter to come to a duel. And it may, for when the young man asked his love directly about Luc, she burst into tears. You can imagine how that looked to him, Mrs. Tarrant, and now he wants Luc's head. In fact, he's hot enough from the reports I have that we should none of us be surprised if we see him galloping up Wensley's drive to call out Luc."

Gwen did not know how much of the story to believe, though parts did ring true. She did not doubt, for example, that Warrick was often away from his home at night, visiting his mistress, or one of his mistresses. But had he really been away on that particular night? Would he ruin a girl of good family for momentary pleasure and have his mother lie for him in order to escape the consequences of his act?

Gwen knew Miles Dacre would do such a thing.

But would Warrick? She did not know.

Devil it! She wanted to scowl outright, though she'd have startled poor Lord Sheffield. She did not care for her uncertainty and not merely because she did not respect equivocation.

Only a week before she'd have been certain the marquess was capable of encouraging a young girl to come to his house well after midnight, swathed in cloak and mask. Miles Dacre would have, counting on the protection of his name and position, and Warrick's name and position were, respectively, older and considerably higher than Miles's.

True, he had said young girls were not to his taste, but he might well have said that just for her ears. Or he might consider a brazen young girl an interesting exception to his rule of taste.

But when she tried to imagine Warrick sweeping even a seductive young girl off to his town house, and then discarding her the next day like an old, used piece of clothing, her imagination failed her.

And the failure alarmed her exceedingly. Was she giving Warrick the benefit of the doubt on his merits? Was he a step or so above Miles Dacre? Or had his abundant charm and unfair good looks insidiously oozed their way beneath her defenses?

She felt ages older than the green girl who had been taken in by a reprobate's lies at the tender age of seventeen. But dear heaven, Warrick was entire staircases above Miles Dacre when it came to attractiveness. She had thought Miles special only because she had had no one with whom to compare him.

With rather deplorable grudging, Gwen did grant she did not care to be unfair to anyone, including a marquess. Her jurors would remain in their deliberating room until they'd more evidence. She would have to be patient, but in the meantime, she would not lose sight of what she did know. Whatever Warrick would or would not do with a young girl, he would use an older, presumably experienced woman—her, for example, and discard her the moment he grew bored, though, of course, he would give her a generous payment as recompense for his exit.

Chapter 9

Lord Sheffield, of course, entertained none of Gwen's uncertainty about Warrick. Having followed his own line of thought, he said suddenly with unexpected forcefulness, "Gossip has always swirled around Luc, of course! I suppose it's inevitable with a man like him, and one could even argue half of the tales actually add to his stature rather than diminish it. He, himself, has never paid the least attention to anything said about him, but I am not half so lofty as Luc. I am infuriated when people attribute the worst sorts of behavior to him. He's really the devil of a fellow." The viscount nodded emphatically. "It's only that most people don't know him as I do. They weren't at school with him. He stood up for me, you know. Never was much good with m'fists." Sheffield shrugged philosophically. "Knuckles always swelled. But after Luc took my place two or three times, I never had to take a beating again, you see."

Gwen thought she did see very well. The viscount would not have been so different as a boy. He'd have been pudgy, unathletic, and a marvelous target for sharper, harder boys. That Warrick had not allowed him to be bullied was unquestionably a mark in the marquess's favor.

The good mark, coming as quickly on the heels of her internal debate vis-à-vis said marquess, very nearly persuaded the hung jurors which way to vote, but Gwen, in her role as judge, stepped in quickly. A testimonial from his closest friend was not the most impartial evidence. She must have time, quiet dispassionate time, to decide what Warrick had or had not done with the young girl.

Meantime, she desired a new subject, Warrick having grown wearisome. "If the marquess was good to you, Lord

Sheffield, I don't doubt you returned him the favor. You must have entertained all your friends at school with your funny stories."

Sheffield looked very pleased. "Well, Luc and Suddy have always said I've a great way with stories. But my principal contribution to their well-being at school was the food I managed to smuggle from the kitchens. Early on I found an accessible kitchen window just wide enough for me to squeeze through." He chuckled, shaking his head. "Got stuck once, though. I forgot to take off my coat."

As the viscount described his predicament, stuck in a narrow window several feet from the ground, feet flailing and arms waving, Gwen began to smile. "How did you get loose?"

"Very suddenly," he observed so drolly, Gwen laughed outright. She laughed some more as he described how, when his coat had ripped suddenly, he'd shot headlong into the very tart he'd been trying to reach. "Deuced sticky stuff, cherry filling," he finished with such mock solemnity, Gwen was wiping tears from her eyes.

"Well, I see you are being well attended, Dickon." There was nothing in the lazy drawl to cause Gwen's good humor to die completely, but if Lord Sheffield was unthreatening company, his friend, returned from fishing, was not. "You make a liar of me, Dickon," Warrick continued, coming to stand behind the couch upon which Gwen sat with the viscount. "I warned Tony and Frances, here, that you might be at death's door, but it would seem that you have dried out nicely. May we attribute your well-being to the excellent nursing you've had?"

Though he asked the question of the viscount, it was at Gwen Warrick looked. She could not read much in his expression, but there was no highwayman's gleam dancing in his eyes.

"Excellent nursing! Excellent!" Lord Sheffield agreed jovially, addressing not only the marquess but the two ladies of the party who accompanied him.

Mrs. Sudbury was smiling pleasantly, but Lady Langdale looked, to Gwen at least, magnificently bored, though for just a second she thought she'd detected a flicker of something like curiosity in the woman's eyes. Able to think of nothing Lady

Langdale might find the least puzzling about her, however,
Gwen dismissed the thought. A little less successfully she tried
to dismiss any comparison of her plain afternoon dress to the
fashionable rose jaconet muslin concoction Lady Langdale not
only wore, but wore to excellent advantage.

Failing, she admitted wryly her dress looked a rag in comparison to the silk. The exaggeration amused her, and she was
able to say with unfeigned lightness to Lord Sheffield, "Actually your cure has been self-administered, my lord. You took
your brandy all on your own."

"But you suggested the cure, Mrs. Tarrant! And, besides,
what truly restored my spirits was the way you did not turn up
your nose in disgust when I entered the house, looking like a
drowned rat."

Even aware as she was of Warrick, and the two women as
well, studying her, Gwen made no attempt to school herself
against a smile. Sheffield was too genuinely nice. "Well, we
are quits then my lord, for if I helped you, you did the same
for me. I have not passed a more pleasant afternoon in some
time. Thank you."

"And my aunt, I wonder if you know how she does, Mrs.
Tarrant?"

The question could not but be ironic. Gwen shot a swift
glance at Warrick. Perhaps he was not so expressionless, after
all. Now, after that question, she thought she detected a certain
flintiness in his eyes. Surprisingly that coolness took her
aback. However little she might desire it, she had, it seemed,
grown accustomed, to warmth in his eyes.

Still, she returned him a level look. "I know very well how
she does, Lord Warrick. Your aunt is sleeping."

Mrs. Sudbury, glancing uncertainly from her cousin to
Gwen, leaned forward. "Mrs. Tarrant, Aunt Vi does usually
nap at this time? I mean this is quite normal for her, isn't it?"

Gwen was surprised to find she was half relieved to have
reason to look away from Warrick. "It is normal for Lady
Chumleigh to nap in the afternoons, yes," Gwen agreed, but
somewhat slowly. Not to her surprise, Warrick noted her hesitation.

"But?" he said, frowning.

Now she could detect only concern in his expression, and

she wondered a little distractedly, if she had quite misread his mood before. Perhaps he'd only been worried for his aunt. Whatever was the case, Gwen responded readily to Warrick's worry. "Lady Chumleigh did not sleep well last night, my lord. That is not terribly unusual, you understand. She is sometimes restless, but she is not usually as difficult the next day as she was today. Just to be safe, I sent for Dr. Hobson."

Warrick's brow shot skyward. "You sent for her doctor and said not a word to me?"

Gwen had the grace to flush slightly. "Dr. Hobson was to come tomorrow anyway. I did not consider it out of the ordinary to ask him to check on her a day early. He found nothing wrong, but I shall gladly notify you in future, should you wish me to do so, my lord."

"I do."

Now he both sounded and looked arrogantly accustomed to obedience, both of which put Gwen's back up. How was she to know when he wished his pleasures to be interrupted? Though she did not tell him he was offensive, she allowed her gaze to cool. "Your aunt has also decided against accompanying you this evening. She has sent her excuses to Sir James and Lady Godolphin, explaining that she wishes to husband her energies for her ball." So saying, Gwen stood.

"You will not stay for tea with us, Mrs. Tarrant?" Warrick asked, and now the irony in his tone could not be mistaken. Apparently he had guessed the cause of her cool look.

Gwen inclined her head toward the ornate French clock on the mantle and said with a little too much innocence, "It is four o'clock, my lord, just the time I was to relieve Finch upstairs. Thank you, though." Turning to Lord Sheffield she produced a real smile. "Thank you again, sir, for your entertaining stories. I fear my attention would have been sadly flat without them."

"My pleasure, Mrs. Tarrant! I assure you! Greatest pleasure!" Lord Sheffield was on his feet, bowing deeply.

Gwen inclined her head to the company in general, then she took her leave before anyone could say the least thing about excusing her.

Warrick looked in on his aunt before he and the others left for the Godolphins that evening. Gwen was not present. She was dining with Mrs. Ames in the housekeeper's rooms as she sometimes did, but she was made aware of his visit. When she had left Lady Chumleigh, the elder lady had been half dozing by an open window. When she returned, Lady Chumleigh was brimming with good spirits, demanding a card game and rattling on about what a charmer her nephew was.

Distressingly enough for Gwen, Mrs. Ames had spoken in much the same vein over their dinner. The housekeeper had begun by shaking her head over the effect Warrick had upon the younger maids. "They'll make any excuse to go to his lordship's rooms, and they nearly come to blows over which one will take up the tea tray or the claret or whatever else has been called for. He could have any one of 'em, I'm ashamed to say, yet he's never taken advantage of a girl on the staff. 'Course he's little need to," she added frankly. "There's always some proper lady thrustin' herself at him. This time 'tis Lady Langdale. I can't say I know the sleeping arrangements on the second floor. I go to bed before midnight, but I can say I know she's the one after him, not the other way around. Why, 'tis almost a scandal the way she looks at him."

Gwen knew she should not gossip with the housekeeper, but she reasoned that she was not the one doing the talking, and if Mrs. Ames wished to unburden herself, then it was not her place to stifle the woman. Also, she was trying to think if she had noticed Lady Langdale regarding Warrick scandalously. With something less than pleasure, she realized that when she had been in company with Lady Chumleigh's guests, it had not been Lady Langdale who had captured her attention.

"But I suppose I ought not to judge her ladyship or any other," Mrs. Ames continued, a womanly twinkle in her eye. "His lordship is the devil's own to look at, I'll grant. And when he smiles!" She turned a little pink, smiling herself. "I'll confess to you, Mrs. Tarrant, I'd be hard put to deny him if he turned that smile on me."

The conversation had definitely gone beyond the bounds. Gwen was not prepared to discuss Warrick's smile, or its effect. And besides, it was the second time in one day she had to listen to Warrick's praises sung. When she returned to Lady Chumleigh and had to listen to a third verse of the same song, she wanted to throw up her hands in frustration.

Failing that, it was difficult not to admit the day had seen an alarming shift in regards to her judgment of the Marquess of Warrick. So many people had spoken well of him! He had defended the viscount at school; did not trifle with Mrs. Ames's maids, though they were willing to be trifled with; and he took time to charm his old aunt. It was difficult in the face of such praise, and even evidence, not to think better of Warrick.

Thinking better is not vindicating entirely. The jurors, by order of the judge, continued to deliberate, and the next morning they received a bit of evidence to balance at least some of the praise the marquess had received. It was not much, and interestingly, Gwen did not take quite the pleasure in what she saw that she might have expected.

After she had done teaching at the orphanage, she stopped in Kingsbridge to purchase a new ribbon for her hair, her old one having given out only that morning. Taking two to a window to judge their color in the sunlight, she happened to look out and whom did she see?—Warrick, carrying several packages, a Godolphin girl on either side of him. Amy was only darting him shy glances, but Jane was smiling brightly up at him, holding his arm as they walked along. And Warrick? Warrick was returning Jane Godolphin's smile.

Gwen could not see from her distance whether there was that highwayman's gleam in his eyes, but she could see his smile from across the street, and she turned away from the window rather abruptly. Lord Sheffield, she thought with enough emotion to heat her cheeks, ought to see the devil now. Then he would put the blame for his slide down the hill above Goodshelter Creek on Warrick alone. The man might complain about young women throwing themselves at him, but as evidenced by this case, he did little to discourage them, and rather a bit to encourage them.

What a man! A scandal brewing in town; Lady Langdale in his bed at night Gwen suddenly did not doubt; and now broad smiles for the elder Godolphin girl. It was a wonder he'd the energy left to spare to pursue her.

She sent her little trap fairly flying over the road back to Wensley, but happily for Gwen, when she arrived, she was given something pleasant to replace Warrick in her thoughts. Tim O'Rourke came to help her down and asked her if she'd a moment for a charming sight. She was careful to withdraw her hand from his, but said, with perhaps an odd emphasis, that she would very much like to see something charming. O'Rourke's surprise was a new foal nuzzling its mother.

The wobbly little thing was utterly endearing, and Gwen stayed for some while with O'Rourke, listening to the details of the foal's birth and watching it take its first steps. Grateful for the respite, she thanked the Irishman with one of her warmest smiles, when he was finally called away to another duty.

Still smiling, she turned to go herself after a moment, but found her way blocked. Even before she took a step back, Gwen knew the man, though with the light of the door behind him, his face was in shadow. She recognized him instantly by his height, by the negligent ease of his stance, and by something as subtle and intimate as his scent.

Almost frightened by her familiarity with him, she spoke unpleasantly. "Oh! You might have made yourself known."

"And miss your smile, Mrs. Tarrant?" Though she could not see Warrick well enough to gauge his mood precisely, she thought there was a dry amusement to his tone. "Though you've smiles aplenty for everyone else, even a foal, you deny me the pleasure of one."

"Must you have every female in sight smiling at you?" Gwen snapped, resentful of several things but particularly at that moment that her heart was beating decidedly faster than it had been. "I should think you would be satisfied with Miss Godolphin positively beaming at you."

The moment she'd said it, of course, she could have bitten her tongue. Warrick's smile was a flash of white in the shadows. "Have you been spying on me, Mrs. Tarrant? I would be delighted to think so."

"Then you are doomed to disappointment, my lord. Of course, I have not been spying on you. You are the one lurking about in the shadows."

"Lurking about?" Warrick echoed, and Gwen flushed a little, hearing his amusement. He was not, in fact, the kind of man who lurked anywhere.

Too stubborn to reverse herself, though, Gwen lifted her chin in challenge. "How else ought I to term the way you crept up so silently? You have trapped me alone, and I wish you would not do so again!"

Warrick did not dispute her choice of words further, nor did he defend himself directly against the accusation of trapping. "I wonder if you read O'Rourke and Dickon, as well, the same lecture, Mrs. Tarrant? Surely you did not think O'Rourke reluctant to show you the foal when there was not a soul nearby, or that Dickon was eager to rush out for a chaperon yesterday in the library?"

"Lord Sheffield behaved with nothing but respect for me yesterday!" Gwen retorted. "We talked, nothing more. As to Mr. O'Rourke, he could not have known the stables would be empty."

"Does he not, as head groom, assign the chores in the stable yard?"

Warrick might have put the question in the lightest of tones, but Gwen flushed again. "I do not know what Mr. O'Rourke's duties are, my lord, but I do know that I would like to go now. Please excuse me."

Warrick made no move to step out of her path. "I beg a smile in farewell, at least." As her eyes had grown more accustomed to the shadows where he stood, Gwen saw his mouth turn up, when she responded by glaring at him. "No? You are a hard woman, Mrs. Tarrant. What if I said I had not the least notion you were here, when I came? That, like you, I came to see the foal."

Gwen felt the ground slipping out from under her. He had called her a hard woman, but he was the hard one. He was relentless, in fact, with that charm of his. Even had he spoken an unintelligible language, even had she not seen the smile curving his mouth, she'd have known he teased her. His smile was in his voice, lazy and sweet and appealing as warm honey.

"You are being quite absurd, Lord Warrick." From somewhere, Gwen found her brisk, efficient, neutral school instructress's voice. "And now I really must go. Your aunt will need me."

He laughed aloud, genuinely, infectiously amused. "You are not a hard woman, but the hardest, Mrs. Tarrant. I begin to see why Middleman spoke so highly of you. Those boys haven't a prayer of being unruly with you. Ah, well, if I must concede, I suppose I must. Come, I'll escort you to your duties."

"But you haven't seen the foal," Gwen avoided the long-fingered hand he held out to her.

"I've lost all interest in the foal." He grinned brazenly. It was his highwayman's smile, the one that made staid Mrs. Ames blush. "And I wish to discuss Aunt Vi."

Gwen couldn't refuse him that, as she knew he well knew. Little wonder he was grinning like the devil. He moved before she expected, taking her hand and tucking in the curve of his arm. Protest seeming utterly fruitless, Gwen bit her tongue and allowed herself to be led from the stable.

Outside Gwen shot a swift, upward look at her companion, and found him looking down at her, a smile still in his eyes, if not on his lips. Despite herself, she felt the pull of that teasing gleam.

"Your aunt slept through the night," she said, trying to summon the formal tone of moments ago, and found mercifully, when she looked again, that Warrick's expression had sobered.

"Has Aunt Vi been having much difficulty sleeping?"

Gwen shook her head. "No, only now and again."

"Does Hobson know why? Is it because she's changed her routine?"

"Dr. Hobson has only said his elderly patients will often experience restless nights. As to her routine, if you are concerned your visit has upset her, it has not. Her habits are the same as ever. If anything varies, it is her mood. Some days she's a tabby, others a definite tartar."

At the dry remark Warrick chuckled. And before she knew what she did, Gwen smiled back at him. The instant their eyes met, she realized her mistake, but it was too late by then. She had already been caught by the warmth in his green eyes.

The warmth intensified, seeming to dance suddenly.

She jerked her gaze from his. How could she have stared so? Who the devil cared if the man had eyes that reminded her of a spring forest dappled with sunlight?

"Are we racing someone, Mrs. Tarrant?"

Gwen considered kicking his shin. But he wore boots and she did not. "I only wish to return to my duties, my lord," she

responded loftily, but she slowed the pace she'd unintention-
ally quickened.

"What an admirable sense of duty you possess, Mrs. Tarrant. Aunt Vi is most fortunate."

"Thank you, my lord," Gwen said without inflection. "And
thank you for your escort. I shall just go in here, that I may
speak to Mrs. Ames before I go upstairs." She gestured to the
kitchen door, though she suspected Warrick had meant to lead
her around to the terrace and the French windows that gave
onto it from the library.

Half to her surprise, he did not argue. "As you wish," he
said merely, but as he disengaged his arm from hers, he tipped
his head, and before she realized what he intended, he was ad-
justing the angle of her bonnet, a gleam dancing in his eyes as
he presumed without apology.

"My lord!" Gwen tried to back out of his reach.

Warrick only shook his head. "Now you've made me tilt it
absurdly. It won't do."

She'd the furious thought that he would follow her into the
house, still holding her hat, and so she forced herself to stand
still while he completed his adjustments.

"Is that smoke I see coming from your ears, Mrs. Tarrant?"

Gwen was not amused. "Yes."

Warrick laughed. He was like a duck. Nothing penetrated
his feathers! "I didn't want you to look disheveled." Before
Gwen could retort that she would take dishevelment to his familiarity, Warrick was adding, "And because I am feeling
helpful today, I shall perform another service for you, Mrs.
Tarrant. I shall warn you that if you believe you've a chance of
entrancing Dickon into marrying you, you'd be wise not to
dream so. His parents betrothed him at his birth to their neighbor's daughter, and he—"

"Stop there, Lord Warrick!" For a moment Gwen could not
say anything, so many furious words crowded her lips. Her
eyes spoke, though, flashing with such indignation a lesser
man might have flinched. "You, you are abominable, twisting
everything in this way! I sat with Lord Sheffield yesterday because I enjoyed his company. I do not give a fig, sir, if he is a
confirmed bachelor, if he is betrothed, or if he is already married. It is all the same to me. And I shall tell you why so that

you'll not be confused again. Just as I do not intend to become any man's mistress, Lord Warrick, so I never, ever intend to marry again! In the future, sir, I shall thank you to keep your advice and your hands to your abysmal self!"

With that Gwen spun around and marched off as rigid as a tin soldier but for her hands. They were so tightly fisted, she could feel her fingernails digging into her palms though she wore gloves.

Chapter 10

Gwen knew Warrick would not strike back at her for her outburst by tattling to his aunt. He would punish her himself for daring to dress him, the Marquess of Warrick, down. That is he would punish her himself, if he chose to retaliate at all. She did not know if he would. She only feared he might. Most men of his status would have done, but Warrick . . . it frustrated Gwen no small amount to realize she had not the least idea what to expect of him.

She steeled herself for she knew not what, only to realize after a few days that he had decided not only to ignore the incident but to avoid her as well. She did see him, but only at a distance. And that time he was with Lady Langdale, walking in the gardens near the pavilion.

Gwen sniffed disdainfully. Let Lady Langdale have him. They made a handsome pair, and they suited perfectly: both were blond, elegant, and of exceedingly easy virtue.

Besides, she hadn't time to worry about the Marquess of Warrick, and that much was true. All the preparations for Lady Chumleigh's ball that had not fallen to Mrs. Ames had fallen to Gwen. She demanded it be so, for she did not want Lady Chumleigh to tire, and so she wrote the invitations and the place cards; made the arrangements with the musicians; informed Mrs. Ames who would stay at Wensley; and oversaw the decorating of the house.

On the day of the ball, along with all her other duties, Gwen undertook to arrange flowers for the guests' rooms. Not so many people were staying the night as had been the case in previous years, but seeing how busy the maids were, she decided to take the flowers around herself. With Mrs. Ames's hasty directions in her mind, she had little difficulty. When she entered the room of the last guest on her list, she realized Lady Chumleigh had spoken no more than the truth when she had said that Colonel Edwards was a favorite of hers. He'd been given a room almost as large as Lady Chumleigh's.

Two banks of windows afforded a dramatic view, on one side of Wensley's park and an enormous oak close to the house, and on the other of the Channel shimmering in the distance.

The Channel drew Gwen. She placed the flowers on a table near the windows, then went to gaze out for she knew not how long. She missed the sea, she realized. Wensley was near the Channel; she could ride out to the cliffs and see it, but St. Ives had stood on the water that was its lifeblood. From every crook and cranny of the village, she had been able to read its moods and smell its tang in the air.

How Gwen realized after a time that she was not alone, she could not have said. Nor could she have explained how she knew whom she'd see when she spun about, frowning sharply already. But there he was, lounging back against the doorway, his arms crossed over his chest, his legs crossed at the ankles, and smiling faintly.

He had been riding and wore an impeccable hunter's green riding coat, buckskins that fit his long legs superbly, and expensive-looking black boots from the tops of which gold tassels swung. More important for Gwen, though, than the elegant and unarguably handsome picture he made, was the memory of their last encounter. She entertained no regret for the way she'd exploded at him—not one moment's—and she lifted her chin defiantly, just to be certain he knew she did not.

He read her expression correctly, and the light in his green eyes seemed to glint a little more brightly. "You've no right to look daggers at me, Mrs. Tarrant," Warrick drawled softly. "None at all," he repeated when she thrust her rather stubborn chin a little farther into the air in order to be certain he knew she did not care what he thought. "As I do not care for having my entirely well-intentioned advice flung back in my face, I've not the least intention of casting any more of my precious pearls before you. Nor . . ." Warrick went on without pause, though Gwen made a very indignant noise when he likened her, by implication, to a swine and his advice to a valuable pearl, ". . . am I open to the charge of lurking about to trap you alone in a bedroom. I have every reason to be here, and if I am delighted, I must own I am also surprised and exceedingly curious, to find it is you who are lurking about in my bedroom."

"Yours?" Gwen gasped, too taken aback to deny she had been lurking anywhere. All she could think of was how Mrs. Ames had said the younger maids would make any excuse to come to his rooms. Heat stinging her cheeks, she stammered defensively. "I, I thought this was Colonel Edward's room."

"Ah." He smiled lopsidely. "My good fortune is explained. Colonel Edwards is always given the room across the hall from this one."

"I see," Gwen said trying to sound as if she were quite unaffected by either that smile or the awareness that she stood in his bedroom with him. "I beg your pardon for intruding into your private quarters, my lord. I was taking flowers to the guests' rooms." She gestured to the summer bouquet on the table by her, acutely aware all the while that Warrick continued to regard her with lazy humor—and to all but block the doorway with his large, lean body. "I must have misunderstood Mrs. Ames, but there is no irreparable harm done. I'll just take these where they belong."

Taking up the vase, she marched toward the doorway as if it were a matter of course that he would move. But Warrick remained where he was, and finally Gwen had to pull up short or run into him.

Indignant, frustrated, and still very embarrassed, she flashed him an impatient look.

He, of course, smiled as if her mood amused him which only made her the more testy.

"My lord?"

"I have not seen much of you for the past few days, Mrs. Tarrant. How has Aunt Vi been sleeping?"

She approved his interest in his aunt and would have been happy to answer him at length, had they not been standing in his bedroom—his bedroom!—with him blocking her exit.

"But forgive me. You cannot want to discuss Aunt Vi while you hold a vase of flowers. Very nicely arranged, I must say," he added as, deliberately misreading the snapping of her eyes, he swept the vase from her hands and settled it out of her reach on the top of a large cabinet just by him. Gwen was, in fact, more comfortable except that to leave now, she must wait not only for Warrick to move out of her way, but for him to hand her the flowers.

"My lord—"

"Aunt Vi," Warrick reminded Gwen, and if there was a teasing light just at the back of his eyes, his voice was firm. "I wish to take advantage of this chance meeting. Nor can there be any harm done. The door is open."

It was, in fact, but even so, Gwen thought it would not look very good, were she to be discovered in Warrick's bedroom. He, however, was not going to budge, and the sooner she got on with telling him what he wished to know—and what he'd every right to ask—the sooner she would be gone.

"Your aunt has been a little restless, but nothing like she was the one night. She wished her sheets smoothed once, and another time sent me for warmed milk. On both occasions she went back to sleep almost at once."

"Is she ill, do you think, or is it the ball making her so restless?"

Gwen's expression reflected her reluctance to give an opinion on such an important matter. "I am no physician, my lord . . ."

"But you are an intelligent woman, Mrs. Tarrant."

To her dismay Gwen felt a blush rising in her cheeks again. "Thank you, my lord," she returned a little stiffly, "but my grandfather used to say that knowing what one does not know is the measure of real wisdom."

Warrick smiled in appreciation of her grandfather's insight. "He sounds a very wise man, Mrs. Tarrant, but you needn't worry. I ask not for a diagnosis, only for an opinion."

Oddly enough a gleam of some amusement lit Gwen's eye then. The man was a master at cloaking an unbending stubbornness with the greatest charm. Little wonder he got his way so often. "Very well then, my lord, it is my opinion, that Lady Chumleigh's restlessness is due to her ball and also your visit."

"Do you believe all this activity is too much for her?"

"I think it may tire her, but I also think to deny her any of it would affect her far more adversely. Just put yourself in her place. What would you do if your physician warned you might shorten your life by a little, if you enjoyed yourself, but might lengthen it by the same small amount, if you sat dully in your room with only your companion for company?"

Not surprisingly Warrick smiled and said, "That would depend upon who my companion was." But the tenderness of his smile did catch Gwen off guard and perhaps that was the reason she was a little slow reacting when he reached out with one finger to trace a semicircle lightly just beneath her eye. When she did finally stiffen and pull back, Warrick was already letting his hand drop. "I think you've been getting less sleep than Aunt Vi, Mrs. Tarrant. You've circles beneath your eyes."

"Well!" She fought his gentle expression and her undeniable response to it with indignation. "I cannot say I am grateful to be told I look haggard."

A more normal sort of grin curled up the corners of Warrick's mouth then. "There isn't a woman alive wouldn't kill to look haggard in the way you do, Mrs. Tarrant. I only mention your very faint circles, because I am ordering you to sleep late or to take a nap, whichever is more to your pleasure, on the days after Aunt Vi has kept you up late."

It was unnerving to have him look out for her, and to her chagrin, Gwen found she could not quite hold his gaze. "You are very thoughtful, my lord. I shall take your, ah, orders into consideration, of course."

"While you do precisely as you please."

Despite herself she smiled. And looked up at him, too. "Perhaps after the ball there will be more time for naps and late sleeping, my lord. But just now I've many duties that I ought to be about. If you will—"

"You will attend tonight, will you not?" Warrick asked as if he had not heard her speaking.

Gwen nodded. "Yes, of course. Lady Chumleigh wishes me to be near her."

"Of course. Still, Aunt Vi will not need you every second, and as balls are for dancing . . ."

But Gwen, understanding now the trend of his thoughts, shook her head firmly. "No, my lord. Lady Chumleigh's guests may dance as they please, but I am not a guest."

"You are no serving maid, either, Mrs. Tarrant. Aunt Vi will want you to enjoy her ball. And I'll hear none of those choked denials," he insisted when Gwen made just such a frustrated sound. "This is a magical night at Wensley, when it is required that everyone enjoy themselves. On my honor, I swear to you that Aunt Vi will not begrudge you your pleasure." Smiling, Warrick straightened and made a graceful bow. It was the bow every girl dreams her prince will make as he says, as Warrick did, "I hereby request the honor of leading you out for a waltz, Mrs. Tarrant." Only Warrick finished by giving Gwen a distinctly unprincely, hard look. "And don't think to fob me off by saying your waltzes are taken. Sudbury only waltzes with Tony, and Dickon doesn't waltz at all."

"I haven't promised a dance to anyone, including the waltz," Gwen said, struggling to keep her voice from going soft and even wistful. "I cannot dance. Mere farmer's wives don't have dancing lessons as a matter of course."

Warrick stared a moment. Gwen could not tell if he doubted her, or if he were only having difficulty crediting the news that there were entire classes of people condemned to live their lives without the benefit of a dance master's instruction.

She got her answer. He didn't doubt her at all and smiling ruefully said simply, "I regret that, Mrs. Tarrant. I regret that very much."

The sound of footsteps in the hallway came to them both, and Gwen greeted the simple sound with a relief out of all proportion to the moment. Warrick had made no move to touch her. But his rueful, lopsided smile had, and she knew it.

"My lord . . ."

"Yes, Mrs. Tarrant, I know. Your duties are calling." He handed her the vase of flowers, and she left before, she hoped, she had betrayed that impossibly, certainly unwillingly, she regretted the dance they'd not have, too.

Lady Chumleigh's ball fascinated Gwen. Before Lady Llanover had died, Gwen had been to a very few small supper dances with people she had known all her life, but never had she seen anything like the glittering crowd of over one hundred people that gathered for Lady Chumleigh's annual, much anticipated ball.

Every sort of dress imaginable paraded by Gwen where she sat partially hidden by a giant fern but within easy call of Lady Chumleigh. There were dresses of satin, of silk, of taffeta, and of net over everything. Some sported lace flounces, others crepe flounces. Some were demure white, if the wearer was younger, others were of deep, rich hues. Necklines were universally low, though it did seem one or two ladies, Lady Langdale among them, were in particular danger of spilling out of theirs, while waistlines were universally high. Atop their coiffed heads many ladies wore graceful plumes. Others had adorned their hair with jewels; the older ladies sported turbans or soft toques; and a few of the younger ones floated about in long, gossamer-fine veils.

The gentlemen could not claim such variety as the ladies, though they were not entirely colorless thanks to a contingent of military officers stationed in Torquay, who were friends of Lady Dent's nephew, Mr. Edmundson. Other than the army officers and a few older men who clung still to knee pants, most of the men wore dark trousers and coats, waistcoats and stiff, formally knotted cravats. It occurred to Gwen that the gentlemen, unlike the ladies, distinguished themselves from one another more by the physical frame their clothes covered than the other way about.

Which was one reason Warrick was one of the most distinguished men present. Gwen gave him his due, though she had not seen all the men, or even the marquess very often, for seated, she could see only the people who were closest to her, either talking along the sidelines or swirling by on the dance floor. That was how she caught sight of Warrick. He swirled by several times with one or another lady on his arm. The first time he passed, he found Gwen, his eyes meeting hers over the head of the strawberry blonde he partnered.

The moment was over so quickly, Gwen could not say what, if anything, had passed between them. She had the impression he had been looking for her, though she could not say why and even chided herself for an overactive imagination. With all the splendidly dressed women there, it did not seem likely a marquess would be searching out a mere companion dressed in a remade ball gown of his aunt's.

For her part Gwen thought she had conveyed nothing but a

courteous good evening, though she'd a tiny bit of unease on the subject. She'd been prepared for his dress, of course. Like most of the gentlemen he wore black evening clothes, a white waistcoat, and a stiffly starched cravat, but his likeness to the rest stopped there. They lacked his dark gold hair, for example, or his height, or his shoulders. In short Warrick was the only man in the room who looked quite sinfully handsome, and Gwen could not be certain her eyes had not widened like a green girl's at the sight of him.

Whatever had been in her eyes, Warrick did nothing more than incline his head, for which Gwen was immensely grateful. Lord Sheffield and Major Sudbury both came to pay their respects, as did Mr. Edmundson with several of his friends from the army. None of them, however, created the stir that Warrick would have done, had he come to chat with his aunt's companion.

To Gwen's surprise Mrs. Sudbury also took the time to come to speak to her. She'd not have thought Warrick's cousin, who was by the by, related to him on the opposite side of his family tree from Lady Chumleigh, would take time from her loftier acquaintances, but she did, and she proved amusing company, for together they admired the very august picture Lady Chumleigh made.

"I think it is the chair," Mrs. Sudbury remarked, laughing. "It looks remarkably like a throne, don't you agree?"

Gwen could not but agree, though she did not think the chair alone made Lady Chumleigh the grande dame that night. "I think Lady Chumleigh might be sitting on a stool, actually, and dominate the evening. No one else, that I've seen at least, is sporting a king's ransom in rubies."

"They are a magnificent set, are they not?" Mrs. Sudbury sighed rather wistfully. "The Sheridan rubies. I suppose she told you how her husband's father was one of the first Englishmen in India and happened to save the life of one of their rulers? Lud, but he was given a splendid reward! The necklace alone must weigh a pound.

Gwen could attest to that. When Finch had handed it to her, she'd gasped at the sheer weight of it. The set also included a ring the size of a robin's egg, a diadem of rubies and diamonds, a heavy pin, and a bracelet of rubies and diamonds.

"The set will go to Warrick, of course, as he is Lady Chum's heir," Mrs. Sudbury was saying. "Pray he does not marry a redhead who will look absurd in them." Gwen laughed, her companion sounded so earnest, but her laughter faded when Mrs. Sudbury, in her bubbly way, rattled on to add, "Now you would look magnificent in the rubies, Mrs. Tarrant. With your coloring and looks, you'd not only look a Celtic princess, you'd be one."

Marriage to Warrick was not a possibility Gwen would allow herself to entertain even in jest. "And you, Mrs. Sudbury," she said quickly. "You would look rather well in them, too."

Mrs. Sudbury giggled with some pleasure at the thought, but before she could respond, Lady Chumleigh caught Gwen's eye, summoning her, and Gwen had to bid Mrs. Sudbury good evening.

Chapter 11

Several of her oldest friends about her, Lady Chumleigh explained what she desired. "Lady Hinsdale's fan has broken, Gwen. Without it, she is quite unable to carry on a flirtation, even with old Woresham who's been baring his teeth at her all evening."

"Vi! You rascal. I am too old to carry on a flirtation with anyone, and Woresham has not smiled at me once this evening. Has he? Where is he? Let me see for myself."

As Lady Hinsdale peered nearsightedly about the room, Gwen exchanged an amused glance with Lady Chumleigh, then slipped off to fetch the fan. Even did old Lady Hinsdale decline to mesmerize Lord Woresham with it, she could use it to cool herself. Though the windows had been thrown open, the ballroom with its hundreds of burning candles and mob of people was warm.

It was also noisy and hectic, and she paused for a time before an open window near the stairs on the second floor. The summer night's air was gentle and sweet, and by some acoustical trick, though the voice of Lady Chumleigh's guests were muted, the music of the musicians carried nicely.

Absorbed by the lilting music, Gwen failed to hear the man approaching until he hiccuped. Startled, she swung about and recognized a florid, beefy lieutenant, clad in his scarlet regimentals, whom Mr. Edmundson had introduced to her in the ballroom.

She had taken little note of him below, but she did not like that he had crept up on her nor that he was drunk to boot. "You are a long way from the ballroom, Lieutenant Michaels," she said crisply. "May I help you?"

"Helsph me?" he slurred. Gwen would have been more easy

had his gaze been as unfocused as his speech. She did not care for the odd glitter in his eyes. "Yesh, yesh, m'beauty. Couldn't take my eyes off y'at the ball. Followed you, when you left. Had the deuce of a time lookin' for you when you dishappeared, but all's right an' tight now I've found you. Want a tashte of those lips. I like widows, y'know. They're ready and don't need coachin'. Come on then, give old Jack a taste."

He grabbed for Gwen with surprising speed, given his weight and drunkenness. She slapped his hand away angrily. "You are foxed, sir! I shall find a footman to help you to a bed."

"Nay! Don't need a footman for a kish, 'less you like trios." He laughed unpleasantly and caught Gwen as she tried to duck around him. His hot, fumey breath made her gag.

"Let me go this instant!" she demanded, trying to pull free.

He laughed again. "Y'like a fight, eh? Thash good. I like 'em with spirit. Know you're not shy. Musht have had a dozen men with your looks. Do y'want a dance and the niceties first? Ish that it?"

"I want you to release me this instant. I do not dance, but if I did, I would not dance with a drunkard!"

Gwen had ample reason for her anger, but she'd have done better not to provoke the lieutenant. His mood turned ugly, and he'd a brutish strength far greater than hers, despite his condition.

"Drunkard?" he snarled. "Never been in my cupsh in my life. You need a leshon, woman."

He jerked Gwen up to him and shook her when she twisted her head to avoid his mouth. "Stop! Get away from me!" she bit out, thrusting her fists between them and shoving. She took him by surprise and sent him staggering back a pace. Acting immediately, Gwen darted for the stairs, but the lieutenant recovered himself, and growling a vicious curse, hurled himself forward.

Gwen had not been truly frightened until then, when he caught her with the intent to punish her. His fingers dug into her shoulder as he whipped her around.

She thrust her hands up, hitting at his face, and tried desperately to remember where it was old Marta had told her to kick a men to hurt him the most.

Gwen did not want to scream for help. She'd have done almost anything not to upset Lady Chumleigh's grand evening or bring attention to herself. She even considered submitting to Lieutenant Michaels's kiss. Had she been certain he would go on his way after only one, she'd have done it, but when he caught both her hands in one of his and, forcing her against the wall, pressed his body full length against hers, she realized with a flare of panic that he wanted far more than a kiss. Their skirmish had aroused him, and when she felt him pulling up her skirts, she began to twist wildly.

She cried out, too, but he muffled her voice with his hand. Kicking his shin, she opened her mouth to try again, but even as she did, the lieutenant was literally lifted off of her and flung violently to the floor.

Warrick. The marquess stepped between Gwen and her assailant.

"Are you hurt?" he demanded in a voice Gwen had never heard or thought to hear from him.

She was not hurt and shook her head quickly, whereupon Warrick pivoted and impaled the lieutenant with a look that caused the half-dazed army man to cower ineffectually where he half sat, half lay upon the floor.

What happened next, happened so quickly, Gwen hadn't time to intervene, even had she wished to do so. Warrick dragged Michaels to his feet and backhanded him twice hard upon the face. "You sniveling, wretched coward. You don't seem so full of spit and fire, when your opponent's not a defenseless woman!" Warrick jerked the sagging man upright and struck him once more, hard enough to make his head snap backward, then snarled through bared teeth. "I think you've need of a lesson in honor, Lieutenant. Name your seconds. Mine will meet with them tomorrow to make arrangements."

A thin line of blood trickled from the lieutenant's nose. It was the only evidence he still had blood left in him, for he had gone deathly pale.

"S-s-seconds?" he croaked, staring in horror at Warrick, who held him still by the front of his scarlet coat. "I, I admired the lady. That's all. Meant no harm. Had no idea she was under your protection, Warrick. No idea a'tall. I'll apologize!"

"Your . . ."

Realizing Warrick intended to insist upon a duel, Gwen gripped his arm tightly to get his attention. "My lord, I am unhurt," she said, when he looked almost impatiently to her. She tried to speak calmly, but she had never dealt with Warrick in such a mood. Gone was the lazy, teasing cavalier. In his place was a stranger coiled for violence. Even his eyes were unfamiliar, no longer forest green but the color of nearly black jade. "Truly," Gwen insisted. "I am not hurt, and I urge you to consider your aunt. She would be most distraught should an unpleasant incident mar her evening. I do not believe this man is worth upsetting her."

Gwen was not at all certain Warrick would heed her. He stared at her with no change of expression, Michaels's scarlet coat knotted in his fist, and then suddenly he flung the man away so abruptly, the lieutenant staggered backward several paces.

"Leave this house at once," he ordered, his voice low and harsh. "I never want to suffer the sight of your face again, and make certain as well, Lieutenant, that I never hear even the breath of a rumor about this lady. You'll not escape retribution a second time, if I do."

Michaels did not even look at Gwen. He bobbed his head at Warrick as he backed to the railing of the stair. Feeling it, he spun and lurched as quickly as he could down the stairs and out of sight.

Gwen thought the incident closed, until she looked at Warrick. His mouth was set still in an unrelievedly thin, menacing line, and he had not taken his eyes from the stairs. When he took a step toward them, as if he meant to go after Michaels, Gwen again caught his arm.

Her touch seemed to shock him. He jerked his head to look at her, almost as if he had forgotten her presence. Beneath her fingers, Gwen could feel the tension in his arm and realized he was only a hair's breadth from springing after the lieutenant.

"Please, my lord. I would be the subject of a great deal of gossip if you did more than you have. And he did not hurt me, only ruffled me."

Warrick's eyes moved over Gwen, taking in the signs of her battle with Michaels. In her struggle with the lieutenant some of her hair had come lose from the coronet she had braided. He brushed the loose strands aside, and his expression hardened. "These don't hurt?" he demanded tightly, moving his finger with feather lightness over her shoulder.

Surprised to feel pain, Gwen glanced down and saw Michaels's grip had left dark bruises. "Bastard," Warrick growled low and started for the stairs.

Gwen sidestepped, putting herself between Warrick and his objective. "I got those because I couldn't think where to kick him," she said bluntly, hoping to shock Warrick enough to divert him.

The ploy worked to the extent that he paused. "What?"

He snapped the question, as if he had more important things to do than listen to irrelevant explanations from Gwen. "Marta told me once, you see," she said, beginning just the sort of explanation his taut look said he'd no time for. "She said if I were ever in difficulties with a man, real difficulties you understand, I should kick him—or was it knee him? Yes, I think she said I should knee him, but I couldn't think where quickly enough. I . . ."

Through the window, the one Gwen had been standing before, she heard the sound of a horse being kicked into a gallop, and she allowed her breathless explanation to trail off with a shrug. "Actually I did remember, but only after you had thrown the wretch to the floor. Thank you."

Warrick had also heard the rider hastily leaving Wensley. "I think you deserve the wretch's thanks, Mrs. Tarrant. Did you not want him punished?"

"I might have enjoyed belting him myself once or twice, but I didn't much desire to see him pulverized. You didn't have a look of mercy about you, my lord."

At that Warrick smiled a little. The tension didn't leave him entirely, his jaw was still rock hard, but some of the darkness left his eyes. "No, I didn't feel very merciful. He looked prepared to do you harm."

Something tightened in Gwen's throat. Warrick had come to her aid, protected her, when she had desperately needed aid, and he had been angered on her behalf. "Well, he did not hurt me," she said as levelly as she could. "And I may have provoked at least the worst—"

"Nonsense," Warrick snapped, cutting her off abruptly.

"You've the right to walk anywhere in this house without being accosted."

"True, but my tongue can be a bit tart."

Though she smiled wryly, Warrick's expression did not lighten. "Tart it indisputably can be, but deserving of violence, it is not. If I had not happened along, you might have been badly hurt. I'll teach you tomorrow where to knee a man, though I find it difficult to understand how a widow would not know."

The openly curious look he gave her made Gwen flush and find cause to look down to smooth her skirts. She had never seen Mr. Tarrant unclothed, much less spoken with him frankly about his body, but she could not imagine revealing the intimate details of her married life to Warrick. Actually it even embarrassed her to think of them with him watching her.

The next thing she knew Warrick was cupping her chin with his hand and bringing her eyes up to his. "I didn't mean to embarrass you." He looked so earnest and yet puzzled, she felt all the more embarrassed. "Truly," he insisted, seeing her cheeks heat again. "I wish only to assure your safety. Next time, if you prefer, simply scream down the house."

His hand felt very warm and strong beneath her chin, and Gwen had the strongest impulse to nuzzle her cheek against his palm. Immediately she lifted her chin from his hold, but she did smile. "I do have an excellent set of lungs, my lord. And, I . . . I am grateful for your rescue."

"Well at least that is a victory of sorts," Warrick said, a smile finally reaching his eyes and warming them. "If I'd known I would earn such a boon, I'd have come sooner. As it is, I must even share some of your gratitude with Dickon. He's the one who noticed Michaels follow you out of the ballroom, and came to remind me there has been gossip about the lieutenant's behavior when he is in his cups."

"I shall thank Lord Sheffield as soon as I return below, which I must do as soon as I've put my hair to rights. Lady Chumleigh will think I have run away, I have been gone so long."

"You feel up to returning?"

Gwen nodded. "Yes, of course."

Warrick smiled a little, more to himself than at Gwen.

There was not a woman of his acquaintance who would not at least have feigned a profound need to be soothed in his arms.

"Go on then and pin up your hair again. I'll wait for you." Gwen opened her mouth to tell him he need not wait, but Warrick shook his head before she could speak. "Go along," he commanded, but softly.

Gwen didn't argue, and not because he'd have done as he pleased, whatever she said. Though she knew Michaels was well away from Wensley, she really did not want to negotiate a dim, deserted hallway alone again that evening.

When Gwen returned, Warrick was waiting by the window at the head of the stairs. "You look very well, indeed," he said, his eyes meeting hers.

"Thank you, my lord," she replied, afraid her voice might have betrayed her reaction to the caress in his eyes, but Warrick didn't seem to have noticed anything. He was cocking his head as if he listened to some faraway sound.

As it seemed he indeed did, for he said, "Listen."

Gwen saw the faint smile playing about his lips, but though she listened as he had bid her, she could distinguish nothing amusing or even unusual.

Seeing that she did not understand, Warrick smiled with an odd gentleness. "The musicians are playing a waltz, the second waltz to be specific." He held out his hand. "It is an easy dance to learn."

Gwen thought how he had just saved her from a drunkard's pawing. And she thought how it would be curlish to refuse him something so small as a dance.

She did not allow herself to think further than that. She lifted her hand and slipped it into his. It was the first time she had willingly touched him, and despite herself, when he pulled her into the circle of his arms, she stiffened. Warrick, however, had no intention of allowing her to balk completely.

He began to instruct her at once and was careful to sound as neutral as any dance instructor. "The pattern for the waltz is a box. Your right foot leads once to the side and once back; now your left foot will lead to the side and forward. Good. One step to the side, one step back. Another to the side and another forward. Again. Right to the side, right to the back. Good, again. Right, right; left, left."

However successful Warrick was at assuming the voice of a dance instructor, he could not change his looks. Gwen had thought him sinfully handsome before, when he was yards away from her on the dance floor. The only difference now was that he stood close enough to her to rest his hand on the small of her back.

Her eyes crept up and up of their own foolish accord. Proximity ought to have revealed his flaws. Perhaps he hadn't any. She even noticed how absurdly long his lashes were. The soft candlelight caught the tips, gilding them.

How would it feel to brush them with a finger tip? She missed an instruction and stepped on his toe.

"Think nothing of it," Warrick soothed with a low chuckle. "Missteps are common."

Unwittingly he said the correct thing, from his point of view at least. Gwen did not greatly care to have done something "common." Frowning to herself, she strove to concentrate on Warrick's directions.

"That's it. No, don't look down. Learn to feel the dance." Unfortunately, Gwen looked up. His eyes were soft as feather down in the candlelight. When she stepped full upon his foot again, she winced, mortified.

"I am sorry! I fear I'm a poor student."

"I'll not hear such a thing," Warrick replied with lazy amusement, though what he'd have liked to have done was sweep her up in his arms and kiss the chagrin in her sky blue eyes away. "We could as easily say I am a poor teacher as that you are a poor student, Mrs. Tarrant, and as I'm not at all prepared to hear ill of myself, I'll not hear ill of you."

Gwen rewarded Warrick for the self-control she didn't know he'd exerted, by laughing up at him. It was the first time she had turned that smile, the one that lit up her face, upon him, and his breath caught for just a moment.

"You are a very toplofty dance instructor, my lord," she chided teasingly.

He managed to recover. "And you are a very apt pupil, despite your misgivings, Mrs. Tarrant. You have been dancing effortlessly for a full two minutes now."

With that Warrick suddenly whirled Gwen about. She'd not known to expect such a move, and tripping, fell full against him. He ought not to have done it, of course, but the music was ending, and Warrick, quite as accustomed to having what he wanted when he wanted as Gwen believed, thought he deserved at least some compensation for the kiss he'd denied himself.

Nor could he keep himself from holding her to him just a moment longer than he should have. He grinned down at her, too, his eyes alight now with that highwayman's gleam.

Oddly, though, Gwen did not bristle angrily. Perhaps she couldn't be angry with him, given the concern he'd displayed for her that night.

"You are very bad, my lord, to push me beyond my level of competence. Lady Langdale may be able to twirl, but not I. You will let me up now?"

If anything his grin intensified. "I do not much want to."

"But you will," Gwen insisted as confidently as if she had known him all of her life. "You are not a man who would force a woman to anything she did not want."

"Would I, Mrs. Tarrant," he challenged oh, so gently, "force you, that is?"

Gwen became acutely aware of many things all at once: of her breasts flush against his hard chest, of his arms encircling her, of his hands locked on her waist, of his handsome face inches from hers. And most of all, of her blood throbbing heavily through her veins.

"I would regret it tomorrow, if you did not."

She did not know precisely what "it" was—a kiss, perhaps; more, perhaps. At any rate he seemed to understand, for he smiled regretfully. "I'd not have you regret anything," he said and stepped back from her.

Gwen felt oddly lost without him. But Warrick was already bowing formally and thanking her for the pleasure of her company, as if they were in the ballroom with a thousand eyes on them, before he took her arm and escorted her back to his aunt.

If Gwen was surprised by Warrick's restraint, and she was, he was doubly so. He could have kissed her. She'd have yielded him a kiss, at the least. He knew women and had no question of it. Yet, though he'd wanted to have her in his arms since he had met her, he had not pressed his advantage.

Perhaps he didn't know what to do with a woman who said

she didn't want him? He smiled wryly at that thought. Knowing what he wanted to do with Mrs. Gwen Tarrant was not his problem.

In part he really did not want her to regret anything they did, just as he'd said. And in part, he discovered, he did not want her to yield to him out of gratitude for pulling the abominable Michaels off her.

Again Warrick laughed at himself. Most men played the knight-errant to earn a kiss. Gratitude was not what he wanted of this woman, though. Simply, he wanted her to want him. And he wanted her to come to him again and again.

Chapter 12

"I've a note for you, Mrs. Tarrant." A young maid poked her head around Gwen's door, smiling as she held out a battered note. "A boy brought it around to the back. 'Spect he was from the orphanage, but he didna say."

"Thank you, Kate."

The note Gwen saw at once was not from the orphanage. The ornate hand was her father's. Having neither seen the baron nor heard from him since she had delivered his brooch to him, she had thought, even hoped, he had left the county. But if he had left, he'd returned, and he wished her to meet him that afternoon at the shepherd's hut.

Gwen crumpled the note in her fist. Whatever he'd gotten for the last Prideaux heirloom had not lasted him a fortnight! She flung the ball of paper as hard as she could at the wall. Damn him! She was not working to support him, and she would meet him only to tell him he'd not have so much as a ha'penny from her.

Lady Chumleigh had enjoyed herself enormously at her ball, staying up almost until her last guest departed at five in the morning. As a result she had slept all morning, and then returned to her bed immediately after luncheon. Gwen judged she had more than enough time for a brief excursion to meet her father.

She was not the only one riding out that afternoon. Jem, one of the younger grooms, informed her apologetically she could not ride Sir Adolphus, because Lady Langdale had already taken him. Nor could she take Aurora, her second choice, for the marquess had the mare, as his stallion had thrown a shoe.

"There's Buttercup," Jem said. "She needs the exercise,

though I'd not blame ye, if ye didna want her, Mrs. Tarrant. She's stubborn as a mule and cares for naught but eatin'."

Gwen chuckled at the description, given in a thoroughly disgusted tone. "If she's the best you have left in the stables, Jem, then Buttercup will have to do. At least I can be assured she won't lag when we turn for home."

Young Jem grinned. "Nay, she won't tarry, when you turn her toward her oats. She'll run away with ye then, if she can."

Buttercup certainly did not run away with Gwen as they departed the yard. Indeed the mare displayed little inclination to move above a walk, until Gwen used her crop and gave the mare to understand a plodding pace would not be tolerated. It was as well, though, that Gwen was mounted on a slow horse, or she might have missed her father altogether. He was not waiting at the shepherd's hut, but in a clearing in the woods closer to the Hall.

"Ho, there! Gwen! Stop, hinny!"

Cantering on Sir Adolphus, Gwen might never have heard her father's voice, but ambling along on Buttercup she heard him clearly and reined in the mare.

"I thought you said—"

"I did. I did," the baron agreed genially. "But the shepherd's hut is already taken. A fair-haired beauty, riding the gelding you had last time, is trysting there with an unseen gentleman, who rides a fleet-looking roan."

Aurora was a large roan mare, and would look fast from a distance. Warrick was meeting Lady Langdale at the abandoned shepherd's hut.

"Doesn't look as if you like the news, Gwen. Is he someone you know?"

"I know nothing of Lady Langdale's trysts." Gwen shrugged off her father's curious look and made herself smile. "I was only thinking that if she meant to tryst not ride, she might as well have taken plodding Buttercup, here."

"Aye." The baron ran a knowledgeable eye over the stolid little mare. "Buttercup looks rather fond of her feed."

"She certainly prefers her feed to carrying a rider about," Gwen agreed, patting the mare's neck, as she battled to clear her mind of the rendezvous taking place at the shepherd's hut. It did not matter to her that Warrick was with Lady Langdale in that way. She had known he was a rake. Just as she had known her dance with him was only a pleasant moment leading to absolutely nothing.

"Tch, tch, Gwen. You've not listened to a word I said, hinny!"

Gwen jerked up her head, a vision of Lady Langdale entwining white arms about Warrick's neck hovering just at the edge of her awareness. "I am sorry, Papa. What is it?"

"I've been saying, I'll help you down. There's a most delightful spot for a sylvan meeting just a few steps away."

When her father had helped her down, he motioned her toward a clear stream, rushing through the middle of the clearing on its way to join Goodshelter Creek and eventually the Salcombe River and the Channel. Thrusting the shepherd's hut from her mind, Gwen nodded at her father. "It is very scenic here, Papa, but what did you want? I must get back to the Hall soon. Lady Chumleigh is weary from her ball, but she will awaken sometime, and when she does, she'll want me."

"Of course, of course!" He not only sounded jovial, Gwen realized, but looked well pleased with himself. "Actually, I doubt it will surprise you, Gwen, but I wished to see you on a matter concerning what we spoke of at our last—"

"Nay!" Gwen whirled on him. She hadn't any patience at all just then, and knowing in her heart why she was in such a foul mood only made her the more prickly. "Nay, Papa! You can have nothing from me. I have nothing!"

Surprisingly Lord Llanover took no offense at Gwen's outburst. He even chuckled. "Gwen, pet, 'tis fearsome you can look, and that's a fact, but you've no reason to stab me with those magnificent eyes of yours. Here, sit upon this rock. You can take the time to rest a moment. Please. 'Tis tiresome to stand about all the time."

Gwen stifled the retort that they could be sitting in proper chairs in a house, if he were not such a ne'er-do-well. She even submitted after her father made a great deal of wiping the rock clean for her and handing her onto it as if they were at Almack's in London.

But she could not soften her expression. "Now, I am seated, Papa. What is it that you want?"

"Let me see." The baron rummaged in his pockets, while

Gwen observed his patent charade with growing impatience. Then, suddenly beaming and sweeping her an exaggerated bow, he extended a small box on the palm of his hand. Almost warily, Gwen took it and lifted the lid. Inside, to her wonder, sparkled her great-grandmother's diamond brooch.

When she looked up in wary surprise, her father smiled. "It is no copy, Gwen."

"You are returning it to me? How did you manage to keep it?"

Taking a seat beside his daughter, the baron smiled jauntily. "A little luck, my dear. That is all."

Gwen studied the brooch in her hand a moment. He meant he'd made a lucky wager. What if he were not so lucky tomorrow? Would he return for it? Knowing the answer to that question, she asked him another. "What of your creditors, Papa? Did you win enough to pay them off?"

"As it happens, I was able to pay off one or two of the more pressing of my creditors."

"You are free of the threat of prison, then?"

"Not entirely, no," the baron admitted, flushing a little. "But I am closer to being free of it that I was, and having won my stake, so to speak, I wished to return the brooch to your keeping. You make a better guardian of it than I."

Gwen didn't quite trust her father, for it was not like the baron to think of anyone but himself. On the other hand she held the brooch she'd never thought to see again and could not imagine how her father thought to profit from returning it to her.

Perhaps she was too hard on him. Perhaps she had shamed him into acting in something approaching a filial manner. Perhaps. Finally, deciding to give her father the benefit of the doubt, she made herself smile. "I am pleased to have it, Papa."

The baron grinned like a boy. "'Tis a beauty you are, when you smile like that, Gwen, my girl. Any man would want you, if you looked at him so. Tell me, did you smile at any of the young bucks last night at the ball you mentioned?"

Yes, Papa, I smiled at the marquess, who is even now bedding a married woman he brought to Devon to amuse him between flirtations.

Gwen shook her head quickly, shaking Warrick out of it. "No, Papa. I attended the ball to assist Lady Chumleigh."

"Tell me who else attended. I wager I know a few of 'em."

As her father listened dreamily to the people she named, commenting now and again when he recognized someone, Gwen wondered if she'd not stumbled upon the reason he had returned the brooch to her. He seemed so happy speaking of the ball and the people he knew. Perhaps he wanted only some contact with that world, a world that would have been his, had he been even a little less profligate.

"And I suppose they all looked very fine, eh? All got up in their fashionable best?" the baron asked when Gwen had rattled off every name she could recall.

"Yes, it was a glittering assembly," Gwen answered, and thinking it was what he wanted to hear, she described some of the finery she'd seen. "Of course no one looked more magnificent than Lady Chumleigh," she continued. "She decked herself out in her best, which is a superb set of rubies. The Sheridan rubies, they are called. Have you heard of them?"

"Yes, of course," the baron said, shrugging. "Most everyone has heard of the Sheridan rubies. She must keep them in the stoutest bank vault in the country."

"Not Lady Chumleigh," Gwen said wryly. "Priceless they may be, but she keeps her rubies at Wensley in plain sight in her jewelry box. Of course the box is locked, but the key's in the drawer below as every servant at Wensley must know. It is a measure of the regard her staff has for her and she for them, that she has never seen a need for more rigorous security. But speaking of Lady Chumleigh, Papa, I must go. She'll need me soon."

When Gwen had remounted, the baron patted Buttercup. "Take care, Gwen. Don't let this old nag run off on you when she smells the barn. And don't forget, if you've need of me, I am still to be reached by a note sent to the Jack in Dartmouth."

"You are still in Dartmouth, then, Papa?"

"For the time being, yes. I've, ah, met some good fellows there."

Gwen felt a flicker of unease. She knew there were no good fellows in Dartmouth. She almost asked him why he lingered there, but knowing he would tell her only what he wished her to hear, held her tongue. She could not play mother to her father and could only hope that all their future meetings went as well as this, though, in truth, she'd little hope of it.

Gwen thought of her father on her return to the Hall. She thought on Lady Chumleigh, too, and hoped the older lady had not tired herself too much the night before. She composed a letter mentally to her brothers and sisters in Plymouth, and she planned her next lesson at the orphanage. Still, even with so much to occupy her, and there was Buttercup, too, champing at the bit for her bag of oats, still, Gwen's mind played odd tricks upon her.

Midthought, she was presented an image of Lady Langdale entering the shepherd's hut. Warrick was there already, lounging on an oddly luxurious bed. His arms behind his head, he was smiling as he watched Lady Langdale unfasten her dress.

Gwen squeezed her eyes shut, effectively erasing the unconscionable image. He was a rake and a libertine, and he probably was depraved enough to watch a woman undress, but she had no right to think on what Warrick did with his women. And she could not imagine where such a thought had come from, anyway! Mr. Tarrant had never come to her before she blew out her candle, and even then, in the dark, she'd kept her nightgown on. He'd have been dismayed had she not.

Warrick presented an easy target for blame. He was infecting her with his licentiousness. She must avoid him assiduously and be on her guard when she could not.

And when she was not with him, she must keep herself occupied. Upon learning from Finch, when she met the dresser in the kitchens, that Lady Chumleigh was still sleeping, Gwen immediately changed direction and made for the front of the house, hoping a letter from her brothers and sisters might have come with the post.

Gwen heard laughter as she approached the billiards room, but paid little attention until suddenly she realized that at least one of the people laughing on the other side of the door was none other than the decadent man she had been trying to banish from her thoughts.

Just for an instant she doubted the evidence of her ears. It could not be Warrick. Surely she would have seen him, had he ridden from the shepherd's hut to the Hall, but then she remembered he could have taken the path that ran along the cliffs. It was more difficult, but it was shorter, and she'd never have seen him.

A particularly high-pitched laugh came to her then. It was a girl's laugh, not Lady Langdale's, nor even Mrs. Sudbury's. He was closeted with Miss Godolphin.

Gwen quickened her pace, wanting nothing more than to be gone from that place and the sound of that laughter. She felt strangely heavy and unbelievably angry all at once. He could not have left his mistress more than a half hour before, and yet he was flirting with a young girl . . . making her laugh. . . .

The door of the billiards room swung open unexpectedly, and Warrick, himself, strode out, smiling a cheerful, quite innocent smile. Had she listened, Gwen would have heard Mrs. Sudbury laughing now, as well as Lord Sheffield, but she was not attuned to anyone but Warrick.

He saw her and his eyes lit, taking on the color of green moss in the forest that just for an instant is illuminated by a warm, golden shaft of sunlight.

"Hello."

"Lord Warrick." Stubbornly, Gwen did not pause in her progress down the hall and away from him. Nor did she do more than toss him a flinty look, though the way he had said that hello, she might have been a fountain of the clearest water, and he just returned from a week's sojourn in the desert. He obviously had a gift that way. He was able to make every woman he met believe she was the only delight he had encountered that day. But Gwen had the advantage of knowing he'd drunk from at least one other fountain that very afternoon.

"You seem in a hurry, Mrs. Tarrant. Will you not even pause a moment?"

Gwen had expected the surprise, but she could not credit he was truly as stung as he sounded. He had too many other women at hand to care deeply what she did.

"No, my lord. I have been too long absent from Lady Chumleigh," Gwen said, but over her shoulder, and she didn't meet those green eyes again.

He watched her, though. Gwen could feel his eyes boring into her back.

Let him look at her rigid back! Let him see how little his charm worked on her! Let him see how little that dance lesson meant to her—or that moment at the end, when, paradoxically, she had felt like kissing him because he had not kissed her. Fool that she was, she had thought he denied himself. Idiot. He had, she knew not, how many women to amuse him. Well, let him have them. Let him enjoy them. He would not have her.

Chapter 13

"Soon enough death will grant me rest aplenty. Until then, I mean to enjoy my old friends just as I always have."

So Lady Chumleigh belligerently defended to Gwen her decision to rouse herself to dine with those of her guests who had come for the ball and would be leaving the next day. All of Lady Chumleigh's vintage, they were among her closest friends, but Gwen had objected to her employer's decision because she thought Lady Chumleigh looked too tired for company. Though she still believed Lady Chumleigh risked her health, Gwen forbore to argue the matter further. For one thing the argument itself wearied Lady Chumleigh, and for another she suspected what Lady Chumleigh was really saying was that she feared this was the last year she would be strong enough to have her ball and gather her friends around her.

"As you are so firm in your wishes, my lady, let us compromise. Why do you not invite Colonel Rupert, Lady Hinsdale, and the others to dine with you in your sitting room? You'll not be obliged to go up and down the stairs, and your seating will be more comfortable. I will arrange everything."

"Of course you will arrange everything! You are the most managing creature I have ever encountered. Which is saying a great deal as I have lived with myself lo these many years." Lady Chumleigh smiled, and if the effort was rather weary, it was also very fond. "It is an excellent suggestion, Gwen. I dreaded all those steps, actually, and I accept your compromise. It will not be too much for you to arrange after all you did to make my ball go off so splendidly?"

Gwen patted Lady Chumleigh's thin, spotted hand, a rush of affection making her smile with particular warmth. "I am glad you enjoyed your ball so, and no, this will not be too much in the least. I am delighted to do it for you."

And delighted to have something to occupy me, Gwen added to herself, as she went to consult with Mrs. Ames.

Something other than Warrick, she meant. Oh, she had not thought of him and his tryst with Lady Langdale the entire afternoon, but it had seemed to lie in wait for her, so that the moment her mind drifted, she was back to it.

Her preoccupation with the marquess and his affairs unsettled her. She'd no right to be angry or even confused. Warrick had only danced with her, after all. And had once discreetly remarked he would make good any loss she suffered "entertaining" him. She had to credit him, in fact, for his honesty. Certainly he'd never protested he loved her, or was infatuated with her, or even that she affected him more than any other woman. He had said only, if not so directly, that he wished to have an illicit affair with her.

So—he lumped her in with Lady Langdale and all the other women he must have had. And that was his right, as it was her right to dismiss him as a fickle sybarite, possessing enormous charm, dangerously good looks, but no substance. He could not be constant. It was not in his power. She would accept the one dance for what it was, a pleasant interlude, and promptly return to keeping him at a distance.

She set her mind to arranging Lady Chumleigh's dinner for her and succeeded nicely. The old woman's friends, all aged too, were delighted to lounge about in padded chairs, footstools at the ready, as they dined. Tired as their hostess, they were also happy to make a short evening of it and trooped off to their own rooms rather early.

Lady Chumleigh was not done with visitors, however. Gwen was in Lady Chumleigh's bedroom, arranging the pillows on her employer's bed as it seemed she was the only one who could get them just right, but the door to the sitting room was open, and Gwen had no difficulty hearing Warrick's voice.

It was not an unusual voice, really. A stranger would not have stopped, arrested by the sound of startlingly clear tenor chords or some such. Nonetheless, Warrick's merely well-modulated and thoroughly pleasant voice had the power to hold Gwen still for an interminable moment, feather pillow in hand.

"And how do you do, Aunt Vi, after all of your revels? You've not enjoyed yourself into illness, I hope?"

Lady Chumleigh made some reply. Gwen heard only the pleasure in the old woman's voice, not the words. She was waiting intently for Warrick to speak, to learn if he meant to stay.

"Shall I pour you a glass of sherry, Aunt Vi?"

He meant to stay, but perhaps Lady Chumleigh would be too tired. No. Lady Chumleigh chuckled.

"I should dearly love a glass of sherry, Lucian, my boy, but you will have to defend me to Gwen. The chit takes Hobson all too seriously and tries to deny me my pleasures."

"Are you not to have sherry, then?"

Gwen wondered sourly if he were already handing Lady Chumleigh her glass, and only inquired because he wished to know how thoroughly bad he was. But she had misjudged him, for she heard Lady Chumleigh say grumpily, "Oh, give that glass here! Of course I may have a glass of sherry."

She ought not to have several, however, as well as claret with dinner. Gwen considered storming into the sitting room and informing his lordship what a bad influence he was upon his aunt. The old woman ought to be in bed, not up carousing with him.

Gwen did not, of course. Lady Chumleigh would not take an insult to her precious nephew well. Nor would she meekly accept being reined in. In all likelihood, were Gwen to argue the issue, she'd toss off another glass of sherry in sheer defiance.

Gwen lingered in Lady Chumleigh's bedroom, rearranging the already arranged pillows, then stopping to straighten the items upon Lady Chumleigh's night table. She didn't know what else to do with herself. Lady Chumleigh had not dismissed her; as a companion she could not invite herself to join Lady Chumleigh and her nephew even had she been so inclined, which she most emphatically was not; and yet, she could not simply go to her room. Lady Chumleigh had not dismissed her, but had, in fact, required her to remain close at hand in case she was needed. She had not minded biding her time in Lady Chumleigh's room earlier, with only the older people in the sitting room. Then she had not been so wary that someone might look in on her and find her rearranging a perfectly orderly night table.

With a sigh of exasperation aimed entirely at herself, Gwen collapsed into the chair in which she sat to read to Lady Chumleigh. The lamp by it had been lit long before, and at random she picked up the first book in the stack beside it. She did not much care for *A Pilgrim's Progress*, but it required concentration, and attending to it, she could not attend to every word said in the next room.

If Gwen did not hear all that the marquess said to his aunt in the next room, still she knew the instant Warrick stepped into the bedroom.

She could not pretend ignorance, either. Her head jerked up, and before she could even think, she was glaring at him. He, as usual, though she knew very well the lamp by her illuminated the militant expression, was smiling, albeit faintly.

"I am not creeping in to attack you, Mrs. Tarrant." Gwen heard a certain wryness in his voice, but there was, distinctly, puzzlement as well. "I've come to advise you that Aunt Vi wishes you to bring her shawl. She did call for you, but you were, I expect, too absorbed by your book to hear. I wonder what book you find so interesting."

Before replying, Gwen rose to fetch the shawl. With her back to him, she knew he could not see her flush, and she could, therefore, say, as if everyone read it, "Why, *A Pilgrim's Progress*, my lord."

"*A Pilgrim's Progress*?" Warrick repeated in just the arrested, highly amused tones she had expected. "I confess to surprise. You don't look a Puritan at all, Mrs. Tarrant."

Gwen pounced then, spinning about with Lady Chumleigh's shawl in hand. "However I may look, my lord, I am thoroughly Puritan at heart."

Their eyes held. Something flickered in Warrick's green ones. She did not think it was amusement. It might have been anger, even, or perhaps it was challenge, for then he said softly, "Puritans don't dance, Mrs. Tarrant, much less waltz."

"Everyone errs," Gwen shot back, but defensively and she could feel her cheeks warming. Abruptly, wishing only for him to be gone, she held out the shawl for him to take to his aunt, but Warrick shook his head and smiling now, bowed her before him into the sitting room.

Gwen suffered an impulse to fling the shawl at his smug expression, but she resisted such an outright admission that he'd gotten the better of the exchange.

Sailing into the sitting room, chin aloft, she arranged the shawl about Lady Chumleigh's shoulders while the elder woman grumbled about old bones that took a chill even in summer. From across the room Gwen heard Warrick inquire if she would like a glass of sherry.

She finished attending to Lady Chumleigh before she turned to answer him. She had not noticed before what he wore. She had not seen him in deep burgundy. In the better light of the sitting room she could not but remark that the color suited him extremely well. It was as warm as his gold-streaked hair—warm enough to touch.

"No, thank you," Gwen said more sharply than she had intended.

Lady Chumleigh seemed delighted with the curtness Gwen regretted instantly. The old woman chuckled. "I told you she has no vices, Lucian. You may as well give up trying to lead her astray."

The reprimand did not appear to affect Warrick, though Gwen felt herself go hot again. "If that will be all, my lady—"

"No, it isn't all. Sit and have some sherry, blast it, then you won't be looking daggers at me for mine."

"For your several do you mean, my lady?" Gwen asked so sweetly and smoothly that it took a moment before Warrick threw back his head and laughed. More accustomed to her companion, Lady Chumleigh scowled at once.

"You are too pert, Mrs. Tarrant! I'll rap your knuckles with my fan, if you don't swallow that impertinent tongue. See if I don't." Warrick placed a glass of sherry by Gwen, but she ignored him in favor of inclining her head with every evidence of obedience in the direction of his aunt.

As Warrick disposed himself comfortably in a chair across from Gwen, Lady Chumleigh snorted belligerently, "That meek expression don't fool me, gel, and don't think it does.

And you, scamp that you are,"—she rounded on her nephew—"you are grinning like a Cheshire cat."

"Do you know I have never seen a Cheshire cat," Warrick returned with such a perfect mixture of seriousness and innocence that Gwen had to bite her lip to keep from smiling. "But if I am smiling like one, then Cheshire cats must delight in the sight of a woman with her blood up, for you, my dearest aunt, are positively sparkling, and I do like that sight very much."

Lady Chumleigh hurrmphed. "You were born with a golden tongue, Lucian!" Gwen seconded the opinion, but she could not object terribly at least then to his ability to charm a bird out of the trees. Lady Chumleigh had not been so animated all evening. "And I cannot understand why you waste it upon me. I'm not in line to be one of your mistresses, and you know already all I have will go to you."

His dark gold head resting back on his chair, Warrick smiled lazily. "Are you angling for a compliment, Aunt Vi? If so, I will confess that I exercise my golden tongue on you for the simple reason that I am exceedingly, even excessively fond of you."

"Exceedingly even excessively? Pshaw! You've gotten me confused with one of your light-skirts," Lady Chumleigh scoffed, but her cheeks had turned a pleasant pink.

"I think I'll not touch that remark, Aunt Vi," Warrick remarked with a wry grin. "Instead I shall tell you why I've come to look in on you, other than to see that you are well, of course. We've decided upon an expedition to Start Point tomorrow, and wish you to accompany us." Start Point was some fifteen miles from Kingsbridge at the tip of a small peninsula jutting out into the Channel. Higher than Prawle Point, which overlooked the Salcombe estuary, Start Point afforded a magnificent vista of the coast to the east. "Tony is determined to walk the ridge path to the lighthouse again," Warrick continued. "She did it last the year she married Sudbury, and she wishes, in my opinion, to show her handsome major that she has not grown too old for youthful pleasures."

"I can think of other youthful pleasures I would far rather taste again," Lady Chumleigh said dryly. "But do you mean you would have me crawl along that narrow ridge top with all of you young ones?"

"Not at all. Dickon will not exert himself to see a mere lighthouse, however friendly the keeper. He will watch our progress from the inn where the footpath begins. You know the one, the Dancing Mermaid. They serve a delicious bread pudding as I recall."

To Gwen's surprise, Lady Chumleigh seemed to consider Warrick's invitation. In the end, though, the old woman shook her head regretfully. "Can't do it! The mention of that bread pudding had me for a moment, but thinking of the carriage ride made up my mind. I'm too old to bounce and jostle for an hour or more."

"I regret that you'll not go," Warrick said seemingly, for Gwen studied him from beneath her lashes, sincerely. "It was you first dragged me out along that path, Aunt Vi."

"Dragged you?" She snorted dismissively. "As I recall, 'twas you, scamp, who positively yanked me along. Lud, I thought we would fall half a dozen times."

His eyes twinkling, Warrick laughed. "We very nearly did go over when that gust came. Uncle Simon was so angry that we hadn't ducked down behind a boulder, I thought he meant to beat us right there with his walking stick."

Lady Chumleigh chuckled softly at the memory. "Simon always was the greatest worrier."

A comfortable silence fell then. Lady Chumleigh sipped her sherry half smiling to herself as she remembered other times, and for a moment Gwen considered lifting her untouched glass of sherry to Warrick. If he couldn't take Lady Chumleigh to Start Point, he had brought the Point to her and made her the happier for the memory. But even as she had the thought and eyed the glass she had refused for reasons of pride, Warrick, himself, broke the soft spell he had woven.

"If you'll not go to the Point, Aunt Vi, you still must allow Mrs. Tarrant to accompany us. She deserves a reward for all the work she did upon the ball. I hope you do realize how much all of us appreciated your efforts, Mrs. Tarrant?"

What Gwen had only considered doing, Warrick did. He lifted his glass in salute. She inclined her head in acceptance of praise, but not so soon he did not see her vexed expression. She didn't quell him, though. His eyes glinted with amusement, and for the second time that evening, Gwen had an overwhelming desire to fling something at her employer's nephew.

"Gwen knows she worked wonders with the dratted ball, Lucian," Lady Chumleigh reproved, not so well pleased now with her nephew. "I told her this morning. Did I not, gel?" She frowned darkly at Gwen, as if daring Gwen to deny her.

But Gwen had no intention of denying her. "You did, my lady, and as I did then, I shall say now, I did no more than my duty. Certainly I am not fatigued from my efforts."

Lady Chumleigh chortled with sudden good humor. "There's your answer, Lucian! The gel don't want to go. She's being subtle about it, but Gwen's like that."

As if he merely mused aloud, Warrick rejoined oh so innocently, "You could order her to go, Aunt Vi. For her own good, of course. Everyone needs a little time away from duty. The people in your employ have some time to themselves during the week, do they not?"

"But I don't need them as I do Gwen," Lady Chumleigh snapped. "And anyway, she don't need to go traipsing about over sharp, dangerous rocks for naught more than a lighthouse! I wager she's seen lighthouses all her life in that heathen Cornwall. Haven't you, Gwen?"

"Actually there was only one lighthouse in St. Ives, my lady, but I visited it innumerable times." Gwen did not allow her gaze to waver from Lady Chumleigh's, though she was acutely aware of Warrick's eyes on her. "And, truly, I have no wish to see another one here in Devon. I am certain it works much the same way."

A laugh of little humor came from Warrick's direction. Lady Chumleigh turned on him at once. "You've had your answer, Luc, and a proper one it was, too. I'll not hear more from you on the subject. The color's up in Gwen's cheeks, if you hadn't noticed, and that means she's furious, which I can tell you from experience, is a most tiresome state. Now go, boy! Get! You've made your invitation, and she's rejected it. I'll hear no more. I am too tired."

In fact there was a lively sparkle in Lady Chumleigh's eye, but Warrick obeyed her and rose from his chair. Perhaps because she was seated, Gwen, watching him covertly, felt as if she had never realized before just how tall he was—nor how well made. He crossed to his aunt and kissed her wrinkled cheek. "I enjoyed our coze, Aunt Vi. Rest well tonight. I shall see you tomorrow before we leave."

Still holding his aunt's hand, he turned to Gwen. Oddly, for she'd done everything to create it, Gwen found it difficult to meet the speculation, even outright question, in his eyes.

"Good night to you as well, Mrs. Tarrant. If you should change your mind and decide an outing to a scenic spot with people who wish only to enjoy your company would be pleasant, you've plenty of time. We won't leave before eleven, if I know Tony and Dickon."

"I shan't change my mind, my lord, but of course, I thank you for the invitation."

"But of course."

She'd gotten what she wanted. The irony in that last had been as cool as it would once have been amused. Nor was there a dangerous gleam dancing in his eyes. Gwen was pleased. The twinge of something like regret had been for the outing she would miss. She'd have liked to see Start Point, had anyone but Warrick issued the invitation, of course.

Chapter 14

Gwen ought to have realized that Warrick would not long be content to speculate to himself about why she had all but turned to ice the day after the ball. Still, even had she expected he would demand some explanation, she'd not have expected the confrontation as she returned from breakfasting with Mrs. Ames in the housekeeper's quarters.

She was not even thinking of Warrick as she passed the room that had served Lord Chumleigh as his study. It was not a room with which she'd have associated him. Lady Chumleigh's estate manager went there to make entries in his ledgers, total accounts, write his reports to Lady Chumleigh, and in general conduct the business of the estate, and Gwen did not believe that Warrick interested himself in anything but pleasurable activities.

But suddenly there he stood, filling the doorway of the study and observing her through slightly narrowed green eyes.

She was not so startled by his sudden appearance before her that she failed to note he'd dispensed with his coat and cravat and wore only a lawn shirt, open at the throat.

"Mrs. Tarrant. Just the person I wished to see. Come in, please."

Warrick stood back, accustomed to having his commands obeyed without question, but Gwen did not move an inch. She did not want to be alone with him. He was an unprincipled libertine, and he was not even fully dressed. She could see his chest, see even a bit of the springy, tawny hair covering it.

"Unless you've extremely important business, my lord, I must decline your invitation. This is the only time I have to prepare my lessons for the orphanage, and I am behind on them, due to the distractions of Lady Chumleigh's ball."

"What I have to say will not take so long that your lesson for those ruffians cannot wait."

He was the Marquess of Warrick, then. Still, though Gwen saw she must concede, given the imbalance in their positions, she did not give in to Warrick with good grace. Chin high and back rigid, she stalked by him, twitching aside her skirt as if touching him might defile her.

She proceeded to the far side of the relatively small, comfortably masculine room, aware of little but the sound of the door closing the two of them in together.

"Won't you have a seat, Mrs. Tarrant?"

Now he was polite, gracious, and concerned with her desires, now he'd gotten his way.

"I would prefer to stand," Gwen said coolly from her position by the window. "You said we would not be long."

Her challenge was underscored by the angle of her stubborn chin and the snapping light in her blue eyes.

Crossing his arms over his chest, Warrick smiled as he leaned back against the door. "Has anyone ever told you, you don't need a whip to flay a man, Mrs. Tarrant, only those magnificent eyes of yours?"

"Yes. Dozens of trounced men, my lord. Now, what was it you wanted of me?"

Her quip had made Warrick's eyes gleam, but her question doused the light, and he studied her soberly for a moment that seemed overlong to Gwen before saying with unsettling quietness, "I had not thought you would flay me the next time we met."

He had caught her off guard. She had not, of all things, expected him to reproach her in the tones of an injured friend. He almost made her feel at fault.

And what was she to say: that since he had dragged the soldier off her during Lady Chumleigh's ball, she had discovered him to be an adulterer and a womanizer? She had known him to be both all along. She was piqued . . . no, she was not piqued! To be piqued, she must care for him.

"Of course, I am grateful, my lord, for your assistance the night of the ball," she said carefully.

"Are you?" Warrick continued to study Gwen thoughtfully. "If so, I must have done something to offend you mortally since then. You glared daggers at me every time we met yesterday, and I think I've a right to hear the charges against me."

"This is absurd! What can it matter how I look at you?" Gwen could feel the heat rise in her cheeks. For reasons she did not care to examine at that moment, she knew she would not tell him it was his tryst with his mistress that had made her colder than ever toward him, and it incensed her thoroughly that though he was the one in the wrong, she was the one embarrassed.

Warrick gave her a sardonic look. "Come, Mrs. Tarrant. I know you are not so slow-witted as to require an answer to that question. You are being disingenuous. What offense have I committed? You've not got a pet bird I inadvertently let loose, have you—or a favorite dress I did not compliment?"

His mouth was beginning to curve. Gwen found herself watching the corners lift and felt something weaken in the core of her.

But she could not weaken now, alone with him and unsettled as to why, really, she had been so infuriated to learn he trysted with his mistress. Damn the man, she cursed him beneath her breath. If she knew him to be a rake of the first order, he was also devastatingly handsome and so full of charm she felt like a fascinated bird about to fly down from the treetops.

"My lord, this conversation is beyond the bounds, for I am naught but an employee in this house. I apologize if I have offended you, I, ah . . . " Gwen bit her lip. She could not say she had not intended to offend. She would be lying then. "Please!" she half groaned. "You must see that I cannot be more to you than your aunt's companion."

His green eyes glinted suddenly with a new intensity, giving Gwen to understand that "must see" had been an injudicious choice of phrase.

Warrick underlined her error, challenging softly, "Must I?" More ominously, he pushed off from the door and began crossing the room. "In fact I cannot see that at all, my dear Mrs. Tarrant."

When Warrick reached the middle of the room, Gwen sidestepped to put a tall wing chair between them. Her eyes fixed on his, she decided it was time to be direct. "There is no point in our being friendlier. Your only purpose is a night, or perhaps several, of lovemaking, and I will not be your mistress, my lord."

Sheltering behind her chair, she reminded him of an animal of prey. He slowed his progress toward her and asked as casually as if they were discussing nothing more controversial than the weather. "Do you refuse to be any man's mistress, or only mine?"

"Any man's!" she said and fiercely.

Warrick did not blink. "Why?"

Gwen did blink. She had expected arguments, blandishments, protestations, not the single, respectfully put question.

"In marriage," Gwen said carefully after a moment, "the woman is equal to the man in at least one set of eyes, God's. As a mistress she is the man's equal in no one's eyes."

"I beg to differ." Warrick did not smile or cajole or otherwise seek to charm Gwen to his point of view. Indeed, he looked as serious as if he were arguing a point of philosophy with his tutor at Oxford. "Of course she is her lover's equal. They have come together for reasons of mutual interest and affection. A wife can never be certain she was chosen for herself alone, but a mistress can. She brings neither property nor family name to the man she honors. Only herself."

"She brings a price," Gwen said tartly.

Still Warrick did not smile. "And a wife does not?" he demanded, his green eyes steady on hers. "Marriage settlements can run for pages."

"There are marriages that involve no settlements," Gwen replied, speaking, obviously, from experience. But then she waved off her own remark, conceding him his point about his own class. "This is all neither here nor there. It is wrong for men and women to be together outside of wedlock."

"Of the marriages I know, only the Sudburys' and one or two others, are marriages of which God would approve. I do not think He would judge freely given love harshly, considering all the other sins of the world."

"Oh! You twist logic for your own convenience. You know full well for all your argument, that society censures the women, if not the men, who have relations outside of marriage. They are considered disreputable and are shunned."

At that Warrick did smile a little. "In a small fishing village in Cornwall, perhaps, but not in London. Depending upon the woman, she may be considered quite the thing there. But none need know anything you do not wish them to know. I do not mean to set you up in town and flaunt you in the Park, unless you should wish it, of course. I only mean to please you and give you a little security. You say you will not marry again. What do you intend for yourself? To eke out a cold, lonely, isolated existence, serving tyrannical old women until you die?"

"No! I've plans. I've . . . "

Gwen's voice trailed off. She had been so fascinated by the smooth flow of his practiced words that she'd let down her guard. While she argued reasonably, he'd closed the distance between them, effectively trapping her in her corner.

If, a moment before, Gwen had felt secure enough to be willing to argue—theoretically—the relative merits of being a wife as opposed to being a man's mistress, she was not now. She felt skittish as a wild colt that suddenly finds itself in new, unknown, and definitely threatening circumstances.

"Stop there, Lord Warrick!" She backed a step, holding to the chair, as if she meant to overturn it in his path. "You press me too much. I do not care for it. Nor can I understand it!" she admitted in a burst of exasperation. "You scarce know me at all."

Warrick knew when to press his case, and when to ease back, though truth to tell, he'd seldom had to back away from a woman. He leaned his shoulder casually against the wall. True, he still blocked her exit, but he guessed she'd be easier without him looming over her, and with some satisfaction he watched the deadly grip she had on the wing chair relax.

"Not know you?" he echoed, smiling suddenly. Gwen blinked a little at the strength of that smile. Because she had read Milton to Lady Chumleigh so often, she instantly thought of the poet's fallen Lucifer. Surely the archangel's smile could have been no more beautiful than Warrick's nor, she was deadly certain, any more laden with dangerous promise. Though she had reason to be armed against Warrick, still she felt her pulses leap.

And his words were no less dangerous, no less beguiling than his smile. "But I know a great deal about you, Mrs. Tarrant," Warrick insisted, his voice so soft it seemed to curl around her ear. "I know you are beautiful enough that Dickon, no poet, would have you descended from Celtic royalty. I know you to be an intelligent woman. I have seen you be both compassionate and humorous with my aunt. I have found you to be quick-witted, and, from the first, spirited enough to take my breath away. I know, too, that whatever his merits, your husband taught you little of the pleasures men and women can give one another. I would, Gwen. I would delight you. . . . "

Warrick made a mistake then. He wanted her more than he realized and acted before he thought, reaching out to feel for himself whether the skin of her cheek was as satiny smooth as it looked.

Gwen jumped back from his hand, and pulled hard upon the chair. It scraped only a few inches across the floor, enough to put a corner between them, no more. Still, her reaction was enough to bring Warrick's hand down.

He'd never had a woman shy away from him like a skittish colt. His women came to him, opened for him of their own accord. He wanted Gwen that way.

"I must go, my lord."

It was more a plea than a demand. Her voice emerged too low as she stared up into Warrick's green eyes. The sudden intensity in them shocked her, held her breathless for the endless moment it took him to answer her.

"I wish you were less dutiful."

His words may have been what she wanted to hear, but Warrick stayed where he was. To Gwen, standing in suspense, it seemed he fought a battle with himself.

And then slowly, he stepped back.

She moved instantly and had gotten by him when he said unexpectedly, "Oh, Mrs. Tarrant."

Turning, Gwen found Warrick had moved with her. "You looked trapped," he said. She'd understand later what he meant; then he was already taking advantage of her confusion. Cupping her chin with his hand, he kissed her full on the mouth.

Oh, could minds shatter, Gwen's did, into a thousand shards of sensation, all centered upon her lips. His mouth stroked hers, velvety warm and even sweet. Her lips were swelling, her chest constricting. And inside, in the center of her, like a bud ripening into flower, an aching bloomed into life.

That aching, rising need startled her, bringing her to her senses. She jerked back violently to look up at Warrick with impossibly wide, shocked eyes.

He wasn't smiling. He looked almost grim in fact, his eyes as dark a jade as if he were angry. But, of course, he wasn't angry. He'd gotten his way! And he couldn't be as rocked as she was, damn him. He was a practiced lover, who knew exactly how to render her, or any female, breathless.

"You—!"

"It was time you understand what you deny yourself," he interrupted, his voice as low as the look in his eyes was intense. "If you do not wish me to show you again, and in greater depth, what you'll miss if you live your life without a lover's touch, you had better go."

Inexplicably something in the husky timbre of his voice sent a ripple through Gwen. She hesitated, uncertain even if she could tear her eyes from him.

"Mrs. Tarrant . . . "

She whirled then, at that low growl.

Warrick stared for a long moment at the door she had closed behind her. Mrs. Gwendolyn Tarrant was no Celtic princess, but a Celtic witch. He had meant to show her how little her husband had taught her of lovemaking. Perhaps he had. He had no idea, really, what she'd learned, he'd been too busy learning his own lesson. Gods above, she affected him. He'd not been rocked by such desire after only one kiss since he was a young boy.

And he had let her go.

Nay, he had sent her away! Dear heaven, was he growing old? A grim laugh erupted from him in answer. Judging from the desire singing through his veins, he would say he was growing younger.

And becoming more, not less, the romantic! He knew why he had all but pushed her and her soft, delicious lips out the door. She was not ready to come to him.

He stood there awhile longer, thinking about all the women who had come to him so easily. Then he laughed, thinking perhaps the gods had sent Gwen as redress. Had they thought he could benefit from a lesson in frustration? They were teaching him well, if so. But he wasn't done, by any means. She had responded. He began to smile slowly, remembering. Oh yes, she had responded—and been so sweet. Perhaps the lesson was that there were prizes worth waiting for. He grinned then. Perhaps, and if so, he would welcome the end of the lesson.

Chapter 15

Returning to her room, Gwen encountered both Finch and Mrs. Ames. They each said the expected things, greeting her and remarking on the weather, for it had turned quite warm. Gwen scarcely listened. She searched their faces, despairing almost about what they might see in hers.

Evidently she did not look wild or even remarkably flushed. And she made sensible responses, it seemed, though even as she repeated rote pleasantries Warrick's kiss teased the corners of her mind, popping up on this edge, then that, and once or twice surfacing in the middle of her thoughts.

Gwen recovered each time. Through sheer force of will she pinned her attention on Finch, then Mrs. Ames, and cut off any recollection of the taste of Warrick's mouth, its melting, drugging warmth—its softness.

She even managed to complete a lesson. She had to have it for the next day, and necessity armed her against Warrick, his kiss, and the scene in the library.

But the moment Gwen laid down her pen, her mind was free. Free to shout at her, and it did. You let him kiss you, she fairly screamed at herself. The weight of the accusation caused her head to droop. He had caught her by surprise, she tried to protest. It was true. Despite what she knew of Warrick, Gwen had not even remotely suspected, after he stepped aside to allow her her freedom, that he intended to touch her. After all, he had restrained himself the night of Lady Chumleigh's ball.

But then! When he had touched her . . . Gwen squeezed her eyes shut for a half second. She couldn't strangle the memory, though. So very clearly she remembered how still she had stood. Not long. She had been the one to break away, but for just a moment she had stood still for him. There was reason—

reason aplenty. The instant his lips had touched hers, she'd experienced such a riot of the sweetest, fieriest sensations, she'd not been able to think.

She'd been able only to register, chaotically, the feel of him, the velvety warmth of his lips; how they teased hers; how they made her lips almost hurt and swell and . . . It had all been so new! Gwen gave a frustrated groan. Mr. Tarrant had kissed her, but his kisses had been dry pecks, sometimes upon her lips, more often on her cheek. And Miles Dacre . . . strangely she could scarcely remember his kisses after all this time.

Perhaps he had not had Warrick's expertise. Perhaps he'd not been able to hone his skills on quite so many willing pairs of lips as Warrick had.

The thought that she had become just another conquest for Warrick, another dalliance between trysts with Lady Langford, drove Gwen from her room. She would gain nothing by berating herself over and over for her foolishness. But most certainly, she would not allow it to happen again.

Gwen avoided the area of the house near the study. That was not difficult. She used another set of stairs, and came down near the breakfast room, a sunny room on the eastern side of the house overlooking the park. She did not want to encounter Warrick so soon and particularly not with the possibility of an audience. She would need time to meet him with anything like composure. However she thought it safe to assume he'd breakfasted before he went to attend to whatever he had been doing in his uncle's study. Instead, Gwen hoped to find Lord Sheffield in the breakfast room. She did need lessons, and she hoped he might have more information about the constellations for her.

Warrick was not in the breakfast room, but neither was Lord Sheffield. It was Lady Langdale, looking very modish in a lilac walking dress of figured silk, who sat idly sipping a cup of coffee, a plate of mostly ignored toast points before her. She did not smile in greeting when Gwen entered, but then neither did Gwen.

In answer to Gwen's question, she said languidly, "Sheffield's breakfasted already. He said he would amuse himself in the library until we are ready to take ourselves off to admire the windswept wonders of Start Point."

"I see, thank you."

As Gwen turned to go, Lady Langdale spoke, halting her. "I really think I must take advantage of this rare moment alone with you to tell you how much I applaud your unusual tactics, Mrs. Tarrant."

Gwen regarded the woman in surprise. She'd not have termed the expression in Lady Langdale's brown eyes admiring. "I beg your pardon, ma'am?"

Lady Langdale smiled. It was a knowing smile that looked quite right on her. She was a worldly woman, as well as beautiful. Little wonder she would be attractive to a worldly man—to Warrick, for example.

"Yes," Lady Langdale was saying in a smooth drawl. "I am not so petty I will not tell you I think you a very clever woman to play at denying Lucian. He's so seldom been allowed the pleasures of the chase, he's riveted. For now, that is. I think I ought, woman to woman, you understand, to warn you, though, that you'll get no further with him than anyone else. Dozens and dozens and still more dozens have tried to bring him to the altar, and I suppose someone will eventually, but she will be very young, I think, and untouched, and of course, well connected. If you want him, and of course you do, you will have to share. . . . "

"Thank you, Lady Langdale," Gwen cut in coolly. It took an effort to be so collected, but she'd have died before she betrayed any heat to the sophisticated woman who was so obviously trying to needle her. "I shall be quite certain to keep your remarks, and their source, of course, in mind."

Gwen left then, satisfied, at least, that she had managed to erase that worldly, condescending little smile.

Why would Lady Langdale have made the speech, though? She had had at least one tryst with Warrick and likely others. Had she hoped to put Gwen off Warrick, because she wanted the marquess all to herself? Gwen smiled sourly to herself. If so, the lady was doomed to disappointment. Warrick had not been born to be faithful.

Riveted. The word popped into her mind before Gwen could catch it and tear it up in little pieces. This she really did not want to consider. But the word lodged in her mind. She'd not have understood, fully, what Lady Langdale meant before that morning. But now she did. He had been riveted that morning. Just after the kiss, when she had pulled back. Dear heaven, he had looked at her so intensely, she went breathless even now, thinking of it.

And the rough, husky edge in his voice! Gwen clapped her hands over her cheeks to cool them. But she couldn't slap away the memory. That note had resonated through her, making her tremble. Making her go hot, too, and so strangely languid. Her mind had felt as thick as honey and as murky. She'd forgotten to go.

He had taught her his lesson!

Now she knew, as she had most definitely not before, how desire looked on a man's face and how it sounded in his voice. And she knew, as she had not wanted to know, that his desire could stir hers.

But of course it was all natural. If men did not desire women and desire stir desire, human history would have been decidedly short. So. She had had her lesson, and she would profit by it.

She would avoid Warrick, she repeated and not for the last time. And particularly she would avoid Warrick then, when the memory of his desire was so very clear in her mind. And she was blushing fiercely at the admission that his desire had tempted her.

Around her the servants were stirring, making preparations for the excursion to Start Point. Gwen flew to her room, and did not come out again until she had seen Warrick canter down the drive, Major Sudbury at his side, and the carriage with Lord Sheffield and the ladies behind him.

She felt on edge all day, then tensed fiercely late in the afternoon, when she heard the crunch of horses on the drive. She was in gardens in the open-air pavilion with Lady Chumleigh, who had insisted upon tottering out upon the arm of her strongest footman. As Gwen heard the sound of voices and then footsteps on the steps to the terrace, she found herself squeezing her hand into a fist.

But it was a lackey who came into sight, not the marquess, and the lackey had surprising news. At the inn near Start Point, where they had had luncheon, Warrick and the men had learned that a mill between two of the most renowned pugilists in the country was to be staged that very evening in the small town of Totnes, not far from Start Point and half way between Exeter and Plymouth. Immediately they had changed their plans. The men had hied off to the mill, while the ladies had been induced to accept their desertion with the promise that they would be met the next day in Plymouth for shopping and any other town pleasures that presented themselves. Mrs. Sudbury and Lady Langdale had gone on to Plymouth to stay with good friends, the Ragsdales, and had sent the lackey to inform Lady Chumleigh of their plans, and of course, to collect their baggage.

It was a surprising turn of events for Gwen, but not for Lady Chumleigh, who said that Warrick and the others usually did make a short visit each year to the Ragsdales.

The indefiniteness of Warrick's absence unsettled Gwen. After three days she did not know if she was glad or sorry he continued to stay away. At times she felt as if she must have dreamed his kiss and the moment after it, the encounter seemed so at variance with her cloistered, uneventful life. Yet at other times the memory of that kiss would burst upon her so vividly, she thought she must see Warrick immediately to make clear such a thing could never happen again.

Gwen knew when Warrick returned, but not because she heard the stir of the servants or the rattle of the carriage's wheels upon the drive. Lady Chumleigh had sent her to the attic to unearth a sewing box that had the particular shade of blue thread Lady Chumleigh needed for her needlepoint. A remote, insulated place that seemed to cover acres, Wensley's attic housed a dusty array of treasures, and Gwen took her time. She studied old portraits deemed unworthy of the portrait gallery; held up creased, outlandish dresses; tried headdresses with tattered birds and wilting flowers in them; and spun not one but five children's tops she discovered.

When finally she found the old walnut sewing box Lady Chumleigh had described, containing the very thread Lady Chumleigh had remembered it to contain, Gwen bid the attic good-bye and returned to her room. The first thing she saw when she entered was the soft pink perfect rose in a vase on her nightstand.

Gwen leaned back against her bedroom door and stared

blankly at that rose. No one had ever put a flower in her room. Perhaps, she thought, Mrs. Ames had ordered it. Perhaps, but Mrs. Ames did not worry herself with flowers. She'd too many more mundane matters to concern her. It was Lady Chumleigh who thought of the amenities like flowers. Perhaps Lady Chumleigh had had it brought to her room. Perhaps, but there were no pink roses in the gardens at Wensley. Lord Chumleigh had admired only red ones.

Gwen even thought of Tim O'Rourke, but then she heard a shout outside, and looking out her window, saw Major Sudbury with his wife. They were hailing someone closer to the house.

It was Warrick. Gwen's heart missed a beat, as he strode into her view. The breeze ruffled his hair, lifting it for the sun to catch and turn a tawny lion's gold. It was an apt image. He moved as gracefully as a cat, lithe and sure and powerful, too, somehow.

He had given her a rose.

Gwen gritted her teeth against a sudden leap of her pulses. Damn him! He could not do this to her.

The difficulty was that Gwen could not simply summon Warrick to her and tell him that he could not leave her gifts nor, certainly, take kisses as he pleased. And because she could not, she might even have to meet him in company with the rose and that kiss hovering between them.

Agitated with Warrick and frustrated by the limitations of her position, Gwen paced until she could not bear the confines of her small room. Catching up her straw bonnet, she went in search of Finch, who promised to listen for Lady Chumleigh's bell until Gwen returned from a walk.

Using the servants stairs, Gwen let herself out on the opposite side of the house from that on which Warrick walked with the Sudburys. She chose a direction that would bring her soon to the woods, where she could hide until she found a way to be certain she could confront Warrick alone.

The day was a pleasant one, for though the air was warm, there was a breeze that smelled of salt and the sea. When she came to one of the small lakes Lord Chumleigh had had put in, Gwen was glad to rest upon a thoughtfully provided bench.

She was just telling herself for the third, perhaps even the fourth, time that she must return to the house when the man with whom she had argued in her mind for days spoke behind her.

"A penny for your thoughts, Mrs. Tarrant. Unless you are thinking of me. Then it's a pound."

At least he was back to addressing her properly as Mrs. Tarrant.

She leaped to her feet and turned about all at once. Warrick smiled. It was his boy's bright, irresistible smile.

"Hello, Mrs. Tarrant."

Gwen tried to meet that smile and unnervingly soft hello with a cool look. It would have helped had Warrick not been quite so amazingly attractive. Seeing him stand before her so large and solid and real, his green eyes alight, and his dark gold hair lifting in the breeze, Gwen found it nearly impossible to recall all the words that had been in her mind only a half second before.

"Sir," she said, getting a grip on herself. "You may not bring me flowers."

"Flowers, Mrs. Tarrant?" he asked, all innocence but for the gleam in his eyes. "I know nothing of flowers."

"Flower then," Gwen snapped, emphasizing the singular as Warrick had the plural. "I cannot accept flowers or a flower from you."

"Why ever not?" Warrick challenged without admitting to the crime. "Is there a rule about such things?"

She wanted to shake him. Though, even as she had the impulse, her eyes strayed to the lock of tawny hair that had fallen onto his brow. "You will get me dismissed with tokens that you know only embarrass me!"

"Dismissed?" Warrick shook his head authoritatively. "There is no chance of that at all."

"Lady Chumleigh . . ."

" . . . adores you. She thrives in your care, and she knows it." Warrick looked as if he were trying hard to be serious. "Aunt Vi would never spite herself over a flower or even flowers."

"Spoken with the assurance of a man who has never been dependent on others for his living! Please, I do not wish you to send me tokens of interest." Gwen heard the pleading note in her voice and added suddenly, angrily, "Damn it!"

The curse might have been an endearment, given the affectionate way Warrick laughed. "There's the Mrs. Tarrant I know. Damn, but it has been a long four days." Gwen made a choking, at-her-wit's-end sound, and he smiled the lopsided smile that despite everything made her heart tumble. "I should be the one chiding you, not the other way about. You are quick to blame me for this offensive flower, and yet anyone might have picked it for you."

"It is pink! And you know as well as I there are no pink roses at Wensley."

"Pink?" He cocked his head, so obviously teasing her Gwen didn't know whether to throw up her hands or throw something at him. "A soft blushing pink the exact color of your cheeks when you are angry?"

Abruptly Gwen swung away. She could feel her cheeks heating with the blush he'd just described so . . . tenderly. Frustrated beyond words—with herself as much as him, for she'd not felt half so alive in days—Gwen strove to remind herself of Lady Langdale. Had he shared his bed with that lady each night in Plymouth? Or another?

"You may not bring me flowers!" she insisted stubbornly, staring unseeing over the light blue waters of the little lake.

She ought not to have turned her back on him. Warrick simply came around the bench to her. And took her hand. At that, Gwen jerked her head up.

"I'll not have you regret so small a gift as a single rose." He looked more the marquess now than the gallant of moments before, though there was nothing angry about him. "There is no harm in the gift. Aunt Vi might toss me out on my ear, if I brought you sapphires to match your eyes, mayhap, but she won't object to a flower to match your cheeks. Is there to be nothing light and pleasing in your life at all? Ought I to have found sackcloth and ashes for you? I'll take the liberty of answering you. No. You deserve a tribute, and I thought that delicate pink rose fitting, though truthfully I did not do you justice. You are a very beautiful woman, Mrs. Gwen Tarrant."

His voice had softened, as had the look in his eyes, and she felt the effect of both to her toes. Dear heaven, she was afraid she might sway into him. Before she could think twice, Gwen jerked her hand from Warrick's and said almost gruffly, "The flower, itself, is quite secondary. I ought to have been saying all this time that I'll not allow you to press your kisses on me again."

Their eyes held, hers blue and stubborn and wary, his green and softer, but for the gleam just at the back that reminded her of the highwayman who would get his unprincipled way. "I will promise you this, Gwen. I will never do anything you do not want me to do."

He was utterly serious. She could see that she could trust him to keep his word, and she ought to have felt quite relieved. That she did not; that she felt a vast relief when Lord Sheffield trotted up, intruding on their tête-à-tête, was testament both to Warrick's powers of persuasion and her own understanding of her susceptibility to same.

Chapter 16

Mrs. Sudbury was visiting with Lady Chumleigh, Gwen found, when she went to her employer's rooms. She'd have left the two women to themselves, but Lady Chumleigh saw her at the door and waved to her.

"Come in, Gwen. Tony's not saying anything you cannot hear. In fact . . . well, she was just saying that the Langdale decided against returning to Wensley in favor of staying on in Plymouth with the Ragsdales."

Not at all sorry to escape the significant look Lady Chumleigh was directing her way, Gwen turned to Mrs. Sudbury whose bright expression gave no hint she deemed Lady Langsdale's exit in any way related to Gwen. "Frances adores Sally Ragsdale, but I think it is possible her decision was influenced by one Sally's guests, a lieutenant Frances met the night of the ball at Wensley."

"How impulsive of Frances to turn her eye to a chance-met acquaintance," Lady Chumleigh murmured, her shrewd eyes slow to stray from Gwen.

"In truth Frances was not impulsive at all, Lady Chum," Mrs. Sudbury protested with a wicked giggle. "Lieutenant Thornton called at Wensley the very day after the ball. They went out riding together."

When she wagged her eyebrows significantly, Lady Chumleigh chortled. "I take it you mean they rode more than horses, Tony?"

"Well." Mrs. Sudbury grinned, so plainly unshocked by Lady Chumleigh's archness that Gwen, who was, felt the veriest child, "I cannot say definitively what they did, but I can say that Frances made mention of an abandoned shepherd's hut somewhere near Prawle Point."

Gwen betrayed her surprise with a start. Lady Chumleigh caught it and demanded instantly, "Does this news mean something to you, gel?"

"No," Gwen lied with a steadiness she knew ought to shame her. "I saw the old hut once. That is all."

"With someone?" Lady Chumleigh shot back, watching Gwen closely.

Gwen almost smiled, thinking how surprised Lady Chumleigh would be if she told the truth and said she saw the hut with her father. "No," she lied again, but with little regret, for she knew Lady Chumleigh had really been asking whether Warrick had escorted her to the hut. "I found the place on my own."

That much was quite true, and she could look Lady Chumleigh in the eye. Her steady regard evidently convinced the older woman. "Hmm. Well, see that you don't go there with anyone in future. It's been a place for trysts since time out of mind."

Gwen nodded meekly, but did not listen closely at all as Lady Chumleigh and Mrs. Sudbury gossiped enthusiastically about the secrets the shepherd's hut could tell, were it to find a voice.

Gwen did not care who had trysted there in the past, she only cared that one man had not trysted there recently, Warrick had not been the man with Lady Langdale. She knew she ought to feel remorse for how unfairly she had thought of him and behaved toward him. And she did. Of course, she did. She could not but regret such unfairness. She knew, too, that it did not really matter whether he had been with Lady Langdale or not. What he asked of Gwen was the same, either way. He still wanted her for nothing more than his mistress.

Nothing was changed, and yet she felt such lightness suddenly. She was afraid she might be smiling. She was afraid why she might be smiling.

" . . . thrown off my numbers, Gwen . . . " Gwen suddenly focused on the sound of her name. " . . . you must take the jade's place, and for the life of me I cannot regret it. She had nothing in the least amusing to say. How could she? She was far too busy casting languishing looks at Warrick."

Gwen made some remark; she knew not quite what. She

was too distracted by her reaction to the news that she would be in Warrick's company again soon. Coming so close upon her response to the discovery that he had not been at the hut, it shook her to her toes that she would feel such a leap of excitement, and it was simply impossible, though she'd have liked to, to fix Lord Sheffield or Major and Mrs. Sudbury as the cause of that quickening.

It did nothing for Gwen's peace of mind that the moment she entered the drawing room with Lady Chumleigh she knew where Warrick was, though he stood off to the side of the room, speaking to Lord Sheffield. Likewise she could not derive much comfort from her reaction when he finally turned and saw her. The swift, unalloyed pleasure that lit his eyes, though she wore, again, the same blue evening dress, caused more than a quickening of excitement in her. In fact it was all Gwen could do to return him a level greeting and turn away to chat with Mrs. Sudbury.

Still, though she was acutely aware of Warrick—and could not seem to cease repeating Mrs. Sudbury's revelation to herself—Gwen managed to enjoy herself that evening. Without Lady Langdale, the group was more relaxed. There was a great deal of talk about other summers, especially the more hilarious contretemps into which they had all fallen at one or another time, and Gwen found herself laughing as she had not done before with the group as a whole.

It was Major Sudbury turned the conversation to present-day matters. Gwen had learned earlier from his wife that the major had returned from Plymouth with a new mount. She learned that evening that the Godolphins had also been in Plymouth, and that Sir James had purchased a roan at the same sale.

"There must have been a surfeit of good 'uns if Sir James bought, too," Lady Chumleigh remarked. "Are the horses equal, Suddy, or are you a better judge of horseflesh than Sir James?"

Major Sudbury laughed. "Shame on you, Lady Chum, you would have me boast on myself. But you won't be in doubt long, actually. Sir James challenged me, and Luc, too, I might add, to race tomorrow."

"Splendid!" Lady Chumleigh exclaimed, looking to her

nephew who smiled at her enthusiasm. "You will do your racing here as always?"

"We hoped you would not mind," Warrick remarked with an ironic twinkle in his eye, and then explained to Gwen that it was a tradition to hold neighborhood races at Wensley because the semicircular drive was exactly half a mile long.

"The drive makes a perfect course," Lord Sheffield chimed in. "As there are no trees on the inside, the spectators have a perfect view of the entire race."

"We must invite Squire Bentham," Lady Chumleigh mused. "He loves a race, and, of course, Hermione and young Edmundson."

At the end of the evening, when the plans for the race had been completed, Warrick walked Lady Chumleigh to her room. Her guard down a little, for he had directed no undue attention to her the entire evening, Gwen was not prepared, when, after he bid his aunt adieu, Warrick took her hand and raised it to his lips.

"Now, now, don't stiffen, Mrs. Tarrant," he chided softly. "If I must report I could not even persuade you surrender so little as your hand, I fear I stand in grave danger of losing my reputation as a nonpareil."

"I think you fear quite needlessly, my lord. I very much doubt such a disaster could befall you," Gwen replied, trying for tartness, but failing so utterly, she teased instead.

She also made no effort to wrest her hand from his. Warrick kissed it, never taking his eyes from hers, "I enjoyed the evening very much, Mrs. Tarrant."

He did not say it, but his eyes conveyed he had enjoyed the evening because Gwen was there.

She inclined her head, and said what she had not meant to say at all, "So did I, my lord."

The atmosphere before the race was festive indeed. Close to twenty people had gathered on Wensley's front lawn to see who had made the better purchase in Plymouth and whether either mount was as swift as Warrick's Ares. Mr. Edmundson singled Gwen out at once. She received him politely enough, for he was a pleasant young man, but he was not so nice that she did not murmur something vague about a duty she must perform for Lady Chumleigh. With some amusement, Gwen observed that Mr. Edmundson took his dismissal in stride. He went directly from her to another eligible lady.

Seeing that he chose Amy Godolphin over her elder sister, Gwen decided Mr. Edmundson was no fool. Since the beginning of the afternoon Jane had had eyes for only one man.

She was an appealing girl, with curly brown hair, and large, bright hazel eyes. More self-confident and sociable than her sister, she talked easily with everyone present, but Gwen saw whom Jane Godolphin's eyes followed as Lady Chumleigh's guests enjoyed refreshments before the start of the race. And Jane seemed to be the only guest not disappointed when Warrick announced after a hushed consultation with Tim O'Rourke that Ares could not race, as he had been favoring his hind right leg since he'd been exercised that morning and had not improved.

While everyone else groaned, Jane went to Warrick to protest how sorry she was but with such patent falseness she was almost amusing. Then she slipped her arm through the marquess's and said more convincingly, "But I am glad, at least, this means we may keep you with us."

Gwen felt an unpleasant catch in her chest when Warrick smiled down at the girl. It was obvious he liked her. His smile was not forced. Did he consider Jane for his wife? Gwen could only note that whether he did or not, Warrick did not remain with her long. Within a few minutes he detached himself from her and went off to speak to Squire Bentham and his wife.

Soon after, amidst a great deal of shouted advice and last-minute wagering, the two horses that would race were led out to the drive. Excited, Gwen stood to judge them for herself and did not realize Warrick had come up behind her until he spoke almost in her ear. "Were you racing today, Mrs. Tarrant, I'd wager on you to win, even were you mounted on nothing better than Sir Adolphus."

Though, or perhaps because, her heart had leaped when Warrick spoke, Gwen kept her regard on the horses, "I imagine I would have some chance to win, my lord, so long, of course, as I suffered no interference."

He laughed aloud. Gwen could almost see the flash of his white smile, but Lady Chumleigh harrumphed that while they were amusing themselves sparring, they were neglecting her and she could not see, as she could not stand without aid.

"That is precisely why I have come, Aunt Vi," Warrick responded good-humoredly. "I am going to take you to the steps, where Mrs. Tarrant had the foresight to arrange an excellent place for you. You'll be able to see the entire race from a comfortable chair."

Lady Chumleigh was delighted with the arrangement. Because the steps were higher than the lawn, she would not have to stand, but perhaps because she wished to separate Warrick from Gwen, she gruffly sent her nephew back to her guests across the drive. "If you do not return, Jane Godolphin will follow you here, and she prattles so, I'll miss the race. Go on now, and while you are there you might advise the chit to help her brother's nurse mind his children, for her charming nephews would be badly hurt, if they got in the way of one of these horses."

The boys were rolling a ball to each other at the back of the crowd. Gwen could just see them with their nurse. She also watched Warrick say something to Thomas Godolphin's wife, rather than Jane Godolphin, but then Squire Bentham blew a horn, calling the contestants to the starting line, and she dismissed the boys and even the marquess from her mind.

Lord Sheffield stepped forward, cocked the starting gun, then pulled the trigger and the two horses leaped forward as if they had been hit. They were well matched. If Sir James's roan looked a little stronger, Major Sudbury's chestnut stallion was younger and fresher.

Neck and neck they rounded the first turn, cutting across the lawn at the far end of the drive, avoiding the public road where there might be traffic. Major Sudbury began to edge ahead as they galloped back up the drive toward the starting line, but Sir James used his crop and the roan strained to meet the challenge.

Her eyes upon the horses, Gwen did not see anything amiss, until Lady Chumleigh clutched her hand and cried aloud, "Oh no! Dear God! Doesn't someone see him?"

Looking where Lady Chumleigh pointed, Gwen saw that the oldest Godolphin boy had toddled away from his nurse, who was watching the race. He was drawing dangerously near the drive, and she yelled frantically, but no one heard her over the thunder of the horses and the cheers of the onlookers. As Gwen watched in horror, the little boy stepped out on the drive itself, perhaps because he wanted to get a better look, she didn't know. What happened next happened so quickly, she could scarcely take in what occurred.

Sir James saw his grandson directly ahead of him and tried to pull up. At the unexpected jerk on the reins, the roan reared wildly and would have come down right on the boy, but from nowhere, as it seemed to Gwen, Warrick dove for the child, and managed to fling him out of the path of the horse's hooves. To avoid the hooves himself, Warrick rolled when he hit the ground, but he was not entirely successful. The roan caught his shoulder, stunning him so he lay senseless.

Gwen flew across the drive to Warrick. She thought the horse had struck him on the head, he lay so still, and her breath caught in her lungs until she got close enough to see blood oozing from a jagged tear across the shoulder of his coat.

She was the first person to reach him, but soon all the race-goers crowded around him. Gwen looked up from where she knelt and fastened upon Lord Sheffield. "Your neckcloth, my lord." The viscount was undoing his cravat before Gwen had done speaking. She applied it to Warrick's wound, pressing hard as Dr. Penryw in St. Ives had taught her, but there were so many people pushing close, she found it difficult to work.

Gwen looked up swiftly. "Stand back! Lord Warrick must breathe."

She'd authority in her voice. The crowd stepped back as one, and those who did not retreat far enough found Sheffield almost pushing them. Only Mrs. Sudbury remained, kneeling on the opposite side of Warrick from Gwen. "My lord?" Gwen leaned down to look at Warrick's face while with careful fingers, she explored his head for an unseen cut or swelling. Beneath his light tan, he looked very pale. "My lord?"

"Mmm?"

Though he sounded sluggish, Gwen drew a breath of relief that he was at least conscious. He moved. She saw his back expand as if he took a deep breath, and then he heaved himself up and sat back on his heels.

Gwen held out the neckcloth and gestured to his shoulder.

"You are bleeding, my lord." Understanding, he took the neck-cloth and applied it to his injury himself. "Can you walk to the house?" she asked, watching him carefully. "Or do you need to be supported?"

Gwen discovered then that Warrick was not so injured he could not meet her eyes and smile, if faintly. "I would be delighted by your support, Mrs. Tarrant," he managed to say, lessening Gwen's anxiety for him significantly, though she could see his quip required a good deal of effort, and his smile faded almost as quickly as it appeared.

"Actually I do believe I need some assistance to stand," Warrick said a moment later with something like surprise. "Dickon?"

Lord Sheffield held out his hand at once and though Warrick grimaced, pulled the marquess to his feet. Immediately the crowd, virtually everyone who had come for the race, pushed forward, talking all at once to inquire about him, and in the case of the Godolphins, to express their most fervent thanks as well as their deepest regret.

Gwen watched Warrick. He tried to smile and dismiss his injury as nothing, but when he swayed visibly, she stepped forward without apology. The man was hurt.

"Lord Warrick, your wound should be cleaned at once. You risk infection otherwise."

Gwen did not think she imagined that Warrick's expression softened momentarily, but she could not have said for certain, and anyway she'd other things to think of when he nodded. "Lead the way, Mrs. Tarrant."

Without a second thought, Gwen did just that, causing the crowd to part as she made briskly for the steps. She did not look back, but hearing several pairs of feet crunching upon the gravel, guessed that Lord Sheffield, and perhaps even Major Sudbury, accompanied Warrick. Inside the house Gwen left the three men to make their way to the marquess's room, while she went to gather the things she would need.

When Gwen entered Warrick's room, accompanied by two maids bearing the supplies, she did not mark that he was alone. He sat back on his bed, supported by a raft of pillows, and she studied him anxiously. Though his color was more normal, his set expression indicated he was in considerable pain. Someone had helped him take off his ruined coat and shirt, but concerned with his injury, Gwen gave little thought to Warrick's state of dress.

Lifting away Sheffield's bloody neckcloth, she saw that the edge of the stallion's shoe had caught Warrick at just the right angle to rip a long tear along his shoulder. But as she told him, he was lucky. Though there was considerable bruising and his shoulder would be stiff and sore for some time, the cut was not deep enough to require stitching.

Working in silence, Gwen washed Warrick's wound and then began to apply basilicum powder to it. "I am sorry to hurt you, my lord," she said when she saw him wince, "but it is necessary to clean the wound."

"And I thought you might enjoy dealing me a little pain." Warrick's strained expression lightened into something approaching a smile, when Gwen looked a little taken aback. "I was only making a very poor joke. Please continue. I would rather be hurt a little now than suffer an infection. And you've a very soothing touch, Mrs. Tarrant."

It was then, as their eyes met and held, that Gwen realized how quiet the room was. Abruptly her hands suspended over his wound, she looked about. "Where are Major Sudbury and Lord Sheffield?"

Warrick chuckled, albeit softly. "You needn't look so wary. My condition does not lend itself to amorous advances at the moment. As to Sudbury and Dickon, they were fretting so I sent them away."

Gwen simply hadn't the heart to make an issue of their being alone together. He was in pain with a badly bruised, torn shoulder, and if Lady Chumleigh was displeased, she would simply tell the older woman she had thought it more important that she attend to Lord Warrick than to the proprieties.

Chapter 17

It was one thing to maintain that Warrick's injury made it perfectly acceptable, and safe, for her to be alone with him, but quite another for Gwen to return with a mental snap of her fingers to thinking of him as nothing but her patient.

As she leaned over him, looping a bandage over his shoulder and under his arm, she caught a faint scent of sandalwood, and for as little reason as that Gwen became truly aware how he was dressed, or not dressed as it happened. He still wore his buckskins, but above the waist Warrick wore nothing but a dressing gown someone had draped over his good shoulder.

Beneath her fingers, his bare skin felt smooth and supple and warm enough to invite stroking. She took in the breadth of the shoulder on which she worked and then her eyes slipped to his chest. She'd a full view now of the tawny, curling hair she'd only glimpsed that day in the study. From nowhere a curiosity about how that springy hair would feel to her finger tips popped into her head, then guiltily she jerked her gaze away. It landed upon his back, which she saw tapered to a V at his waist. She had known Warrick was lean. She had seen him in the lawn shirt, but she had not known of the long straight furrow his spine made.

A leaping impulse to run her finger down the length of that furrow sent Gwen's eyes flying back to the bandage she had nearly completed. She needed only to tie it and managed to do so, though her fingers seemed suddenly thick and clumsy as boards. In the quiet of the room, she became acutely aware of her own breathing. It sounded embarrassingly loud and rapid. By contrast, her voice, when she asked how his bandage felt, sounded so low she had to clear her throat.

Warrick lifted his arm, flexing it to test the bandage, and

Gwen's mouth went a little dry as she watched the play of the muscles beneath the sleek skin of his back.

"It feels right," Warrick said. "I thank you, Mrs. Tarrant." He looked up at her, but Gwen reached behind him to find the arm of his robe and hold it out for him.

As Warrick shrugged into it, she stepped away to pick up the tray with the bandages and basilicum powder. When she held the tray before her, and only then, did she face Warrick. He had not belted the robe. It hung open, revealing a chest that was as powerful and clearly defined as any statue of a young Greek god.

Swallowing, Gwen controlled herself, forcing her eyes up to Warrick's. He was not smiling at all. Nor were his green eyes dancing.

"I wish you to stay with me," he said directly.

Gwen had to think to breathe evenly. She did not want to go; did not want to leave the hushed intimacy of that room with that man looking at her in a way that made words superfluous.

"You stayed alone with Dickon," Warrick argued as if he were privy to the argument swirling in her brain, which he might have been, given the intent way he watched her.

"Sitting in the library with Lord Sheffield was not the same."

She only stated the obvious, though in truth it was her differing reaction to the two men that made the situations so utterly unalike.

"I will move into my sitting room."

But Gwen was already halfway to the door and did not reply to Warrick's offer at compromise. "Shall I send anyone to you? Major Sudbury and Lord Sheffield? Or your valet?"

"No," Warrick said to her slender back. "They'll only flutter around me like hens, and my head aches too much for that."

"Your head aches?" Gwen swung about at the door. "Does it hurt badly?"

A gleam flared in Warrick's eyes, but then he smiled ruefully. "In truth? It hurts very little, I fear."

Gwen had the greatest difficulty untangling her gaze from Warrick's then. She had not meant to look back at him: had done so because in her concern for him she'd forgotten her resolution. Now, there he sat, his sun-streaked hair mussed and falling over his brow, his chest bared for her pleasure, and his eyes, beneath the wry self-amusement in them, connecting with hers in such a way she thought he would reduce her to a ball of malleable putty.

"I trust you will feel better soon, my lord."

Her voice was too soft to her ears, but at least it had the effect of breaking through whatever spell held her fast. Outside Warrick's door, a maid waited to tell her Lady Chumleigh and the others were in the West Saloon.

Half an hour later, Gwen returned to Warrick's room. She had reason. Lady Chumleigh had appointed her Warrick's nurse. "I have sent for Hobson, but there is no saying when the pompous fool will get himself here," Lady Chumleigh had fretted. "He's underfoot when he's not needed, but if he is needed, then he's in the furtherest corner of the district delivering a squalling brat. Until he comes, I wish you to look after Lucian, Gwen. You've more knowledge of doctoring than the rest of us, and I daresay, you're the only one he'll mind."

Gwen flushed at that, particularly as Lady Chumleigh voiced the opinion before everyone who'd gathered to hear how Warrick did. But she did not argue against her new position. For one thing, she thought Lady Chumleigh correct to say Warrick would be more obedient for her than anyone else, and for another, Gwen suspected she'd have gone back to Warrick's room to check on him whether Lady Chumleigh had sent her or not.

His remark about his headache had begun to worry her. Perhaps he hadn't really been teasing her. Perhaps he'd been trying to spare her worry by denying the headache. It was quite possible she had missed something, when she had examined his head just after he'd been struck.

Before she returned to Warrick's room, Gwen made an infusion of hops and chamomile flowers that Dr. Penrywn had used to counter pain. Carrying the tray herself, on her hip, she knocked at Warrick's door before she entered.

He called out brusquely, demanding who disturbed him, but when he saw her, he stared in surprise. Gwen smiled, pleased to have caught him off guard for once. But her smile faded almost as soon as it had come, for she saw he was sitting on the edge of his bed, obviously readying himself to rise.

"I don't think it would be wise for you to move about yet, my lord." She frowned as she went to put the tray on the table by him.

Warrick frowned back at her. "Resting here with no company, all I have to do is inventory every pain and ache. I would rather be up."

He sounded like an ill-humored boy. Gwen bit her lip against a smile. "I'd have sent someone to you, had you wished, but now I have brought you a tea that I hope will ease the pain in your shoulder."

He did not give the medicinal tea much thought. "Will you stay while I drink it?"

Now he looked a mischievous boy. "Yes, I will stay." Warrick grinned and started to rise. Gwen supposed he thought she would insist he must take his tea somewhere other than his bed, if she were present. Shaking her head, she stayed his progress. "I have come to help you rest better, not to agitate you. Lay back against your pillows."

"You want me in my bed, Mrs. Tarrant?"

She made a face. "I see you are not so ill, my lord, that you lack the strength to try and provoke me. And yes, I want you resting against those pillows." When he rested as she wished, Gwen quickly examined his head again, and finding no evidence of a wound or even soreness, exhaled a heartfelt, "Good! I did not miss anything."

"You were worried for me?"

Gwen thought his green eyes would be twinkling, but could not, mercifully, say for certain, as she was pouring the tea she'd made. "Of course I worried for you, my lord. Lady Chumleigh has appointed me your nurse until Dr. Hobson arrives. Were she to learn, I had overlooked a wound, she'd turn me off for certain, and if it were to fester . . . " Gwen finished the sentence with a grimace, and Warrick gave a rather smug chuckle.

"Yes, I can see you will have to be very attentive . . . but what is this?" His smile faded as he sniffed the steaming cup she handed him.

"An infusion of hops and chamomile flowers. The doctor in

St. Ives had my mother dose us with it, when one of us had an ache or pain." Warrick took a sip. "How is it?"

"It tastes like peppermint."

"Mrs. Ames said you did not care for much sugar in your tea, and so I thought to use peppermint to help the taste."

"And you put sugar in it."

Gwen smiled wryly. "Mrs. Ames said you would notice, but hops are bitter without a sweetener, and so I took the chance you would not mind."

"I like it," At her obvious surprise, he grinned. "Well, almost." Gwen blushed. He was humoring her. Warrick grinned again, "Perhaps I wouldn't have obediently sipped mineral oil, had you brought it, but I am glad you returned."

"Your shoulder is hurting?"

"My shoulder has little to do with why I am pleased to see you, Mrs. Tarrant, but, yes, it does hurt. Are you the oldest?"

It took Gwen a moment to get her mind off the teasing gleam warming his eyes, and then, well aware her cheeks heated again, she turned away with the excuse that she needed to find a chair. There were two by the window, large, heavy things it would take all her strength to drag to his bedside.

"The foot of my bed is not taken."

At the so-idle suggestion, Gwen glanced to the foot of Warrick's bed. Because he was sitting up against his pillows, his legs did not reach quite so far. Without looking at him she sat down gingerly upon the very corner of the bed. Just behind her, she could feel the bedpost.

If Warrick was not grinning outright, his eyes were grinning for him, when Gwen met them. In the face of those dancing eyes, she lifted her chin, and scooting back against the bedpost, drew her legs up under her skirts on the bed.

He smiled outright. "I think if I do not say something provoking about having you in—or—on my bed at last, I'll burst."

She laughed, her embarrassment lanced by his brazenness. "You are an incorrigible man, my lord."

"And you, you were the eldest, Mrs. Tarrant?" he reminded her of the question that had gotten lost while she resolved the dilemma of where she would sit.

"How did you guess?" she countered, settling back more comfortably.

"How did I guess?" he mused, touching her with eyes that were warm and to Gwen, surprisingly gentle. "Your behavior today held clues enough. You felt my head as if you'd done it before, and according to Suddy and Dickon, you sent the lot of race-goers scattering, even men at least twice your age, with only a word or two."

"Lady Chumleigh maintains I've a managing nature," Gwen admitted wryly.

Warrick's grin held more admiration than humor, really. "I'll not make the mistake of commenting upon that, Mrs. Tarrant, but I will say, I was eternally grateful for your quick understanding today. I could not seem to find the words to say that my shoulder ached too blastedly much for idle conversation."

"They ought to have realized as much for themselves," Gwen observed tartly, then seeing Warrick was finished with the tea she'd made, reached forward to take his empty cup, to save him from having to move his shoulder.

There was nothing suggestive in the movement. Gwen simply leaned forward with an economy of movement, nor was there anything provocative about the dress she wore. Of muslin of only middling quality, it was plain and neat, and it buttoned to her neck. Still, as it was highwaisted, it was gathered just beneath her breasts, and when she leaned forward as she did, the material across the bosom of the dress stretched very tight indeed.

"Wo . . ."

Gwen began to ask Warrick if he wished more of the herbal tea, but looking at him, she saw where his arrested glance had fallen. At once she leaped from the bed.

"I should leave now and allow the tea to take its effect," she said, busying herself with straightening the items on the tray, "If you need anything, you have only to . . ."

Before she could lift the tray and go, he caught her hand and tugging, pulled her around to look at him. Her cheeks were flushed, but her eyes were wary.

"You are the most desirable woman I have ever seen. That is no excuse, but I want you to know that I did not mean to offend you. My eyes wandered. They will not again, if you will stay."

Gwen could scarcely believe he was speaking so frankly to her. No man ever had, including, nay especially, her husband. But then Warrick had spoken frankly to her from the first. Now he said he would not allow his gaze to wander below her neck, if she stayed. She almost smiled. She did not know if he were making a threat or a promise.

She was even less certain that it had been offense his straying glance had given her in the first place. Indignation had not been foremost among the emotions she'd registered when she had found his eyes upon her breasts. Her breath had caught in her throat, and beneath the touch of his eyes, her breasts had swelled, hardened even, with an inexplicable fieriness.

"Come," he ordered softly, tugging her hand again. "I've promised to school my eyes, and heaven knows just now I'm not feeling up to more than looking, though I would not object if you offered to hold you while I fell asleep. To all your other attributes, I must add that you smell good."

He said it with such a whimsical smile, Gwen found herself smiling, too. "Would you like another cup of the tea?" she asked, ignoring both the compliment that was at least slightly improper and the suggestion that was definitely out of bounds, but also, somehow, infinitely appealing.

"Hmm, I suppose," Warrick agreed idly to the suggestion of more tea. "I am feeling better, but I am not certain it is the tea that is responsible."

"Now, now, I'll not have you disparage Dr. Penrywn's special tea. He is a very wise man."

"I think I am jealous," Warrick teased, sipping the tea Gwen gave him, as she sat down again upon the very end of his bed. "You sound as if you admire this doctor too much, but before you reprimand me and tell me he is sixty odd, tell me instead if I am right to believe that there were not many children in St. Ives who dared tease your brothers or sisters."

As she thought of her brothers and sisters, Gwen's expression softened. "You are right again. You see, I am not only the eldest but the eldest by six years, as my mother lost two children between us."

"And did you fix the bullies well?" he asked smiling sleepily as he rested his head against his pillows.

It was an odd moment, the two of them sitting on his bed alone in his bedroom, and feeling, at least on Gwen's part, an unexpected companionableness. She laughed at a memory Warrick's question had triggered.

"I fixed Seth Pollard at least. He used to tease Arthur, who was often sick as a child. The day I found little Arthur sobbing in a field, because Seth had beaten him in front of his friends, I was so incensed, I ran to the docks and seized the first weapon I saw. Unfortunately it was a bucket of fish, and when I dumped the bucket's contents upon Seth, I also threw away an innocent fisherman's livelihood."

Warrick laughed. "Did you suffer a consequence?"

Gwen nodded. "My grandfather was very strict in his way. I had to make up the loss by assisting Mr. Turgo's wife with their six children for the duration of the summer. But I didn't mind. Seeing Seth Pollard covered in slimy pilchards was too great a pleasure."

"I think Arthur was very lucky to have such an incorrigible sister," Warrick approved, a lazy light in his eyes.

That teasing and something-more light was enough to unsettle Gwen. It caused her to entertain, without warning, a vision of herself curled up by his side, her head resting upon his good shoulder. It was time and more that she go.

"What of your father, Mrs. Tarrant? Did he not discipline you, too?"

Oh yes, it was definitely time to go. Carefully Gwen said, "My grandfather raised us, my lord, from the time I was seven or so."

"I see. And does he still live in St. Ives?"

"No. My mother and grandfather died a few years ago."

At last the second cup of Dr. Penrywn's tea began to take effect. Warrick's eyes drooped almost gracefully, and he only vaguely heard the whisper of Gwen's muslin skirts as she rose from the bed. He heard her bid him farewell, and he thought he responded, but the only coherent thought playing in his mind as his eyes fell closed was that now he understood why a woman of her beauty had married a mere farmer. To support herself and her brothers and sisters, she had had to accept the first offer she received. He wondered how young she had been, but couldn't think quickly enough to ask her before he heard the door click shut behind her. He did, however, have the clarity of mind to vow to himself that she would never find herself in such dire straits again.

Chapter 18

Lady Chumleigh made much of Gwen's abilities as a nurse, her ability to handle the crowd at the race, and her ability to manage Warrick, who had never to Lady Chumleigh's knowledge, taken a nap in his life. Gwen protested she had neither done anything extraordinary, nor even "managed" Warrick, but Lady Chumleigh, no stranger to stubbornness, continued to declare her a miracle worker and to insist she take dinner with her and Sheffield and the Sudburys.

The afternoon's near tragedy was under discussion yet again when Warrick, himself, strolled into the West Saloon before dinner. Instantly Lady Chumleigh swerved about to cast a triumphant look at Gwen. "Did I not say you were the best of nurses, Gwen? Indeed, I did! And here's the proof. Lucian's up and about before any of us looked for him to be."

Certainly Gwen had not looked for him to be up by that very evening. Warrick smiled at her as he sank carefully into a comfortable chair. "You look as if you doubt my recovery, Mrs. Tarrant. Perhaps you wish to take my pulse?"

He looked so teasingly hopeful, she couldn't but smile back. "I don't think taking your pulse is necessary, my lord. You are the best judge of your stamina, though I must say I am surprised to see you."

"It was that herbal brew you gave me, ma'am. I slept so soundly that I feel entirely refreshed now, though I will admit I am still a trifle stiff."

"A trifle stiff?" Mrs. Sudbury exclaimed. "I should imagine you are painfully sore, Luc. Lord, but you were brave to dive beneath that stallion's hooves!"

"Brave or idiotic!" Lady Chumleigh declared gruffly. "I

thought you might never raise your head again, Lucian, and I vow your heroics took a decade off my life."

"But Luc performs such feats daily, Lady Chum!" Sheffield protested, demonstrating his relief at Warrick's escape from serious injury by teasing him. "I assure you, it's true. He must impress the ladies, you know."

"He's no other means to do so," Major Sudbury added in quite the same vein. "With all of Luc's handicaps, he must throw himself beneath the flashing hooves of a racing stallion, if he's to gain attention."

The two men even drew Lady Chumleigh and Mrs. Sudbury into their raillery, but though Gwen understood why they made light of the incident, all she could see was the heavy iron shoes of the stallion coming down inches from Warrick's head, and she could not bring herself to laugh.

She did not think anyone noticed her reserve, until she chanced to look Warrick's way. He was watching her, a very keen, and not a little pleased, look in his eyes.

What her own eyes might reveal to him, Gwen did not know, and was therefore grateful that Lady Chumleigh chose to remark again how fortunate Warrick had been to have Gwen at hand.

"Hobson would have cupped you, had he come. He's a positive fiend for the treatment! Bah! I think it is nonsense to draw off a substance God gives you. I'll not allow him near me with his lancet, but luckily we were spared by Gwen's abilities from arguing with the old fool. I hope you gave her proper thanks."

"I hope I did as well, Aunt Vi. Did I thank you properly, Mrs. Tarrant?"

He was, Gwen thought, as incorrigible as the gleam dancing so mischievously in his eyes. "You did, my lord," she said primly.

"Ah well," he sighed. "At least you do know that I am grateful."

Fighting a smile that would only encourage his play, she inclined her head. "I do."

It was not quite the last exchange they had on the subject. When they went into dinner, Warrick managed, though Lord Sheffield was nearer to her, to escort Gwen, and he leaned down to whisper provocatively, "Aunt Vi has caused me to feel most remiss, Mrs. Tarrant. I really believe I should proclaim my gratitude to you tangibly."

"No, indeed you need not, my lord," Gwen protested in equally hushed, if somewhat emphatic, tones. "Your good health is all the reward I desire."

Warrick made a very gratified sound. They were passing into the dining room, and he'd no time to be more eloquent, nor had Gwen time to regret the statement she'd made. It was the truth, anyway. She did desire his good health, and when, the next day, upon her return from the Chumleigh orphanage, Dabney greeted her at the door with a strained look on his face, her heart sank at the thought that she had failed to cleanse Warrick's wound adequately enough, and he'd become terribly ill.

"It is her ladyship," Dabney said, relieving Gwen of the one worry, anyway.

"She is awake, Dabney?" Gwen remarked in surprise.

"She awakened only moments ago, Mrs. Tarrant, and complains of being feverish. Finch is with her now."

Above, Gwen found Lady Chumleigh tossing in her bed, her brow hot to the touch and moaning about how her head and joints ached.

"Perhaps it is the rheumatism," Finch opined as Gwen lifted Lady Chumleigh's hand to feel for her pulse.

"Perhaps," Gwen replied, distractedly. "I am not able to say. We must send for Dr. Hobson. I shall stay with Lady Chumleigh, if you will see to it, Finch?"

No sooner had the dresser hurried away than Lady Chumleigh suddenly gripped Gwen's hand with surprising force. "You're sending for Hobson?" she demanded, wheezing with the effort it took her to get a breath. When Gwen nodded, she rasped harshly, "I'll not be bled! Don't let him cup me! Swear that you won't!"

Concerned Lady Chumleigh was so overwrought she might harm herself, Gwen tried to appease her. "I shall do my best, my lady. Dr. Hobson—"

"Is a fool! No bleeding! Swear it!"

Gwen took her hand and held it firmly. "Do not fret yourself, my lady. I've no authority to prevent Dr. Hobson treating you as he deems best, but I shall consult with Lord Warrick."

Lady Chumleigh slumped back upon the bed. "Yes, yes. Get Lucian," she said, as if she had forgotten her nephew was visiting. "He'll agree."

When the maid announced that Warrick awaited her in Lady Chumleigh's sitting room, Gwen was conscious of a start of relief, but it was not until she actually saw him standing before her, tall and handsome and assured, that she realized how Lady Chumleigh's feverish countenance had catapulted her back to the time she'd nursed her grandfather and her mother with only a superstitious, old country woman to share the responsibility.

The first words out of her mouth, indeed, were an expression of her relief. "I am glad you are here, my lord!"

"What has happened, Mrs. Tarrant?" he asked with a calmness that immediately steadied Gwen.

"Lady Chumleigh has taken ill. She is feverish, complains of aching everywhere, and is breathing hoarsely. I have sent for Dr. Hobson, but when Lady Chumleigh heard his name, she became most distraught. She wanted me to vow that I would not allow him to bleed her. My lord, I haven't the authority to do such a thing, nor can I even say I believe it would be for the best. Truly I do not know, though I can say the treatment would distress her deeply."

"Odd that she should have spoken of how little she cares for bleeding only last night," Warrick said, frowning as he considered. "She was adamant then. And you have no opinion on the matter?"

"I've no opinion as learned, surely, as Dr. Hobson's will be," Gwen said slowly. "I can say, though, from my own experience, that bleeding helped neither my grandfather or mother."

Warrick took her hand and squeezed it, responding to the pain that briefly clouded Gwen's expression. The quick, spontaneous gesture caught at her heart, and she found herself returning his gentle pressure.

"Do you believe Aunt Vi has contracted what they had, Mrs. Tarrant?"

Gwen shook her head hastily. "No, thank heaven. Though

she's a fever and she aches, she has no rash as they did. I have looked. I only meant to say that cupping is no guarantee of recovery."

"I see." Warrick raked his hand through his hair, as he expelled a long, considering breath. "Well, as there is no guarantee, it seems unwise to upset Aunt Vi by insisting upon it."

Though he had made his decision, two grim lines bracketed his mouth, and Gwen was struck more than ever by the realization that Warrick cared deeply for his combative old aunt.

"I commend your decision, my lord," she said quietly, wanting to ease the lines about his mouth and the one etching a groove down the middle of his brow as well. "I think cupping would upset Lady Chumleigh more than the treatment could help her."

"Pray God we are right," Warrick said, and this time it was Gwen found herself reaching out to touch his hand reassuringly. It was amazing to Gwen that so little could rout the grimness she'd felt, but her step was altogether brisker when she returned to Lady Chumleigh, and Warrick went to apprise Lord Sheffield and the Sudburys of the turn of events.

The interview with Dr. Hobson did not go easily. A careful man with a keen appreciation of his own knowledge, the doctor was deeply offended when Warrick questioned his professional judgment.

"But fever is a symptom of obstruction in my lady's vessels, Lord Warrick! Her blood is heated due to the excessive pressure. We must relieve her of that pressure, or she will never improve! Indeed, she will decline."

"If she begins to decline, we shall reconsider," Warrick declared in a tone that conveyed he did not care to be disputed. "Until then, however, we shall abide by her wishes."

"But Lady Chumleigh is feverish, my lord! She is raving! No one desires to be cupped. It is natural for a patient to object."

"Mrs. Tarrant, did you think Aunt Vi raved when she begged not to be cupped?"

"No, my lord."

Warrick looked back at Dr. Hobson. "She will not be cupped, sir. If you've nothing but a lancet in that bag of yours, you may as well leave now."

Seeing the doctor begin to quiver with wounded dignity, and perhaps with dismay for the look in Warrick's eyes, Gwen stepped forward, smiling, she hoped, bracingly.

"Though it is not possible, at least at this juncture, to cup Lady Chumleigh, I am confident you have other remedies for us to try, Dr. Hobson. I have told Lord Warrick how successful you were with the elixir you administered to Lady Chumleigh in June, I believe it was."

"Ah, yes, it was an elixir of rhubarb." Dr. Hobson appeared much gratified by the reminder of his success, and perhaps, too, by the smile Gwen gave him. He was not so middle-aged, after all. "Her blood was thin and slow then. Rhubarb would not do at all now. Mastic is called for now; olibanum, too; and licorice root for her cough." He paused to consider further treatment. "You must close the windows in Lady Chumleigh's room, Mrs. Tarrant. We do not want her to take a chill when we apply the cold compresses to her. Ah! And I shall also instruct Mrs. Ames to infuse parsley and parsley roots in water. The parsley may help to cleanse her in place of the cupping. It may, but I cannot be certain, you understand, my lord?"

"I do understand, Dr. Hobson," Warrick said, all charm now the doctor was doing what he wished. "And I greatly appreciate your effort to cooperate so completely."

Dr. Hobson looked almost comically gratified. "Of course, of course, my lord! Now, Mrs. Tarrant, allow me to instruct you precisely how and when to administer the treatments to Lady Chumleigh."

If Dr. Hobson had hoped the marquess might leave him to do his work unsupervised, he was denied the wish. Warrick settled down to listen to all the particulars about cold compresses, hot air, elixirs, powders, and possets that the doctor related to Gwen.

"Well, I think that is all," Dr. Hobson said finally. "If there is a change for the worse, and there may well be—Lady Chumleigh is old—send for me at once. Otherwise, I shall return tomorrow morning. Will that do, my lord?"

"Very well, indeed, Dr. Hobson. Thank you again. I hope you will stay for luncheon, if you have time. We've guests who would like to hear from your lips the diagnosis you have given to Mrs. Tarrant and me."

"I would be honored, my lord."

"Then we shall have a footman take you down." The alacrity with which a footman responded to Warrick's pull of the bell rope indicated he had been waiting just outside the door. "I shall join you in a moment, Dr. Hobson," Warrick said as he delivered the doctor into the footman's hands. Closing the door, he swung around to fix Gwen with a piercing look. "Have you heard of these treatments before, Mrs. Tarrant? Is he reliable? Or ought I to send to town for my father's physician?"

"Olibanum and mastic are frequently used for fever, my lord. As to sending for your father's physician, I imagine he, too, would urge you to allow him to bleed Lady Chumleigh."

Warrick acknowledged the observation with a vague sound of assent. "Well then, we shall stay with Dr. Hobson whose ruffled feathers you smoothed so well. Thank you."

The wry look he gave her made Gwen smile, and for just a moment the tension she felt over Lady Chumleigh eased. "I think you do not like to be denied your way, my lord."

"I suppose not." He grinned suddenly, unexpectedly. "Perhaps you will remember that, Mrs. Tarrant, and act accordingly."

She flushed a little beneath the power of that smile but still managed to say with credible aplomb, "I assure you, my lord, that I rarely forget how determined you are to have your way, but I am undaunted, for I strengthen myself with the reassuring thought that I am providing you a unique experience."

He laughed outright. "Minx." It was all he said before Gwen, smiling herself, returned to his aunt's bedroom, but the single, teasing syllable played over and over in Gwen's mind the afternoon long.

Or at least Gwen thought of it often during the earlier part of the afternoon and evening. As time wore on, she'd little energy for thought, pleasant or even unpleasant. Lady Chumleigh's condition worsened. Dr. Hobson had warned them that her illness might only be beginning and to expect her temperature to increase, her chills to come more often, and her coughing to deepen.

By dinner time Lady Chumleigh's was weak with coughing and her brow felt hotter than ever to the touch. She tossed restlessly in her bed and when her gruel and the healing concoctions Dr. Hobson had prescribed were brought, she pushed weakly at Finch's arm.

The faithful maid was nearly in tears when Gwen returned from supping off a tray in the sitting room. Seating herself upon the edge of Lady Chumleigh's bed, Gwen brushed gray wisps of hair back from Lady Chumleigh's forehead, quieting her.

"Gwen? Gwen, is that you?" the elder woman queried in a thin, ragged voice that tugged at Gwen's sympathies.

"It is, my lady, and I've an elixir for you to swallow."

"I ache so! And my head. My head hurts."

"You've a high fever, but you'll soon be better. Now quickly, and it will be done."

Patiently, Gwen coaxed Lady Chumleigh into swallowing her elixir, her posset, and even her gruel. Finch, worn and fearful, told her she was a miracle worker. Gwen said she was only stubborn, and sent Finch off to her dinner and bed.

"You must take care of yourself, Finch. I can manage the evening."

"But there is so much to do, Mrs. Tarrant. There are the cold cloths when she is hot, and the blankets, when she is chilled, and Doctor Hobson's medicines."

"I shall call one of the maids to help me, Finch. I wish you to conserve your energies that you may take my place tomorrow morning."

Finch understood that not only was she needed, but that she was as well being spared the most difficult part of nursing, having to sit with the patient through the night. She patted Gwen upon the shoulder. "You have only to call me if you need me."

"I know, Finch. I think Lady Chumleigh very lucky to have you."

"It is we who are lucky, I think," the aged dresser said, weariness and sentiment bringing tears to her eyes.

Gwen's evening and night were as strenuous as Finch had predicted. Lady Chumleigh alternately tossed with fever, needing the cold compresses Dr. Hobson had ordered, or shook with chills, needed to be bundled in heavy blankets.

Warrick did not desert Gwen. He took dinner below with

his guests, but he came afterward and stayed to help until Lady Chumleigh realized who it was applied cold cloths to her chest and fretfully sent him away, saying he'd no business in a lady's sickroom.

Warrick left, but he frowned down at Gwen before he went. "I do not like to heap all the burden for nursing Aunt Vi upon you, Mrs. Tarrant."

"You have not, my lord. I've the maids to help me. However I would like to consult with you. Dr. Hobson left a tincture of opium to be used, if absolutely necessary. I should like to administer a little to Lady Chumleigh, if she continues to complain of headaches and muscle aches. Do you approve?"

"I do. It should help her to sleep, I think."

"Yes." Gwen nodded. "She must rest."

"As must you, if you are not to become so ill, you cannot nurse her. Promise me, you will call a maid to relieve you during the night."

She felt warmth pool comfortingly in her chest and knew its cause. She liked his concern. "I shall call in a maid, if it is possible, my lord."

"And call me, if there is a crisis."

"Of course."

He looked as if he were about to say something else, but Lady Chumleigh's quavering voice, calling for Gwen interrupted them, and all he said in a quiet voice was, "Thank you, Mrs. Tarrant."

Warrick came the next morning at dawn to find what he had expected, that Gwen had not given her responsibilities over to one of the maids. She slept curled in a chair with a blanket over her, her head slumped awkwardly to the side as if the heavy plait she has made of her hair for the night, weighed her down.

Beneath the flush caused by the unnatural heat in the room, he could see she was pale with fatigue and had dark circles beneath her eyes. Something tightened in his chest as he thought how she had kept watch over his gruff old aunt, and it seemed the most natural thing in the world to waken her by leaning over her chair and gently slipping his hand beneath the confined mass of her black hair to massage her cramped shoulders and neck.

Gwen came awake with a start to look up into Warrick's watchful face. Her mind muddled from lack of sleep, the only thing that came to her was something akin to a sigh for how handsome he was, the early sun streaking his hair to gold, and his eyes so green.

He said nothing, only continued to trace the column of her spine down her neck, creating a tingling warmth where there had been only stiffness, and Gwen did more than let him continue. She sagged forward, sighing aloud, too weary and too grateful of the service to even think to protest the familiarity of it.

"You have disobeyed me about having a care for yourself, Mrs. Tarrant," Warrick remonstrated softly, watching her neck arch gratefully in response to his ministrations. "You did not sleep, but napped and even that infrequently, I suspect. You had best have a good reason for your disobedience."

Gwen stretched with an unself-consciousness born of fatigue. "Thank you, my lord, that felt heavenly. As to my sleeping arrangements, Lady Chumleigh had a difficult night. She called out a great deal, needing someone. I finally gave her another dose of the tincture of opium about an hour ago. That is why she is so quiet now."

"I see. Well, if she is opiated, she will tolerate my presence. You will go at once to your room and to sleep."

His arrogance made her smile. "I can think of no command I would rather obey," she said, rising to stand before him without thought for what she wore, or that the light from the windows behind her shone through her cotton nightgown and robe to reveal the outline of her body as plainly as if she had stood naked before Warrick.

It was not his chest that tightened at the sight. "Go to bed," he ordered his voice sounding unusually gruff.

She did not notice. "Yes, my lord, but would you awaken me when Dr. Hobson comes? I wish to consult him about a treatment Dr. Penrywn used on occasion."

Warrick did not give an answer. He did not have to, Gwen was already drifting through the door to Lady Chumleigh's dressing room, which in turn led to the door to her own room.

He sat down to watch his aunt, but thought of the woman who had just left the room. It seemed that every day he saw a new side of her, and it disconcerted him to realize that the more he saw of her, the less he could imagine doing without the sight of her.

Chapter 19

Rather than awaken Gwen when Dr. Hobson came, Warrick invited the doctor to stay until she awakened on her own. He offered the enticement of tea, but even had he not, Hobson would have stayed. Warrick was not a man easily refused.

Gwen did not sleep long. She awoke after only two hours, a sense of urgency bringing her instantly alert. There was reason for her anxiety, she learned when she went to Lady Chumleigh's rooms. Not only was her ladyship's fever as high as ever, but she suffered from a severe nosebleed.

Dr. Hobson direly warned that she was not progressing because he had not been allowed to bleed her, but Gwen, having listened to Lady Chumleigh fret again during the night about the treatment, said with a curtness caused by lack of sleep and worry, that she thought the nosebleed would have thinned Lady Chumleigh's blood quite enough.

"I have another treatment I wish to discuss with you, Dr. Hobson," she continued, taking care not to look at Warrick, who had, she believed, actually grinned at her impatient reaction to Hobson. "Our doctor in St. Ives had some success when he dosed his fever patients with an infusion of elderberry leaves and pearl barley. He was not so learned as you, though, and I wished to consult you as to whether you believe the concoction could cause Lady Chumleigh harm."

His professionalism neatly appealed to, Dr. Hobson gave Gwen's suggestion careful thought, and in the end allowed he thought the elderberry leaves might help alleviate the headache of which Lady Chumleigh complained. As to the pearl barley, at the least, it would do no harm.

When the doctor departed, Lord Sheffield and the Sudburys came to the sitting room. Believing the staff at Wensley ought to concentrate solely upon Lady Chumleigh, they had decided to depart, but they were not removing far.

"We'll be at Randall's near Plymouth, should there be need of us," Lord Sheffield explained.

Abstracted with her own concerns, Gwen did not realize for a little that he meant they were staying close in case Lady Chumleigh did not survive. The thought braced Gwen as no other could have. She did not want to lose another person to fever. In fact she was determined not to and marched back into Lady Chumleigh's room with her energy renewed.

Warrick made her take lunch and dinner with him in his aunt's sitting room, and he forced her to leave the sickroom for a walk. They said little at those times, but Gwen did not need to talk. She needed the comfort and support his mere presence lent her.

Perhaps it was the pearl barley and elderberry water that caused the improvement, but that night, Lady Chumleigh slept a little better. Though she was still weak and feverish, she did not ache as she had, and Gwen was able to sleep with only a few disturbances upon the couch Warrick had had made up as a bed for her.

If he came again at dawn to check upon his aunt, Gwen did not know, she slept so soundly, but when she did awaken, a maid delivered the message that his lordship requested her presence as soon as possible in his study. Alarmed, Gwen hurried to make herself presentable, though she did take the time to select a lime green muslin she considered the most becoming dress she owned. She justified the choice by telling herself it was for herself she wished to look attractive. After two days in a hot sickroom, she deserved to feel cool and collected.

Whether Gwen believed what she told herself or not, the first thing she thought of when she entered Warrick's study was that the last time she'd been in the room, he had kissed her.

Kisses were not on Warrick's mind that morning, however, or at least not openly. "How is Aunt Vi, Mrs. Tarrant?" he asked, rising from his seat behind the desk. He had been working on a ledger, Gwen noted with surprise, Following the direction of her gaze, he smiled a little. "I do not spend all my time on pleasure." She flushed, and not only because he had read her thoughts so accurately. The word "pleasure" on War-rick's lips had a tempting sound.

Turning from the thought and from the smile with which he eyed her blush, Gwen lied outright. "I did not think you did, my lord. As to Lady Chumleigh, she slept better last night than the night before."

"Her fever is broken, then?"

She shook her head, sorry to disappoint the hopeful note in his voice. "No, nothing so good as that. But she does not com-plain of aching as she did, nor was she so fretful in the night. I feel some hope."

"I am glad to hear it!" he said with such relief Gwen feared she might have overstated Lady Chumleigh's improvement.

"I do not mean to give you false hope, my lord."

But Warrick shrugged off her concern. "Hope is just that, hope, and not certainty."

He came around the desk and without the sun behind him, she could see his face better; could see specifically the lines about his eyes and mouth that indicated he had slept as poorly as she. Her heart went out to him, and she thought to touch his hand comfortingly, as he had hers, but a knock sounded at the door.

"Come in, Dabney," Warrick called out, and when the but-ler entered before two footmen bearing trays, Warrick pointed to a low mahogany table between two comfortable chairs. "That table should do." To Gwen's look of mystification, he explained, smiling faintly, "It is breakfast. I decided it was time you had a change of scenery when you ate, and uncertain I could lure you to the formal dining room, I chose my study because, I am saddened to admit, it was convenient for me."

He had meant, at the least, to make her smile. She gratified him immensely by laughing. "It smells delicious. I had not re-alized how hungry I was."

"That is because a sparrow could have eaten as much as you did last night. The way you picked at your food is what prompted me to remove you to a new dining site. I don't want you flagging midcourse due to lack of nourishment."

Gwen took that in the spirit it was intended, and because she really was hungry, fell to her breakfast with a will. In other circumstances she'd have been reluctant to remain alone with

Warrick in his study, but circumstances were different with his aunt lying so ill above. And, too, he set himself to entertain her with stories that did not even obliquely hint at passion or pleasure or desire.

He had finished his breakfast, though she had not, when Dabney came to announce that Dr. Hobson had arrived. Warrick, saying he was perfectly up to dealing with "his lordship, the doctor" alone, bade her stay and finish her meal in leisurely fashion. "If you put in an appearance upstairs in less than half an hour, I shall find some means to punish you."

Feeling very well looked after, and not reluctant to bask in that rare feeling, Gwen answered by leaning back in her chair and lifting her cup of chocolate. "I promise to be very lazy, my lord. Do go gently with Dr. Hobson, though."

"Yes, Mrs. Tarrant," he said in dutiful tones that were entirely belied by an amused smile.

It really was refreshing to be away from Lady Chumleigh's rooms, and Gwen was just savoring another cup of the hot chocolate, when she heard voices in the hallway. She thought they heralded Warrick and Dr. Hobson until she realized it was Dabney's voice she heard calling out sharply and a stranger replying angrily before, suddenly, the two burst into the study.

The stranger was a young man, dressed in army scarlet. His belligerent expression more than his uniform gave Gwen a suspicion as to his purpose at Wensley.

"Who are you?" the young man demanded, drawing up short when he encountered a strange woman where he had expected to find Warrick. "And where is Lord Warrick?"

Though she guessed he was older than she by several years, he looked a boy, for he'd a smattering of freckles dotting his short nose and his rounded face was free of lines. Noting the angry flush mottling his smooth face, Gwen cautioned herself not to take him lightly. However young he was, he meant Warrick harm, and as an officer in the army likely had the skill to inflict that harm.

"Lord Warrick is above," she said, as if young men stormed in every day to disturb her breakfast. "He is conferring with the physician who is attending his aunt. Lady Chumleigh is very ill just now, I fear. I am her companion, Mrs. Tarrant. Why do you not come in and sit down?" Gwen went on, nodding over his shoulder to indicate to Dabney that he need not stay. "There is coffee, and you may as well be comfortable while you await Lord Warrick."

Some decisions are made with great care, others simply come. In this case Gwen did not even in passing question her decision to involve herself in Warrick's affairs.

The angry young soldier looked a great deal less angry of a sudden and a great deal more uncertain. "Lady Chumleigh is ill?" he repeated.

Gwen nodded as, taking the decision from him, she poured him a cup of coffee. "Yes. She awakened the day before yesterday with a fever and an inflammation in her chest. Cream? Sugar?" The young man nodded perfunctorily. Indeed he looked dazed. Gwen took the added step of stirring his coffee for him. "And your name? I cannot go on calling you sir. Or I suppose I could, but I don't particularly care to."

That brought him out of his abstraction. Gwen guessed he was accustomed to more retiring ladies. "I, I am Captain George Dacre."

She nearly dropped the cup she had extended to him, and staring at George Dacre, searched for some resemblance to Miles. There was the straight, auburn hair, and perhaps something similar about the eyes, now she looked. Nothing more though. Even in his infancy Miles had not had this boy's freckled, open countenance.

Gwen could not hold back the question. "Are you related to Miles Dacre?"

Young George looked at her in surprise. "He is my brother. Do you, er, know him well?"

A cutting retort rose to her lips, something to the effect that she knew Miles well enough to know he was a scoundrel who thought nothing of playing loose with the truth and a young girl's vulnerable heart. Before she ripped up at George on his brother's account, however, she took in how he had stiffened, sitting on the edge of his chair, as if he braced himself for just the retort she had thought to make.

Reminding herself that George Dacre was not his brother, Gwen amended her reply. "I knew your brother only briefly, Captain Dacre. He spent a summer on an estate in Cornwall near the village where I lived. Is he well?"

George Dacre shrugged. "Since you saw him, he succeeded in marrying an heiress and now goes about in the best circles. I suppose he's getting on well enough. It's he who told me Lord Warrick cast his damnable eye upon Daphne. That is why I've come here: to learn what went on between them."

Gwen did not hesitate. Perhaps she intruded into what was none of her business, but she knew both Miles Dacre and Warrick, and it had been a long while since she had thought them cut from the same cloth. So different did she now see them, she did not even have the least question as to whether Warrick would use and discard an innocent girl. The jurors in her mind had come to know him, and in the process had come to their verdict without fanfare.

"I hope you will not be deeply offended if I sound skeptical, Captain Dacre, but I wonder if there is another person to confirm your brother's story. I said I did not know him well. It is the truth, but I knew him well enough to know he is not always sincere."

George flushed scarlet. "He is my brother! Miles would not put me on a false scent."

"And I do not believe that Lord Warrick would ruin your Daphne. Have you ever heard of him debauching a young girl before?"

At her plain speaking, young George shifted uneasily. "I, I cannot say so, no. But . . . "

"And is he so poorly regarded by the ladies of the *ton* that he must stoop to stealing impressionable girls away from the young men to whom they are all but betrothed?"

"No! Of course, not. He's one of the most sought-after men in town. But Daphne even wrote to me while I was in France to say Warrick had asked her to dance twice. It quite put her in alt to be singled out like that by him."

"Surely she'd not have written you of Warrick's attentions, had they been less than innocent," Gwen protested.

But George had a response for her. "I've thought of that, but she is so innocent, she'd never have suspected his ultimate design was to seduce her."

Gwen wisely refrained from questioning the girl's true innocence. Daphne's late night visit to Warrick might have been no more than the youthful indiscretion of a naive girl, but even if she were not so naive or innocent, Gwen knew she would never be able to convince the smitten captain of it.

"What of my earlier question?" Gwen asked him. "Did any but your brother accuse Warrick of behaving less than honorably with your Daphne?"

Reluctantly, George shook his head. "No, but Miles says no one will say a word against Warrick, because he's such a reputation with both swords and pistols. And when I went to question her, Daphne burst into tears, as if the worst had happened."

Unable to tell him precisely why Daphne had burst into tears, Gwen took a different tack, saying tartly enough that she took the captain aback, "I rather imagine she would burst into tears. Did you charge into her home as you have Wensley, making similar, unfounded accusations?"

Poor boy, Gwen thought, watching him turn a helpless red again. She'd have dearly liked, at that moment, to have Miles in range of a handful of rocks again. He had encouraged his hotheaded younger brother to make a fool of himself.

"You needn't answer," she continued more moderately. "I can see you did, but you must see that given her inexperience, she feared you meant to attack her, not defend her. Have you spoken to her again?"

George shook his head, looking rather wretched. "Her parents have sent her to Scotland."

Gwen just bit back an impatient clucking sound. Doubtless Daphne's parents had been thinking of their daughter when they separated the two, but by preventing a confession of the truth, or something near it, they'd all but assured the boy would go after Warrick.

"Well, I've two points to make, beyond the one that I do not believe your brother is a very reliable source when it comes to honorable behavior." Gwen disregarded the captain's stiffening, and leaning forward spoke very carefully. "First, if you call out Warrick, you will make Daphne the subject of even more intense gossip than she is now, and I believe she's the right to be consulted as to whether she desires such notoriety. Second," Gwen went on, though now young George was staring at her as if she had said something startlingly original, "I must repeat that, though I have not known Warrick long and though I cannot say I approve of everything I do know, I can say, categorically, that he would never ruin an innocent girl."

"I must say, though I am heartened by your defense, Mrs. Tarrant, I am not well pleased you were called upon to give it."

Both Gwen and Captain Dacre swung around to find Warrick's tall, broad-shouldered figure filling the doorway. Deep in their discussion, they had not heard him come.

His face flushing hotly, George Dacre found his feet. "Lord Warrick!"

"In the flesh." Warrick strolled into the room, but there was nothing lazy about the narrowed look he fastened upon the young man. "Have you come with your seconds, Captain?"

"Of course, he has not, Lord Warrick," Gwen interjected before Captain Dacre could get beyond Warrick's deadly tone to his question. "Sit, I beg you both. You give me a pain in my neck, looming over me so."

Warrick gave Gwen a cool, unreadable look that did not bode so well, but he did at least lean back against his desk. Captain Dacre lowered himself to sit gingerly upon the edge of his chair. Swiftly, before Warrick could needle the boy again, Gwen spoke.

"Captain Dacre is concerned about a young woman named Daphne, and was given to understand you might have some insight as to why she burst into tears at the mention of your name."

"It was my understanding that Captain Dacre has already accused me of being the reason for the young lady's tears." Warrick parried, fixing his unfriendly gaze upon the boy.

"Well, I—"

"You were accused to him, my lord," Gwen smoothly interrupted the captain's stammer. "And he is in love." As it was intended, the remark brought Warrick's gaze rounding back to her. "I don't know if you have ever been in love, my lord, but it is no easy matter for a young man to be head over heels and posted a body of water away from his love for . . . ?"

She looked a question at George Dacre, who, taking his cue, exclaimed with a perfect touch of anguish. "Eleven months!"

"Eleven months is a very long time to a young man in love," Gwen continued, returning her attention to Warrick, whose mouth betrayed, just at the corners, the first hint of softening. Emboldened, she continued, "Many questions can arise, and there was some mention of you singling out the girl. Can you not help him? You've some connection with her I suspect?"

"On what do you base that suspicion, Mrs. Tarrant? If I may be so bold as to ask?"

Gwen thought the irony, directed entirely at her, an excellent sign. "I shall forgive your boldness this time, my lord," she said with real humor, and then went on to tell him what she had deduced from Lord Sheffield's story, though she did not think it quite the time to mention that she and the viscount had gossiped about the incident long before. "As you have said, young ladies hold little interest for you, I cannot think why you would ask one to dance, unless someone else, someone you likely hold in esteem, begged you to honor her."

Warrick regarded Gwen a minute, before he said, his eyes remaining upon her, "My mother asked me to honor her. Miss Sinclair is her godchild."

"What?" George Dacre exclaimed, his jaw dropping ludicrously. "Lady Grafton is Daphne's godmother?"

"I believe I said just that."

Gwen thought the poor boy might faint, he looked so undone, and to give him time to collect himself, she rose to her feet. "Thank you very much for the breakfast, Lord Warrick. I feel quite refreshed. Is Dr. Hobson still above?"

"He is and waiting to consult with you. Our little drama on the subject of young, hotheaded love caused me, I fear, to forget the good man."

Gwen could understand Warrick's testiness, but she had taken a liking to Captain Dacre. "Hotheaded, perhaps," she conceded, a twinkle in her eyes that made them seem impossibly blue and impossibly deep. "But staunch, too. I think such loyalty deserves a little tolerance."

Warrick did not give Gwen, or Captain Dacre, the satisfaction of any reassurances as to his behavior. His brow lifting at her presumption, he inclined his head. "I shall see you shortly, Mrs. Tarrant."

Reasoning that she had done what she could, and fairly confident that young George would suffer no more than the caustic side of Warrick's tongue, which, she did grant, he probably deserved, Gwen left.

She did not see Warrick until much later in the morning, by which time Dr. Hobson had departed, and Lady Chumleigh had fallen into a light doze. He entered his aunt's room quietly, careful not to disturb her, and motioned with his head for Gwen to join him in her sitting room. She was glad to go for several reasons, not the least of them being that Lady Chumleigh's room had become, with a fire in August, unbearably hot.

It was the first thing Warrick remarked upon, though indirectly. "Your cheeks are red as beets and your hair is as limp as a rag."

"Well!" Gwen's eyes flashed with umbrage. "Thank you very much, my lord, for the compliments. I am sorry I have been in a sickroom half the day."

"That is what you get for interfering in my affairs."

"Your affairs," she stressed the word sarcastically, "all but sat down on top of me."

"The boy needed a thrashing."

"He was hotheaded and impetuous," she conceded, suddenly understanding Warrick's temper better. He had let the boy go unscathed.

"And prepared to ruin my good name."

"I cannot imagine anyone who knows you well would believe that you ruined an innocent girl."

"Ah." He did not look so disgruntled suddenly. "Now we come to the only intriguing point in the affair, that you should be the one to act as my character witness, Mrs. Tarrant."

Suddenly Gwen blessed the heat that had reddened her cheeks. Her confidence bolstered by the knowledge that Warrick could not detect her blush, she assumed her primmest voice.

"I cannot think why you are so intrigued, my lord. Whatever your faults, and I am certain they are legion, I simply do not believe you lack all honor."

She slanted a sideways look at Warrick then, and saw enough to know that he was studying her carefully. "I still find it exceedingly odd that a woman who knows me only a little would believe the best of me, while people who claim to know me exceedingly well have believed the worst sort of slander about me."

Gwen shrugged. "Likely the people to whom you refer are bored and have nothing better to do than pass on stories whether they believe them or not."

Warrick made no reply. Eventually, reluctantly, Gwen had to lift her eyes to his. He was looking at her in a way that made her heart trip.

"And anyway," she said gruffly, rushing to say something. "I know the man who accused you to the captain to be most, ah, unreliable."

"What?" Warrick's expression had turned to one of snapping surprise. "You know Miles Dacre? It was he did the whispering, I'm certain. But how do you know him?"

"Mr. Dacre stayed a summer near St. Ives."

Something hard settled in Warrick's eyes as he searched her face. "How well did you know him, Gwen?"

Having no idea whether his anger was directed at her or at Miles, Gwen took offense. Her chin went up. "I do not think I care for either your tone or your question, my lord."

"Miles could use a thorough beating. I'll administer it without ado if he seduced you. Is that why you married Tarrant?"

Dear heaven, he thought to avenge her. Gwen thought she might actually cry. Quickly she shook her head. "No, no. Miles didn't seduce me. He did try, though, and I was infatuated with him. As you can imagine, he had a great deal more polish than anyone I had ever met." She shrugged, Miles and the hurt he had dealt her seeming, somehow, very distant now. "Suffice it to say he disappointed me, but I managed to give him something of a drubbing, for I pelted him with a shower of rocks."

She had thought to make Warrick laugh, and his handsome mouth did quirk, but only momentarily. "I have always considered Miles Dacre lower than a cockroach. And just now, I would like to crack him in two as a service to humanity."

Perhaps Gwen swayed forward. Perhaps it was just the sudden, suspicious shine in her eyes that caused Warrick to take a step toward her. And she'd have gone to him. Later Gwen would acknowledge that, for the compassion in his eyes alone, she'd have walked into his strong arms. She did not only because Lady Chumleigh interrupted them, calling out in a thin, querulous voice. Instantly Gwen ducked by Warrick, and hurried out of temptation's reach.

Chapter 20

By the fourth night of her illness, Lady Chumleigh seemed improved. Her fever had moderated, and she actually slept, albeit in fits and starts. She was not well enough, however, to do without someone in her room through the night, and Gwen sat reading, though it was after midnight.

When she heard a board squeak in Lady Chumleigh's dressing room, she looked up, aware her heartbeat had quickened. There was only one person who would be up and about so late, unless she had called for a maid, and she had not.

The moment Gwen felt that racing of her heart, she clenched her jaw. But her tightened jaw had no effect on her heart. It continued to beat faster at the prospect of Warrick's appearance. It ought not to, though. Her jaw had it right. Gwen knew she ought to fight her response to Warrick, her growing response. He would only bring her disgrace.

And security and companionship and kindness and affection. She would not say love. She did not think he loved her, but she did believe that he cared for her and more than passingly. He would protect her in any way she needed, and he would protect her with all the grace and charm and courtesy he came by so naturally.

She bit her lip. He was wearing her down, making himself indispensable to her. She would say yes soon, simply because she wanted him to hold her. No, she wanted more than that. At night she dreamed of more, awakening with the feel of his lips on hers, his hands on her body.

Oh, it was absurd! She could not be his mistress. She would die a slow death every time he left her bed for someone else's.

Wife—Gwen's pulses quickened again, but for such a different reason—his wife. Could *she* be his wife? She dismissed out of hand her vow not to marry again. She had not known Warrick so well then. If he asked her, she would marry him.

There, she had said it. She would marry Warrick, if he wished. She had fallen in love with him.

How would he respond if she told him she was a baron's daughter, though? Her fingers drummed excitedly on the arm of her chair, only to still suddenly and finally to fall limp. Her father was not only a baron; he was also a ne'er-do-well who kept company with rogues and smugglers and whose address might soon be a debtor's prison. She couldn't expect Warrick to view her differently on the baron's account, though she knew he would never react as cruelly as Miles Dacre had. No. Warrick would be, in contrast, very careful not to offend her. It made her cringe even to think how polite he would be as he explained gently that her parentage would not do for the woman who would be his marchioness and eventually his duchess.

Gwen had too much pride to listen to such a dismissal, and she glanced resentfully toward the door, almost angry with Warrick, though the scene had not, and never would, take place. But her glare rearranged itself into a puzzled frown when Gwen realized she had been awaiting Warrick longer than it would take him to cross the dressing room to his aunt's bedroom door.

Quietly, she rose and crossed to the door, cracking it only slightly, though she told herself she was being fanciful. But she was not. Looking through the crack, she saw a huge, malignant shadow on the wall and then froze utterly. It was her father's shadow.

A soundless cry escaped her. The baron was not idle in Lady Chumleigh's sitting room. He stood at the dressing table with the jewelry box open before him.

Gwen thought she might be sick. He had come to steal the Sheridan rubies, after learning from her where they were kept.

A sudden, intense fury galvanized her, propelling her through the door, which she pulled shut behind her. At the click of the lock, the baron whirled.

Gwen might have said he looked comically surprised, but that the light of the single candle cast odd shadows on the baron's face, and he looked more grotesque than droll.

"I do work at Wensley, Papa. I wonder at your surprise."

"But you should be in bed!"

"Should I? Lady Chumleigh is sick, and I am sitting with her. Your informant did not keep you well apprised of events here." Bitterly she added, as her gaze fell to his hand and the priceless ruby necklace he held, "Though she did serve her purposes, I suppose. You'd not have discovered where the rubies were kept, and even where the key lay, so easily without her. Now I understand why you returned the brooch."

"Now, Gwen, 'tisn't so bad as it looks!" the baron protested, allowing the necklace to slide off his palm into the jewelry box. "Nothing's harmed. I only wanted to have a look at the rubies. I've never seen their like before and am not likely to do so in the future." Closing the box, Llanover turned the key, then held it out to Gwen. "You see? Here's the key, sweeting."

Gwen felt sick again. That he should try to persuade her to believe he'd crept into Wensley that night for nothing but a glimpse of the rubies . . .

Gwen took the key but stepped back so she stood between the baron and the door. "I cannot allow you to leave this room, Papa, until you empty the contents of your coat pockets upon the table."

The baron went still, even his mouth, just turning up in a smile as Gwen spoke, froze. But he was quick, and only caught off guard half a second. "You doubt your father, Gwen?" He pulled himself up stiffly. "You believe I am a common thief?"

"Not common, perhaps," she said bitterly. "But a thief nonetheless. You'll not get around me, Papa. Should you try, I will call for help. Now give me whatever it is you have secreted in your pockets."

"You'll send me to debtor's prison!" the baron pleaded.

Gwen ignored his pitiful look and retorted bluntly, "Better debtor's prison than the loss of your hand for thievery. You couldn't cheat at cards so easily, then."

The baron went pale, then heaving an angry sigh, he extracted Lady Chumleigh's ruby earrings from his pocket and slammed them down upon the table. "There! I hope you are satisfied when the men awaiting me in Dartmouth cut my neck."

"Now your other pocket, Papa."

The baron stared a long moment, then, unbelievably, he chuckled. True, there was an edge to his laugh, but there was real amusement in it, too. "Damn, Gwen, but you'd have made a splendid highwayman. The dowagers would not have kept a stray pearl from you. There now!" He plunked the ruby ring upon the table. "That does it. Now, come and see what you've made me surrender."

Gwen shrewdly examined her father's pockets as she walked to the table. They were flat. Immediately she scooped up the ring and earrings and lifting the candle, turned her attention to Lady Chumleigh's jewelry box.

"You had best go, now, Papa," she advised, but absently, for she was anxious to return the earrings and ring safely to their proper place. Holding the candle aloft to see what she did, Gwen did not mark that her father lingered beside her, drawn by the opportunity to feast his eyes again upon the magnificent collection of rubies he'd come so close to having.

Gwen stood before the jewelry box, the jewels her father had almost taken in one hand, the candle in the other, when a voice cold enough to drip ice, shattered the stillness of the night. "Well, well. I should say this is an enlightening scene."

Gwen started so sharply, she tilted the candle, spilling hot wax on her arm. "Oh!" she cried, at the pain of the burning wax and at the sight of Warrick standing in the doorway to his aunt's bedroom.

His green eyes were cold and hard as dark jade as he took in her, the jewel box, and the rubies in her hand in a single, lethal look.

For a moment time seemed suspended as, her mouth still caught in an *O* of surprise, Gwen stared aghast into that deadly gaze. Then, from somewhere near her, she heard her father swear and grit out between his teeth. "The candle!"

Without allowing herself time to think, Gwen blew out the room's only light. Her father fled at once. For a large man with a love of good food and drink, the baron could move swiftly when the occasion warranted. And there could not have been an occasion that warranted more speed. No sooner was the candle doused, than he was flinging open the door to the hallway and racing to the room just a little farther down, where he'd found an unlocked window. Just below lay a narrow roof that slanted to another roof that tilted down to meet a trellis. It was no easy series of leaps and scrambles for a man of middle age, but the baron had cause to exceed himself. An image of his arm cut off at the wrist spurred him. Panting hoarsely, he fled to the copse near the stable yard where he'd tethered his horse, and heaving himself on the mount's back, he fled into the night.

Only when he glanced over his shoulder after he was a half a mile away did Llanover realize there had been little need for such haste. No alarm had been raised. Wensley lay dark and silent. But for one room. He knew, none better, it was Lady Chumleigh's dressing room the candle illuminated, and for once in his life the baron found himself actually praying for the well-being of someone other than himself.

It was as well he prayed for Gwen. She was beyond praying for herself. Her mouth was dry and her heart was beating so hard she could scarcely draw breath.

After she doused the candle, she stood absolutely still, listening to her father's escape, the jewels she had sought to protect, squeezed tightly in her fist.

To the extent that she could think, it surprised her that Warrick did not rush after her father or even call out to raise an alarm. Instead, standing numbly in the dark, she heard the sound of a match being struck. When the match blazed to life, she saw Warrick was looking at her as if he had not taken his eyes off her even in the dark.

There was such savagery in his expression as he wrenched the candle from her nerveless fingers that Gwen could scarcely keep her feet from retreating a step or two, out the door even. She ought to have fled with her father! She bit her lip, trying to still her panic. Had she tried to flee with the baron, Warrick would have pursued them. Besides, she was not guilty!

"I was not taking the jewels."

Warrick did not accord her even a glance. He caught her hand and forcing it into the light, pried open her fist. Against the milk white of her skin, Lady Chumleigh's rubies gleamed a deep, damning red.

Clenching her jaw against the cry of dismay welling up in her throat. Gwen tilted her hand, sending the jewels sliding into the jewelry box. "Whaaat . . . " She bit her lip. Her voice shook so she couldn't speak.

Warrick could, standing no more than a foot from her, his every muscle so taut with tension she could almost feel him vibrate with it. "Who was he?"

Too frightened to think whether the truth or a lie would serve her best, she told the truth. "My father."

"What!" Warrick flung her wrist aside and with all the force of his sense of betrayal struck out at the dressing table with his fist. The candle rocked, sending the shadows of the room careening chaotically, and Gwen cried out in alarm.

Good. Let the witch be frightened out of her wits.

"Your father?" And now Warrick's eyes, eyes that had been cold with fury, blazed with it. "Not the lovingly strict grandfather who raised you in your father's place to be such an estimable, devoted, chaste—oh yes, above all chaste—widow?" And then both his hands were upon her, clenching her shoulders so tightly Gwen cried out in pain, but Warrick didn't seem to hear as he began to shake her.

"How long have you planned this? From the first? Did you think of this thievery every time you told me you could not afford to lose this position? Please, my lord," Warrick mimicked, as he rattled Gwen's teeth with the fury of his attack. "I've my standards, and I cannot lose this position. I've my poor, dear brothers and sisters to support. Do they exist at all? Are they lurking below, preparing to steal off with the china and plate?"

Gwen clutched frantically at Warrick's arms, struggling futilely against his strength. "N-no! No! P-please!" She feared he meant to snap her neck, and perhaps he did. "S-stop! Stop!"

He did. Dazed, her heart pounding so fiercely she could not hear, Gwen dragged in a breath, but she retained sufficient presence of mind not to move even slightly. There was too much violence in Warrick still, in the bruising grip he retained on her, in his hard breathing, in the flare of his nostrils, and in his deadly, blazing green gaze.

Warrick did not himself know what he meant to do. He wanted to shake her again, fling her savagely aside . . . jerk her to him. God above, but she was beautiful even now, and particularly now, perhaps, with only her thin robe and nightgown for cover and the thick braid of her hair loosened to wanton disarray by the shaking he'd given her.

Warrick released Gwen suddenly, lifting his hands away from her as swiftly as if she'd gone up in flames.

She stumbled, off balance without his hold, then realized Lady Chumleigh was calling out from her room. Abruptly, flinging one murderous look at Gwen, Warrick wheeled away to go to his aunt.

Gwen did not move. She could not seem to order her thoughts after Warrick's violence. Suddenly she shivered and clasped her arms about her shoulders, one thought crystallizing out of the chaotic swirl: Warrick believed her capable of stealing his aunt's rubies.

And then he flung back into the dressing room, his fury seeming to set the very air about him in turbulent motion. "She needs you. God help you, you conniving jade, but you had best give her the greatest care it is possible to give!"

"Wh-what will you do to me afterward?"

"Damnation!" Gwen, no coward by any means, recoiled at the crack of the oath, certain Warrick meant to hit her. "Get in there!" he snarled. "You will think of someone other than yourself this night, Mrs. Tarrant, and if it torments you to wonder what I mean to do, then so much the better! I trust you will work twice as hard."

Chapter 21

Gwen did not sleep at all that night, but not because Warrick had threatened her. Lady Chumleigh's condition regressed sharply. Once more her fever surged, and with it came again all the aches and restless tossing that made her so uncomfortable.

Throughout the night, Gwen applied cold compresses to Lady Chumleigh's brow, sponged her with cool cloths, and dosed with the elderberry bark infusion as often as she could coax the elder woman to swallow.

Warrick spent the remainder of the night in his aunt's sitting room. Gwen did not know what he did there, whether he slept on the couch or kept watch to see she did not try to escape. She certainly did not look to see. She'd have liked not to think of him at all, in fact.

She could not have wished for anything less possible. Her stomach stayed tightly clenched, and as she wrung out one of the cold compresses before laying it on Lady Chumleigh's brow, for example, she would suddenly relive the instant she had looked up to see Warrick in the door of his aunt's room, or worse, with equally piercing clarity the moment after he had lit his match.

Each time it was as if the memory were fresh, and the anguish as sharp as if she had never experienced it before. With the death of her mother and grandfather, Gwen had lost the two people dearest to her in the world apart from her brothers and sisters, and yet she had not suffered then in quite the way she did that night, while she nursed Lady Chumleigh. In their case she had had the balm of knowing she'd done all she could, and if they were taken, it was Divine Will.

But the dreadful, searing, irreparable scene in Lady Chumleigh's dressing room was her responsibility. Had she only guarded her tongue, it would never have happened! Granted her father was the real rogue, but she had shown him the way, blithely divulging to him how ill-guarded the rubies were and where precisely they were kept. She had not realized, she really had not, just how far beyond redemption he had sunk, but that did not matter. She had had no right to betray the information to anyone.

And Warrick believed her an accomplice! When she thought of that, and of the fury in his green eyes, eyes that had always gleamed with such light for her, she bit her lip until she tasted blood.

She'd no anger to serve as a buffer against him. She knew she could not have looked more guilty than she had when he had found her with his aunt's priceless rubies in her hand, a stranger at her side, and the hour well after midnight.

Gwen clenched her jaw against another welling of despair. She could not bear much more of the regret, the self-directed anger, the if onlys. She must take each moment as it came, and just now she must focus on Lady Chumleigh, who demanded all of her flagging energies. She must not think of Warrick in the next room, waiting to . . . do what to her? Gwen clenched her jaw the harder.

By four o'clock, she had put more compresses on Lady Chumleigh's brow than she could count, repeatedly stoked the fire to the sweltering temperature Dr. Hobson had ordered, and spooned countless sips of the elderberry leaves and pearl barley infusion into her patient. Exhausted, she no longer cared what Warrick might do to her. By dawn, when at long last beads of sweat broke out on Lady Chumleigh's brow, Gwen scarcely had the strength to be glad. An hour or so later, when Lady Chumleigh fell into a real sleep, Gwen was too drained to think of anything at all. Her shoulders slumped, her mind muddled, she sank into a chair near Lady Chumleigh's window and fell asleep.

The next day, when she thought back on that night, Gwen would remember hazily, as if she had dreamed the episode, that strong arms lifted her from the chair, and that when she cried out in alarm, a deep voice bade her "Hush" more gruffly than gently.

When she first awakened only several hours later, however, she did not recall being moved from Lady Chumleigh's rooms. For the first groggy moments she did not even remember the cause of the heaviness oppressing her, and when she realized she had no idea where she was, she was so unsettled she could not think coherently at all.

She lay upon a narrow, unfamiliar bed, really more cot than bed, and could not think why. The room was one she had never seen. Almost the size of a closet, its walls were bare and it was furnished with only the cot and a night table. At the end of the room was one window. From where Gwen lay, she could see only the sky and the limbs of a large oak. Frowning, she recalled seeing the great tree only from . . . Warrick's windows.

Warrick.

Like an ocean wave memory crashed over her. She rolled to her side, curling into a ball and clapping her fist to her mouth. A sob, an endless, "aaeeeee" of regret and loss, rose in her, but she clenched her teeth against it. She had not cried since her mother's death and would not now for fear that she might never stop.

Suddenly, almost violently, Gwen tossed back the sheet and leaped out of the bed. She did not know what she intended, only knew she could not lie in the bed another moment. On her feet she went still again, looking down at herself. She wore only her nightgown. Her robe? She saw it then. It had been carelessly tossed upon the end of the bed.

No maid trained by Mrs. Ames would ever have treated a piece of clothing so casually. Who had brought her to the room and undressed her? It was then she remembered stirring in strong arms and provoking that "Hush."

Warrick had carried her. He had removed her robe, seen her in her nightgown. At another time Gwen would have flushed with embarrassment or indignation. And she might even have been aroused, too, she admitted it, by the thought of him seeing her dressed in only a flimsy piece of cotton. But not that morning. She was too distraught to care how Warrick had seen her. Nor did she believe he'd have been in a mood to look closely at her.

But he had brought her to a new room. Why? Was she confined? There were two doors. She tried the one she thought must lead to the hall. It did not open.

Did he mean to give her over to the magistrate of the county? What would happen to her then? Punishment for theft was so cruel. She had not exaggerated when she warned her father he might lose his hand. Perhaps she would be transported. What a fate to desire! She would never see her brothers and sisters again.

Panic racing through her, she ran to the other door. It opened easily. Her breath lodged in her throat, Gwen stepped through the doorway and recognized the large room instantly. It was Warrick's.

What did it mean that he had put her so near him? She crossed swiftly to his outer door, nearly running. The door handle jiggled, but the door did not move.

He had imprisoned her.

Her hand trembled as she lowered it, and she realized she felt almost sick. Clasping her hands together, she flicked her gaze about Warrick's room, seeking something, anything to steady her. And she did find, at least, something to occupy her.

Like any prisoner she'd been allotted clothes. One of her dresses lay upon a chair along with her undergarments, stocking, shoes, and a comb. Gathering up her belongings, she saw that water had been left for her as well. She held the pitcher and bowl to her hip and returned to the smaller room to make herself ready for whatever lay ahead.

When she was done rebraiding her hair, for no pins had been provided her, Gwen remained there, sometimes pacing to the window, sometimes sitting stiffly upon the cot. Warrick's room would have been more comfortable: the view from his window broader, but she could not bring herself to treat his room as her own, though she acknowledged grimly that the distinction between the two rooms was very fine.

Finally, perhaps an hour, perhaps more, later, Gwen heard a key click in the lock of Warrick's door. Strong strides then approached her room, and she leaped to her feet, for it was Warrick. She knew it.

He flung open her door as if he meant to wake her, if she were not already arisen. Still it did not take him aback to find her fully dressed and standing, hands clasped tightly at her waist, as if she must hold to herself for courage. He raked her with eyes not a whit warmer or softer for the hours that had passed. "I see you've explored your new quarters, Mrs. Tarrant."

"What do you intend to do with me?"

She was proud to hear her voice was even, and that pride gave her the courage to face Warrick's contempt with her chin raised.

"Concerned about your fate before the magistrate, are you, Mrs. Tarrant?" He taunted her with a cruel smile. "You've reason to be, if you are. Squire Bentham's of the old school that holds criminals must be dealt with harshly, as an example."

Gwen's mouth went so dry she could not reply. She could not make a protestation of innocence, however futile it might be, or even ask when the squire would come. There was no question what would happen then. At any trial it would be her word against what the Marquess of Warrick had seen. She'd be found guilty. Her hand . . . she gripped it, going white, her blue eyes staring.

Suddenly a strong hand clamped down hard upon her neck and pushed on her. "Sit, damn it!" Warrick commanded, when she went rigid with fear. "And put your head between your legs. You are about to faint."

Gwen did feel odd, and she allowed her head to sink forward, bowing to the weight of his hand now upon her. Gradually, as she took deep breaths, the darkness that had swarmed at the edge of her vision began to recede.

As if he could sense her recovery, Warrick removed his hand from her neck and himself from her side. Gwen thought he took himself to the window and saw she'd guessed aright when she slowly lifted her head.

He was not enjoying the narrow view the small window afforded, however. He was watching her, and their eyes locked.

"For attempting to betray the trust of an old, helpless woman, you deserve to suffer whatever punishment terrified you merely to think of just then. There's a rub, however. That old woman is in the greatest need of you. For some inexplicable reason, you soothe her as none of the other servants can." Gwen flushed, though not at being called a servant. She knew what she was, but Warrick had never made her feel one before. "You will not escape punishment, however, Mrs. Tarrant. Never think it," he went on, his voice harsh enough to make her flinch. "Perhaps I cannot yet expose you to the world as the thief you are, but I can be certain everyone knows you to be a jade. This will be your room for the remainder of your stay at Wensley. As the room adjoins mine, all and sundry will assume you share my bed at night. They will be wrong, but only you and I will know I keep you here because I despise and distrust you. You may accept my terms, Mrs. Tarrant, or you may try your luck with Bentham forthwith."

There was no question which immediate fate—she had duly registered Warrick had not eliminated Squire Bentham in future—Gwen would choose. Still, she didn't deserve any punishment at all and found, finally, the voice to ask, "You will not listen to my version of the events of last night?"

Warrick gave a savage, mocking laugh. "What will you say, Mrs. Tarrant? That you were merely showing off the famous Sheridan rubies to your father? That he keeps late hours, otherwise he'd have come at a proper hour through the front door?" Warrick snapped his fingers. "Or, perhaps, you will maintain that you intended to prevent him from taking the jewels and that you've no idea at all how he learned where Aunt Vi has safely kept her rubies for half a century?"

What use to repeat what he had already dismissed? Gwen raised her chin and said evenly, "I am innocent. I would not steal Lady Chumleigh's jewels."

He did not pause to draw breath. "I saw you, and I cannot be beguiled twice."

For the next few days Gwen lived by a routine Warrick set for her. She stayed with his aunt from early morning until midafternoon when he gave her a half hour to herself in her room. At exactly four o'clock he came to take her for a walk in the gardens, observing mockingly the first day that even prisoners in Newgate were allowed exercise.

That release from the confines of the house and Lady Chumleigh's stuffy sickroom should have been the best part of Gwen's day. It was almost the worst. Gwen never felt more a prisoner than she did then, with Warrick following five steps back of her, his green eyes fixed coldly upon her.

He could not require a footman to take the duty he so obviously despised, though. The thought almost brought Gwen a grim smile. Everyone at Wensley, by his doing, believed her to be his mistress. What interesting gossip there would have been, had it been thought Warrick, of all men, had to set a watch on his mistress to keep her from escaping him.

For the most part the staff at Wensley was too well trained to react overtly to the change in Gwen's status. Perhaps she did have the effect of putting an end to whispering among the maids when she walked into a room, but Dabney remained quite as formal as ever, and poor Finch was too worried over her mistress to notice much of anything.

Mrs. Ames, alone, approached the subject. The first time they met in the hallway, she gave Gwen a long, thorough look before she shook her head and said cryptically, "Nay, you're too pale. Go on, then, my dear. Whatever has happened, you need rest more than my mouth, I'm thinkin'."

Gwen did need rest. Though Lady Chumleigh had improved gradually since her fever had broken, she still required someone with her at all times. In addition to her day duties, Gwen sat with her employer each evening until a maid came to relieve her for the night. Then she returned to the little room attached to Warrick's, where she was supposed to sleep.

Only she did not.

She could not, at least not easily. Warrick did not allow her to close the door between their rooms. He wanted the servants who came to his room to see the easy access he had to her. At least that was what she supposed. Warrick did not explain himself.

Every night she lay in her narrow bed in the dark, listening to Warrick in his room. Sometimes his valet, Jeffries came with him. A few, low words would be exchanged; Jeffries would turn down his master's bed; the wardrobe might be opened and shut; then Jeffries would depart; and she'd only Warrick's footsteps to follow. Inevitably they came toward her door. Just as inevitably, every night, she went very still, tensing, her eyes fastened upon the shadows playing on her ceiling. Closer, closer, and then, he passed by without pause.

Every night it was the same, until the fifth night, she could not bear it. Warrick's footsteps came again. Tonight he would come into her room. Tonight he would say he had finally realized she could not be guilty. He must! He had won. He had coaxed her into letting him into her heart. And what was the result? She had never known such hurt. He punished her more cruelly than he imagined. The hurt of it all, the loneliness, throbbed inside her, growing every night.

But he passed by again. And that night Gwen broke. She clapped her hand over her mouth. Dear heaven! The sob welling in her hurt so much. She seized her pillow and stuffed it over her head. She could not bear for him to hear! He would be glad. Dear heaven . . . he would be glad. That she could not bear.

Had she but known it, sleep came no easier each night to Warrick than it did to Gwen. He could hear the squeak of her narrow bed each time she turned; could hear the rustle of her sheets; and even, he thought, her soft breathing.

Without doubt he could remember the gossamer fineness of her nightgown from the time he had carried her to her new quarters. The thin cotton had caught on the peak of her breast when he had put her into her bed. He'd tugged it free and felt the firm fullness of her.

Almost, in the hot summer darkness, he could smell her scent. Warrick smiled grimly to himself. He wanted her still.

She was a criminal, a woman capable of the basest betrayal. It did not seem to matter. And the torment went on and on every night. He could not dump her back in her old room. Oh, no, he did not doubt the witch would seek to escape the moment she was unguarded.

God! It was a damnable situation. Lucian tossed restlessly in his bed, counting her sins, hating her . . . What was that? He lay still, listening intently, though in his heart he knew. But perhaps she had gotten up from her bed, meant to escape . . . but no. The noise when it came again was muffled, as if she had hidden her head beneath her pillow. Still, there was no mistaking the ragged, despairing sound.

Something tightened in him, but he thrust that response away instantly. Good, he told himself, instead. She should cry for her sins. She'd shown no other evidence of remorse. She had intended to betray his aunt, an old woman who had taken her in when she needed help and who paid her royally for the work she did. He knew just what her salary was . . . she was still crying. He could hear every shuddering breath even with her head buried.

She cried like this to a purpose, to make him feel the one at fault. She'd fail there, though. She deserved to cry like this, as if . . . God, as if she were coming undone.

He clenched his hands into fists, gripping his sheet as if he thought to hold himself in his bed. And still she wept.

Damn! It was not possible to cry like that at will. And even were it, she was going to make herself sick. Warrick wrenched his sheet aside and stalked into Gwen's little room, savagely intent upon bringing her to her senses. He'd slap her, if need be, he thought, and he did jerk back her sheet.

She gave a cry of fear. It was the wateriest most pitiful excuse for a scream Warrick had ever heard. And it twisted in him like a knife. Her face was awash with tears. He could see them gleaming in the moonlight. And by that same light settled the issue of whether or not her sobbing was contrived. It was a homely detail convinced him. Her delicate nose was a streaming mess.

With an oath he scooped her into his arms. She gave a feeble cry and pushed at him, but she seemed weak as a kitten. He was not even holding her very tightly, but when she struck out at his chest to no effect whatsoever, she gave a wild cry and then suddenly, to Warrick's considerable dismay, curled her face into the hollow of his neck and burst once again into tears.

Holding her, Lucian fumbled for the linen cloth Jeffries left on his washstand each night. It was not the fine linen of a handkerchief, but it would do to wipe her face. He thrust it at her when he sat down on his bed. She could not seem to lift her head, but she edged the cloth between her face and his bare shoulder.

"Sshh, sshh." Lucian heard himself whispering. He was almost afraid for her, to the extent he could be afraid for a woman of her stamp, she seemed so completely undone.

He could feel her trying to halt the wrenching flow. The breath caught in her throat, and her body tightened with the force of the sob trying to force its way out. He found himself rocking her. "Easy, easy," he whispered, and she gulped for air and another sob shook her.

He began to rub her back as he rocked her. She seemed too small and slender for such deep, tearing sobs. He held her tighter, pressing her to him, saying over and over, "Easy, easy. Quiet now."

Finally, after an eternity, when the linen cloth felt wet and clammy to his skin, her sobs grew shallower. She took another gulping breath. And another, and then he heard her sniff into the saturated linen cloth.

He was afraid to move—afraid he might set her off again. He rocked her, holding her, while she sniffed and caught her breath. Then, after a little, he felt her body relax against him.

She was warm and pliant in his arms. And fit, somehow, with the silky cotton of her nightgown smooth against his chest. His chest. Something crackled inside Warrick, jolting him into a new kind of awareness. Until that moment he'd not cared that he had not thought to drag on his dressing gown before he went to her. Now he felt every inch of his nakedness— and hers.

Perhaps she felt him tense. Perhaps she simply came aware herself. He felt her eyelashes fan softly across his collarbone. Her eyes remained open, and her body was no longer so malleable. She lifted her head away from his shoulder.

He could see little but that she regarded him gravely. And then, slowly, so infinitely slowly, she lifted her hand to his cheek.

Lucian drew in his breath sharply. "If . . . "

"No." It was the merest whisper on the night air. "I know this will make no diff—"

He took her mouth before she could finish, pulling her to him with a low, throaty growl.

Chapter 22

Awareness came swiftly to Gwen the next morning—and with it memory. She remembered the taste of Warrick's mouth: the feel of his hands everywhere; where hers had been; how he had felt, the hair of his chest, his long, smooth back, the curve of his hip. . . .

She had known so little. Warrick had been right there. She had had no idea how poor her previous experience had been. There had been everything to learn. And much of it, in the end, about herself.

She edged the border of her pillowcase over her heating face, but her mind, of course, was immune to the childish trick. Though her face hid, her mind conjured for her vividly every searing, swirling moment of her abandon.

She had not had the least inkling how shamelessly she could give herself. It seemed to have been the urgent way he pulled her to him, as if he could not get her soon enough, that had set her ablaze—that and the low growling sound that had come from deep in his throat.

With a groan of her own she buried her face in her pillow. She'd not known . . . lovemaking could be . . . it had been so fierce. They might have been trying to hurt each other even, except that her cries had not been of pain at all. Oh, not at all. They'd been cries of the most intense pleasure.

Again and again they had come together, until Gwen had protested she could not rise to meet him again, but Warrick had proved her a liar and by the by shown her a different sort of lovemaking, lazier and slower, and she'd wanted him again. He had fallen asleep then, just before dawn, but not she. Gwen had watched him until his breathing deepened, and then she had slipped away to her cot. It was one thing to open herself to

Warrick in the dark of night, but it would have been quite another to lie beside him naked and vulnerable in the revealing light of day.

And yet, she'd do the same thing again in the same circumstances. She had never been as drained and weak as she had been after she had leached away all her remorse and hurt with those tears.

Drained of her defenses and in his arms—for he had not gloated, not at all. He'd held her to him, hushed her, rocked her . . . and given her a cloth for her nose. She'd gone limp against his warmth finally, soaking it in, feeling it seep through her spent body like a balm. And it had been the most natural thing in the world, when, after a little, her body had seemed to bloom with a different awareness of him.

If she had it to do over a thousand times, she would again lift her hand to his face in invitation. She could not regret what she had done. As well to regret being born. It had been right to love Warrick so, for she did love him.

And he had wanted her. Oh yes, and fiercely. It had been so heady, the depth of his wanting.

But it was morning now. The sun slanted through her window, promising a hot day, demanding full awareness. And she was aware, had been the night before as she had begun to say to him, that nothing they might do in his bed would change his opinion of her. Today, as he had yesterday, he would want her physically though he still believed her to be the basest of creatures.

Awareness is one thing, acceptance another. After what they had shared, Gwen knew she could not bear to see that his green eyes really would not light for her again.

And there was a good possibility she would not have to see him ever again, if all went well.

He was to attend a garden party at the Godolphins. Lady Chumleigh had been strong enough to sit up in her bed the day before and had mentioned the affair. Gwen had not listened closely. She did not know how long the party was to last, could only hope it would last long enough.

When Gwen went to Lady Chumleigh's rooms, she found the elder lady not only awake but truly alert for the first time in the ten days since she had fallen ill.

"I must say, you are looking very well, my lady." Gwen found a smile for her.

"Well, if I am, I cannot say you are, chit." Gwen actually laughed then. At least she could be assured when she left that Lady Chumleigh was as good as recovered. "You've circles under your eyes," Lady Chumleigh remarked with much of her former spirit. "I find it interesting they match in color and size the pair Lucian sports, though I must say you do not look to be in quite the black spirits he was, when he came to bid me good morrow and inform me I was well enough to do without him until tonight."

"We have both been concerned for you, my lady," Gwen replied, leaning down to fluff the pillows beneath Lady Chumleigh's gray head. Not by coincidence the task removed her from Lady Chumleigh's line of sight. She needed a moment to recover not only from the mention of Warrick, but from the report that their one night had put him in a foul mood. Foolishly she had not thought he would regret it. Gwen clenched her jaw and looked a little stonier as she went to fetch Lady Chumleigh's tea from the tray a maid had brought.

Lady Chumleigh waited until Gwen was seated and also sipping from a steaming cup before she spoke again. "Your bleary eyes are not really what I wished to ask you about this morning, my dear. They are quite your own business, but there is this curious matter of your new quarters. When I wished Finch to fetch you for me a little early, she floundered about in the most helpless way. I did finally ascertain that you no longer sleep in the room I assigned you, but I'd deuced little success discovering where you do sleep now."

Gwen was rather proud that her cup did not rattle against its saucer. Though she had accepted she could not leave Wensley without making an explanation to Lady Chumleigh, she had hoped she would not need to discuss her new quarters.

Carefully she set her tea aside. "Are you strong enough for a most fantastical story, my lady?" she asked, smiling rather raggedly.

Lady Chumleigh frowned. "Whatever my strength, I am not certain I wish to hear your story, child. From the look on your face it is a sad one."

Gwen was not prepared for the tears that stung her eyes. She had thought herself completely composed. "'Tis a very minor tragedy really, my lady," she said, looking away a moment. "Its principal character is my father. He is . . ." she paused a moment trying to think how to characterize the baron without being too bitter or saying who he was. Finally she shrugged and said simply, "He is not the most admirable of men."

It took so little time to tell the story, to own it was she who had so unthinkingly revealed where Lady Chumleigh kept her rubies, and then to tell how she had found her father in the dressing room only to be found in her turn by Warrick. Gwen admitted readily that she'd blown out the candle. "He is my father," she explained quietly. "When it came to it, despite his sins, I could not see him punished for a crime he'd been prevented from committing. I do not say I was right, only that I could do nothing else. Not surprisingly, however, Lord Warrick reached the most damning conclusion. I cannot blame him. I looked every inch my father's accomplice. Because you still needed me, however, Lord Warrick could not deliver me to Squire Bentham for the punishment he believed I deserved, and so he punished me himself. It was he who had my things moved to the valet's closet next to his room. He did not force me into his bed. That was the furtherest thing from his mind, but he did wish to destroy the good reputation to which he thought I had no right."

Gwen paused then. There was only the one bit more to tell, but the words would not seem to come. "It . . ." She twined her fingers tightly together where they lay in her lap. "It was I," she said finally, so softly Lady Chumleigh had to strain to hear, "who went to him, my lady. Quite like all the rest."

"Like all the rest?" Lady Chumleigh echoed disbelievingly. "Don't be absurd, child. He put you in an intolerable situation and without the least authority."

Gwen forced a wobbly smile. "I should say Lord Warrick is his own authority. But you must not misunderstand, Lady Chumleigh. I do not regret what I did, though I know how shameless I must sound. I really do not intend to marry, and . . ." her voice trailed off as she found she simply could not admit to more.

Lady Chumleigh was not so constrained. "But you would rather have had one night with him than none?"

Gwen flushed, but nodded. "Which brings me to my final point. Though I willingly erred the once, I cannot do so repeatedly." She laughed with little humor. "I have some scruples left, it would seem. I must go, my lady."

Lady Chumleigh started. "Do you mean you intend to leave Wensley?"

"Yes, if you will allow me to go," Gwen replied firmly, though the stunned look on the old woman's face wrenched her heart. "I have no notion what Lord Warrick intends in regards to me, but I cannot be certain of my response should he decide I am not intolerable at least once more. Oh!" She wrung her hands, as her cheeks heated. "I had not thought to admit so much, but there it is. I cannot trust myself! I must go, Lady Chumleigh, if, that is, you do not intend to have me brought before Squire Bentham."

"Bah!" Lady Chumleigh dismissed the possibility with a wave of her mottled hand. "I may be old and half dead, but I know who is capable of thievery and who is not. Dear heaven! At the very least you are intelligent enough not to attempt to steal my rubies with Warrick in residence."

Lady Chumleigh's affirmation gratified Gwen so she wanted to throw her arms around the gruff, old dear; but the affirmation hurt, too, for it raised the inevitable question: if his aunt believed in her, why could Warrick not?

"I have it!" Lady Chumleigh exclaimed suddenly. "You will return in a month, when Lucian is quite gone. I shall not tell him, either. I shall tell him, instead, I've hired a prodigiously uninteresting old stick. He'll never think to come and see for himself."

Gwen did not believe she could ever return to Wensley. She did not shrink from facing the servants or neighbors with a ruined reputation. In truth she never thought of them. She thought only of Warrick. Were he to want her still, she could not resist him; and were he not to want her . . . she smiled grimly to herself. His disinterest would be worse. And what if he were betrothed or married? No, she did not think she could return to Wensley, but Gwen knew better than most that the future was impossible to predict.

"I am grateful you give the choice to me, my lady, but in all honesty, I cannot promise I will return. I must have some time to think what to do."

Lady Chumleigh grumbled and even tried to cajole, but Gwen would not be persuaded to a firmer commitment. In the end Lady Chumleigh could do naught but grudgingly agree that they would correspond in a month and go from there.

They did not take leave of one another then. Gwen packed her old valise, then returned for what was a more painful session of farewell than she had expected it to be. As she said simply to Lady Chumleigh, the elder woman had come to mean a great deal to her.

Word had spread in the mysterious way it does among servants, and both Finch and Mrs. Ames awaited Gwen in the hallway outside Lady Chumleigh's rooms. She had not expected them at all, and once more painful tears welled in her eyes. Still, even when Mrs. Ames roughly embraced her, Gwen retained enough control to reply, when she was asked where she would go, only that she meant to go to her brothers and sisters. It was the truth, and if one and all assumed her brothers and sisters lived in St. Ives, she had not actually said it.

Late that night Warrick scowled out the window of his carriage as it rattled over the country road, returning him from the Godolphins. He had stayed to dinner at Sir James's invitation, though he had known the Godolphins would misinterpret his lengthy stay at their home as interest in their eldest daughter. He'd not a whit of interest in Jane, though, only a desire to escape Wensley. Not the house, of course, but the witch in it.

He knew precisely why, finally, she had yielded to him. She had denied it, but she lied as easily as she breathed. Of course she hoped to insinuate herself into his good graces again. He did not know the precise end she sought. Perhaps she hoped for as little as to escape punishment; or perhaps, she hoped to fascinate him so he would take her to London and install her there in comfort, buy her rubies even.

Warrick scowled so darkly, he'd have frightened anyone who did not know him. She was the wiliest jade imaginable. Oh, her tears had been real. He did accept that. No one could feign such shuddering, uncontrolled sobbing, but she'd recovered nicely enough, landing on her slender feet. Or more precisely, in his arms.

And why had she landed where she had wanted to land? Because he had allowed her sobs to touch him.

He ought to have hardened his heart. He had every reason to be glad of her tears, but no, he'd gone to her. And held her, and been lost from the moment he touched her.

Dear God, he grew warm even now thinking how she had felt, all soft and rounded and womanly with only that thin, silky piece of cotton over her. And then when she had touched no more provocative place than his face! He'd never felt such a surge of desire. He'd not been able to control himself, something that hadn't happened to him in over a decade. Nor had he taken her only the once. Oh no. He'd had to have her again and again, as if she were an opiate to which he'd become addicted with one taste.

Above, on the box of the coach, Warrick's coachman heard him laugh and looked over to the groom by him, rolling his eyes as if to say his nibs was acting most peculiar. Had the two men been privy to Warrick's expression, they'd not have been reassured.

If he was addicted, he'd some excuse. She had proved as passionate as she was beautiful. He had known she would not be docile when he at last got her to his bed. She'd too much spirit, but he'd not imagined she would be as abandoned and fiery and sensuous as she had been.

Almost . . . he gritted his jaw and breathing deeply of the night air, sought sanity. He would not be taken in by her again. She had no particular feeling for him. She was simply a good whore—a superb whore. He would take her to London.

There. It had taken him the day to decide, but he had. He wanted her still, and he would have her until he tired of her. He would simply take care to guard his valuables.

His decision made, Warrick strode swiftly up the steps at Wensley, and when Dabney met him at the door, asked after his aunt out of habit more than anything.

His first surprise came then. He had assumed Lady Chumleigh would be asleep, as it was late in the evening, but Dabney informed him not only was she awake, she awaited him.

"Now, Dabney?" Warrick repeated.

"Yes, my lord."

"Has something happened?" A flicker of alarm shot through him when the old retainer hesitated. Something had happened. Something Dabney did not want to tell him. "Never mind, Dabney. I can see you believe Aunt Vi would wish to give me the news."

Dabney bowed low, likely from relief. "As you say, my lord."

Warrick's alarm turned to consternation when he entered his aunt's room. A complete stranger sat by her bed, reading to her.

"You needn't look so baffled, Lucian. We've had a changing of the guard while you were away."

"I beg your pardon, Aunt Vi?"

"This is Miss Smeddley, Lucian, my new companion. Smeddley, you've the dubious honor of meeting my nephew, Lord Warrick. Lucian's not usually so remiss about the social niceties—"

"Where is your former companion, Aunt Vi?"

"Lucian!" Lady Chumleigh looked the very picture of offended dignity. "I can scarce believe you interrupted me. I vow your father would be carried off to his reward were I to report such a lapse in manners."

"I do beg your pardon, Aunt Vi." Lucian gritted his teeth and bowed over the hand of the reed-thin, angular, middle-aged woman whom his aunt had presented to him as her new companion. "And, I beg yours as well, Miss, er, Smeddley. If I have been rude, it is only because I had a matter of some importance to discuss with, ah, Mrs. Tarrant."

"Indeed, Lucian?" Lady Chumleigh said, a provocative twinkle in her old eyes. "Well, whatever you had to discuss with Gwen, I suppose you will be obliged to discuss with me now."

She was toying with him. Lucian's eyes narrowed, and Lady Chumleigh decided it was time to relent. "Oh very well! I can see you are impatient to have a coze this moment. Smeddley, that will be all for tonight. I shall ring for you if I need aught."

"Very well, my lady, Good night. Good night, my lord."

Warrick mustered a curt, brief nod, before he returned his impatient gaze to his aunt. She waited for Miss Smeddley to close the door behind her, then said helpfully, "Smeddley is the vicar's sister as you'll have guessed." Warrick, who had not spared a thought for Miss Smeddley's identity, expressed his impatience with a low growl. "You don't give a whit who she is?" Lady Chumleigh interpreted that sound accurately. "Well, you ought to at least give thanks Smeddley seems to have an unending supply of companions for me. I lost mine today on your account, nevvy."

The news stunned him. For a moment Warrick could only stare blankly at his aunt. "Gwen has left Wensley?" he asked at last.

Lady Chumleigh gave a snort that signaled her supply of patience was not limitless either. "Did I not just say so? And did I not name you the cause of her leaving? Good lord, Lucian, I cannot blame her! You exceeded yourself, dear boy, compromising her as you did. Nay, I'll have my say, thank you. Age before beauty and all that. I've had to sleep half the day away to be certain I'd have the strength for this coze, though sleeping was easy enough to do as she wasn't here to entertain me. But that brings me back my point, which is that as they were *my* rubies she was supposedly stealing, her punishment was mine to decide—not yours!"

Not a muscle moved in Warrick's handsome face. "Where is she, Aunt Vi?"

"Nor," Lady Chumleigh went on doggedly, "when it comes to it, was it your place to decide her guilty. My companion, my rubies, ergo, my right to judge!"

A muscle in Warrick's jaw tensed. "You were not there, Aunt Vi, and did not see her about to hand your gems to her father. I did see her, and as, given your illness, I was the authority in the house, I did as I saw fit. Now where is she?"

"Bah!" Lady Chumleigh scowled ominously. "You reacted in anger, Lucian, because you thought she'd made a fool of you. But if her purpose in being here at Wensley was to steal the rubies, then why did she choose a time when you were not only in residence here, but quite likely to visit my room to check upon me?"

"Not being afflicted with idiocy, it did occur to me to question why she chose such an inopportune time, Aunt Vi, and the answer is not so difficult to see, if one chooses." Warrick returned his aunt's baleful glare without blinking. "Obviously her father could not come at any other time."

"She could have been here years, Lucian," Lady Chumleigh rebutted, though something in her nephew's grim expression made her soften her tone. "He had all the time in the world to make the trip from wherever he makes his home. Not St. Ives, I wager."

"There, at least, we agree. Her father will not be in St. Ives. But where, I repeat, is Mrs. Tarrant?"

"And why are you so eager to know, Lucian? If she's a thief or an accomplice to thievery, I should think you would wish to shun her."

Warrick's eyes narrowed. "You are doing it a bit brown, Aunt Vi. Her morals hold little interest for me."

"Well, they should," Lady Chumleigh snapped, impatient again. "She left because she'd no wish to succumb to you twice."

"Succumb to me? I did not force her to my bed!"

"I did not mean succumb in that sense, Lucian, I know you did not drag her down unwilling. Gwen made clear who made the first overture."

He was a man of thirty, famous, or infamous perhaps, for his affairs, and yet something in the softening of his aunt's voice, when she said she knew it was Gwen had come to him, made Warrick smother a curse. He was too self-assured to betray his discomfort, but he did defend himself to the extent that he said levelly, "She is a jade, Aunt Vi. A beautiful, convincing one, I grant, but a jade nonetheless. She knows how to use the truth."

"Meaning that she has managed to pull the wool over my eyes about the rubies, by telling the truth about going to your bed? Perhaps, or perhaps you misread the scene with her father."

"Very well, then. Let us make a wager," Warrick proposed, deciding the only way he would get the truth from his aunt was to appeal to her gaming instincts. "You tell me where she said she would go. If she is there, I will concede that I may be wrong about her, but if she is not there, you will concede it is you who are wrong."

Lady Chumleigh snorted. "How unfair you are, Lucian! You will only concede that you *may* be wrong, while I must concede I *am* wrong. Still . . . I'll take it. I am that certain of winning, and I want that Tintoretto of yours, too. I've always admired it prodigiously. What do you want?"

At that moment there was only one thing Warrick wanted: a black-haired Celtic witch whose escape had taken him so by surprise he still could not quite credit that she was not lying on that miserable bed in the valet's closet, waiting in the dark for him to come to her.

"Where is she, Aunt Vi?"

"In truth she said only that she would go to her brothers and sisters. It is my assumption they are in St. Ives."

Chapter 23

"Lucian! Can you have been to the far end of Cornwall and back? It has only been four days." Lady Chumleigh studied her nephew for some sign of what he had found on his journey. Her heart sank. He looked grim as well as weary.

"Were there an official record for the Wensley to St. Ives run, I'm certain I'd have broken it." Lucian managed a faint smile as he kissed his aunt's wrinkled cheek. "Almost broke myself as well. The Cornish have a singular tendency to label mere ruts as roads. But it is a most welcome balm to return and see that your health looks to have improved appreciably in my absence."

"I am certain there is no connection between my health and your absence," Lady Chumleigh returned wryly, "but I have progressed. Even went out in the gardens yesterday. My health doesn't interest me as much as your trip, though. You don't look overjoyed, Lucian. Have you lost the Tintoretto?"

"Actually, I have."

With a relief that revealed she'd not been so certain of her former companion's whereabouts as she had claimed, Lady Chumleigh exclaimed, "Gwen was there, then! I told . . . but why are you shaking your head Lucian? If she is not in St. Ives, how can I have won the Tintoretto? Tell me everything."

Lucian could not obey his aunt's autocratic demand immediately. Lady Chumleigh had sent for tea the moment Finch came scurrying in to tell her the marquess's coach was racing up the drive. Finch brought it then, and silence reigned while she poured and handed out the cups. When she left the room, Lady Chumleigh found Lucian lounging by the window, but his back was to the view outside and his eyes were upon the depths of his tea cup.

"I swirled up before the Sailor's Rest in St. Ives very late the second day of my journey," Lucian began without prompting. "My coach and four produced quite an effect, and the inn's host rushed out to greet me with the greatest enthusiasm. The poor devil soon regretted his display of hospitality. As he bowed me into the entryway, I asked him if he knew of a Gwen Tarrant. When he answered in the negative, I am afraid I broke his hall table. It was a spindly thing," Lucian observed, giving his aunt an ironic look, "and easily replaced. At least my intemperate response had the effect of sending the landlord flying off for his wife. As he informed me only belatedly, he was not a local man, but his wife, he assured me with a great wringing of hands, knew everyone thereabouts. I adjourned to the taproom and awaited the good woman's arrival with no confidence whatsoever, nor did Mrs. Trask's appearance reassure me. As broad as she is tall, she was smiling most obsequiously, and I presumed she and her husband had fabricated some tale to please the mad Englishman lest he break every stick of furniture in the inn."

Lady Chumleigh gave a low chuckle, and Lucian looked up from his cup to smile, too, a little. "I really felt half mad by then, and tired and frustrated to boot, but Mrs. Trask proved not to be so negligible as she looked."

Lucian idly stirred his cup, remembering the squat woman, the glass of bitter ale he'd had before him, the smells of the taproom and even Mr. Trask hovering nervously behind his wife.

"Miss Gwen, m'lord?" Mrs. Trask had beamed as she slid into the seat across from him. "To be sure everyone from St. Ives knows her. Her family has lived in these parts since, well, from time out o' mind, if y'understand. She's not here now, o'course, nor any of the Prideaux, and all on account o' that wastrel father of hers, and I beg no one's pardon for callin' him such, neither. He was a bad 'un from the start, m'lord. Why a sweet, gentle girl like Emily Trevelyan ever married him, I'll never know, though he had the devil's own looks and was the Baron Llanover, o'course."

Warrick had been absently following the track of a bead of moisture down his tankard. Abruptly, he looked up to fix Mrs.

Trask with a suddenly piercing look. "I beg your pardon, ma'am. Who did you say was Mrs. Tarrant's father?"

"Why, Baron Llanover, m'lord! In the old days 'twas his family, the Prideaux, owned all the land around St. Ives. You'd have seen the castle on the cliff west of the village as you drove in?" Warrick had nodded slowly, almost reluctantly, for he had indeed marked the great medieval-looking pile of stones that hung out over the sea. " 'Tis Prideaux castle, though the baron's no longer master there. He's the gamin' sickness, my lord. Lost it and everythin' else he ever had in games o' chance. No loss stopped him, though. He may have married a local girl, Emily Trevelyan, or Lady Llanover I should call her, but he was a rare sight in St. Ives. The only reason he ever did return was to get money for himself from her da, and to get her with another babe. She'd have done better to bar her door, but that's women for you.

"Her da was a good man, though. Took her in when the baron lost the castle and kept her and the children. He was like a father to Miss Gwen, I guess. Lord help us, what a time it was for the poor lass when he died first and her mother a few days later. Both of 'em gone and Miss Gwen with nothin' to support herself and her brothers and sisters. O'course the baron was nowhere to be found! It's lucky, she's nothin' like her father—or her mother either, when it comes to it. Miss Gwen's the spittin' image o' her father's grandmama, old Lady Llanover, least that's what my da says. The old baroness ruled like a queen, but for all that, she wasn't too high and mighty not to help if there was a wreck outside the bay there, and sailors needed nursin'. Came herself to the shore, my da says. Miss Gwen did the same—her and old Dr. Penrywn.

"But she'd worse to face than shipwrecked sailors, poor mite. Still, like her grandmother, Miss Gwen knew her duty and had the backbone to do it, even if seeing those little mites supported meant she must marry the first man that asked, and John Tarrant was worlds beneath her. Made tears come to my eyes, m'lord, her bein' such a beauty and so proud and havin' to settle for him. But she never once let on that it hurt her to take John. She put up her chin and made him proud. He was a widower, you know, and older, and never dreamed he'd have the likes of her for a wife."

Lucian continued to stir the tea he had not thought to taste as he reported Mrs. Trask's revelations to his aunt. Watching him, Lady Chumleigh humphed suddenly. "What you want is brandy, Lucian. You've not touched that tea. I don't know why I didn't think to order some."

"You are not supposed to have it, perhaps," he suggested, but his mind was clearly elsewhere, and Lady Chumleigh could guess where easily enough.

"I take it from your expression that for all of the history they knew of her, no one in that cursed fishing village knew where Gwen might have gone from here."

"You take it correctly, Aunt Vi. There was mention of a cousin, a relative of her mother's but there was disagreement where the woman lives. She may be in Truro, Falmouth, or Plymouth. Take your pick."

"I see. Gwen might be anywhere to the west of us. But," Lady Chumleigh continued on a lighter note, "at least we know she is not to the east or the north."

"Yes, there is that."

Lady Chumleigh eyed her nephew a moment. She had never seen him so abstracted and or so grim. Hoping action might be the antidote to his mood, she asked briskly, "Well, what do you intend to do now?"

"Actually I stopped in Plymouth to engage a man John Ragsdale recommended. He's not a Bow Street Runner, but he's the same sort and claims he could find a needle in a haystack."

Well. Lucian had already acted. Lady Chumleigh was left, then, with the second of her theories as to the cause of her nephew's bleak mood. She'd no opportunity to test it, however. Lucian lifted his eyes from his cooled tea to regard her directly.

"Why do you think she did not tell us?"

"Pride," Lady Chumleigh said simply, understanding the question and not having to consider her answer at all. "She did not want us to know how deep her father had sunk his noble family. I think the very last thing Gwen would be able to abide with any grace at all would be pity. Fearing it like the plague, she only acted the baron's daughter."

Warrick's mouth quirked. "She did that."

"Hmmm," Lady Chumleigh agreed, pleased to see he had not entirely forgotten how to smile. "No yeoman's daughter ever held herself like Gwen, nor possessed such spirit. Nor, when it comes to it, do the middling classes produce beauties like Gwen. Their daughters might be pretty, but they do not put one in mind of . . . what did Dickon say?"

"Celtic royalty," Warrick reminded her dryly, and then he shook his head. "But I've no right to mock Dickon. He came a deal closer than I."

"And I," Lady Chumleigh allowed ruefully. "I thought her some nobleman's by-blow."

"To the extent her father is a bastard of the first order, I beg your pardon, Aunt Vi, I should say you were not too far off." Warrick's jaw tensed again. "Could I get my hands on the Baron Llanover, I would throttle him."

Lady Chumleigh's brow lifted. "You no longer believe she was his accomplice, then?"

"No, I do not," he said with a harshness directed entirely at himself. For an instant, seeing his hands tighten on it, Lady Chumleigh feared for the bone china cup he held. "Do you know, Aunt Vi, I never allowed her to give me her version of events? I was so certain I knew the truth, but I hadn't been to St. Ives then. Now it seems clear that the baron must have pumped her somehow or other for information and that she surprised him in the act. And he? He did not merely desert her. He all but threw her at me to divert me. And he succeeded! Do you know I never thought to give him chase? For that, alone, I may never forgive myself."

Lady Chumleigh nodded to herself. Her second theory about Lucian's mood had had to do with self-reproach.

"You misjudged," she agreed as she could scarcely argue the point. "But if it is any comfort, Gwen did not fault you. She, herself, told me the scene in my dressing room could have been no more incriminating to her."

"You believed in her, Aunt Vi."

Lady Chumleigh allowed that she had. "But then I did not actually see what you saw."

"No, but I treated her in the worst possible way."

It was an admission that had been ringing over and over in Lucian's head. Dear God, but he had been so harsh. And she . . . he almost could not bear to think about Gwen's life. Now that he knew her father's history, he understood too well what she had meant when she had told his aunt that she had learned not to depend on men.

Could he wring the baron's neck before he throttled himself, Lucian would. The wretch, absent even at the death of his wife, had left his exquisitely fine daughter to wed a dry, middle-aged stick of a farmer. Oh, John Tarrant had likely been a worthy man, and he had provided Gwen a port, however temporary, but when Lucian thought of her wedding night, he had to clench his jaw to keep from lashing out in a rage. Good God! Lucian knew Tarrant's type, and if he hadn't, he'd have guessed what it was from knowing Gwen. Tarrant and his kind thought a woman sinful did she derive any pleasure from lovemaking. Lovemaking! He'd not have called the marriage act anything so pleasant. He'd have called it mating, and believed its sole purpose, other than pleasuring him, of course, was the begetting of children.

To think of his passionate, spirited, sensuous Gwen as such a man's wife . . . Lucian smiled grimly. His Gwen. When had he begun to think of her as his? Before the trip to St. Ives, certainly. Before the night he'd come upon her with her father, even. Perhaps the night he had rescued her from Michaels's pawing had marked the turning point. He had pulled other men off other unwilling women, but he'd never felt such savage anger as he had that night. He had told himself he reacted so strongly because she was a dependent of his aunt's and therefore, of his. But he'd not have had to be held back from tearing Michaels limb from limb had the lieutenant pushed himself upon one of Wensley's maids.

The thought of Michaels assaulting Gwen nearly drove Lucian out of his mind. Any man would want her, and there were men aplenty like Michaels in the world. Spirited as she was, she was still alone and vulnerable—again, due this time to him, another of the men in her life had done her more harm than good.

He must find her. Pacing his study for the next few days, Lucian tried to recall every conversation they had had, hoping that she'd let slip some hint of where she might go. But she'd guarded her secrets well, and he'd displayed precious little interest in anything but getting her into his bed. He would have to rely on Sanders, the man in Plymouth, and pray for a miracle.

Lucian's miracle came in the least likely form imaginable. Three days after he returned from St. Ives, Dabney knocked upon his study door to give him the card of a gentleman who had come to call.

Lucian marked that there was an unusual gleam in Dabney's old eyes before he looked down at the card. "What?" he all but roared when he saw the name neatly printed on the entirely ordinary card.

"I have put him in the yellow saloon," Dabney offered tentatively. "He, ah, well, that is, my lord, what shall I tell him?"

Warrick might have wondered what Dabney had been going to say, but he hadn't even heard the hesitation. "You need tell Baron Llanover nothing, Dabney," he said through clenched teeth. "I shall see to him."

Rather more slowly than Warrick proceeded to the yellow saloon, Dabney made his way to his post near the front of the house. Three maids, two footmen, and even a groom had all found reason to busy themselves in the area. Dabney gave them a censorious look that sent them scuttling at least out of his sight, but in his heart, he did not really fault any of them. There had been a storm of gossip about Mrs. Tarrant after his lordship had had her things moved to the valet's closet by his room, and her abrupt departure followed by the marquess's dashing journey into Cornwall had served only to intensify the speculation to a feverish pitch. Now a Baron Llanover, bearing an amazing resemblance to Mrs. Tarrant, appeared. It was only natural that the servants would be in a frenzy to know if there were a connection between the two. Could she be a baron's daughter? Dabney thought it eminently possible. He had long marked that Mrs. Tarrant had the manner of a lady, despite the farmer's name she bore.

The real question in his mind had to do with whether or not the baron's appearance would improve Lord Warrick's mood. Dabney exhaled a sigh. He certainly hoped so. His lordship had been most difficult for nearly a fortnight.

Dabney would not have been much heartened had he been

privy to Lucian's expression as he let himself into the formal room where Llanover awaited him. He'd the look of a hunter who has sighted his prey.

The baron, who made what living he did by reading men's expressions across a card table, went a little cold when he looked into the Marquess of Warrick's face. Nonetheless, he summoned a blustery smile as he leaped to his feet.

"Lord Warrick! I imagine I am the last man you expected to see."

He got no response at all, only a steely look from a pair of narrowed, singularly green eyes. Understandably the baron's cravat began to feel a little tight. He restrained an impulse to pull at it, though. The marquess looked like a man who might pounce if he discerned weakness.

"I know we met under most unusual circumstances, my lord, and that my, ah, behavior must have seemed most unusual—"

"We did not meet at all that night, Llanover, and your behavior was first criminal and then craven."

The baron swallowed with difficulty. Warrick was going to be as difficult as he had anticipated. "Ah, well, actually I only came to have a look at—"

Warrick pushed off from the door and took a menacing step toward the baron, silencing him. "Spare me your fiction, baron. It is tedious. You came to steal the rubies."

"There are some men in Dartmouth to whom I owed money. They are not gentlemen at all and would not accept my notes. It was they suggested I make good—"

"And now spare me your excuses, Baron," Lucian interrupted as ruthlessly as he had a moment before. "They are as pitiful as you are. I know all about you now, Llanover. I've been to St. Ives. I've seen the castle you lost. I know how you honored and cherished your wife. I know how well you protected your children." Lucian reached out and grabbed the hapless baron by the lapels of his coat. "What I want to know, and succinctly, is why the devil you've returned to be charged with attempted robbery."

"Oh." It was a pitiful little squeak, but the baron could produce nothing hardier with Warrick holding him, promising to murder him with his eyes, and threatening charges of attempted robbery. "Well, I, ah, I cannot breathe, my lord!"

Realizing the punishing grip he had on the man, Lucian relaxed his hold, but he did not let him go entirely and he shook him for good measure, shouting, "I say, why the devil are you here?"

"For Gwen!"

"For Gwen!" Warrick flung the baron away so violently, Llanover reeled off balance, bumped into a couch, and sat down hard. Instantly Warrick was over him, one hand on either side of his head and his teeth bared in a snarl. "You've never done anything for anyone in your life. Why are you here?"

"I, I really am here on her account, my lord. I'd not have come on any other. There has been talk in the neighborhood, not about the rubies, of course, but that you took her to your bed first and then threw her out. I . . . could not let her suffer on my account."

"You abandoned her that night without a second thought!"

Llanover flinched, but he managed to hold his gaze steady on Warrick's. "I will never forgive myself for that."

Warrick wrenched away, furious with himself for being in any way affected by the wretch. "You desert her to face me alone and expect me to believe you have some concern for her? Do you think I am that great a fool?"

"I know you not to be any sort of fool, my lord," Llanover said, taking out his handkerchief and mopping his face. He had thought Warrick meant to beat him. "And I know, too, that I'll not go to my grave famous for heroism. The opposite, I suppose, but she . . . she is the best thing I have in the world. I realized I could not simply stand by and let her come to harm for something I did."

"It has been over two weeks, man!"

"Quite, my lord." The baron's eyes fell and his shoulders sagged so that he looked little like the man who had greeted Warrick with such bluster. "You have not had her transported, have you?"

Warrick regarded him a long moment, but with little pity. "No, small thanks to you, I have not had her transported. She left of her own accord. But I want her back."

Knowing what he did of Llanover, Warrick was not astonished to watch the man's bearing alter in the twinkling of an opportunist's eye. Up went the shoulders and the head, and the blue eyes, too like Gwen's for comfort, lit. "I, ah, cannot blame you for that, my lord."

"No, I am sure you cannot. But I should remind you that as her father, you ought to be inquiring in what capacity I mean to have her back."

"I do not believe I am obliged to ask, my lord," the baron replied slowly. Amazingly he even began to smile, albeit tentatively. "She'd not stay with you unless you made her your wife."

"How astute you are, Baron. I wonder why you have not done better at the gaming tables. But that is a subject for another time, should there be one. The subject that must occupy us now is Gwen's whereabouts. Where is she?"

Only once in his life had Llanover been dealt a royal flush. He felt the same almost sensuous thrill now, knowing Warrick wanted something of him. "As to my being charged . . . "

"I'll not have you charged like a common criminal, Llanover. You are Gwen's father. But I will beat you to a pulp. With pleasure. Now, where is she?"

The baron could do nothing if not bend with the prevailing winds. Later he would find some way to profit from the remarkable turn of events he had, he could not but mark it, predicted. Now he would please his future, and so very immensely, marvelously wealthy son-in-law. "She would likely be in Plymouth with her mother's cousin, Miss Esther Trevelyan. I am not well acquainted with the woman, and do not know her address. . . . "

"Her name is enough. Now, Baron, what am I to do with you?"

"Ah, must you do anything with me?"

"I cannot leave you here. I can't be certain what you would do."

The baron's first impulse was to stiffen with outrage, but he curbed it wisely. And then, ever pliable, he found himself smiling. "But you may trust me entirely, my lord. I am too clever to offend Gwen's future family."

Warrick almost smiled himself. The man was the most redoubtable rogue he'd ever encountered. "No, I don't suppose you would. What of the men in Dartmouth?"

"Most fortuitously, a, ah, business transaction came to belated fruition, allowing me to repay them all I owed."

Warrick did not know precisely what Llanover meant, but the only business in Dartmouth was smuggling. He gave the baron a hard look. "If you enter into any more such transactions, Llanover, I shall have you sent to the hottest, dustiest state in Australia, and do not be foolish enough to doubt me. You may be Gwen's father, but you have done her precious little good as far as I can see. Now, come along. I shall take you to my aunt. She will keep you in line until I return from Plymouth."

Chapter 24

Warrick left for Plymouth that afternoon though it was already four o'clock. The next morning he contacted Mr. Sanders, and by one o'clock he was riding to Miss Esther Trevelyan's house. It was a small thing, cheek by jowl with dozens of others much like it, in a part of Plymouth that might most kindly be described as neat and clean. Warrick was not at all surprised. He had learned from the baron that Miss Trevelyan was a spinster who eked out a spare living on a pension she had inherited from a great uncle.

The street was busy. Vendors walked along, calling out a description of their wares; housewives came out to inspect the items for themselves; children ran about playing tag or hide-and-seek; and there were the usual assorted men hurrying about on indeterminate errands. Mounted on Ares, Warrick picked his way carefully through the crowd and pulled up at number twenty-one, keenly aware of his heart pumping in his chest.

A tall, thin boy broke away from a group of older children nearby and pelted up to him. " 'Tis a prime piece of horseflesh, sir! I'd be honored to walk him for you."

The boy had brown hair, not black, freckles, and a thinnish mouth unlike Gwen's. But he'd high, refined cheekbones, and his eyes were celestial blue.

He also regarded Warrick openly, unlike a typical street urchin who knew to pull his forelock and duck his head meekly.

"You wouldn't be Arthur, would you?"

Warrick had expected the lad to gape, but the opposite occurred. His expression became guarded, and he parried with a question. "Who are you?"

"I am Lucian Montfort, a, ah, friend of your sister's."

"She hasn't mentioned you."

The boy's chin went up in a gesture that squeezed at Warrick's heart. Arthur might not be Gwen's image, but there was no question he was her brother—and feeling very much the man of the family, it seemed. Which, Warrick realized, he was in his father's absence.

"It is a rather involved story, Arthur, but I think it fair to say that your sister and I had a very great misunderstanding. She has some responsibility for it, but I have the most, and I offended her deeply. Now I have come to make amends as best I can, even to tell her that I love her. However, I think I must admit that I am not certain Gwen will welcome my arrival. She's not easy for me to predict."

Surprisingly young Arthur seemed not only to understand but even to sympathize, for he nodded. "Aye, Gwen's always had a mind of her own and been stubborn as a mule to boot."

For the first time since he'd discovered Gwen and her father with the rubies, Warrick heard himself chuckle. "Well, at least I know we are speaking of the same woman. Is she at home?"

"No. She's at the hat shop where she's to work now. She took Meg and Annie with her, but they'll be home soon. It's half day today."

It was Wednesday, the day most shops closed at half past one. "Is there someplace I may stable my horse?"

There was a mews back of the house. Arthur showed Warrick where it was, then took him inside to the kitchen, where Miss Trevelyan was just taking some gingerbread out of the oven. A small, cheerful woman with bright eyes, Miss Trevelyan had Warrick sit down at her kitchen table and taste her gingerbread. He was pleased to comply, for he realized he had had little breakfast and no luncheon at all. Tristan came bursting through the back door, eager to report there was a strange, black horse in the stable. Arthur, with a loftiness natural to an older brother, informed Tristan not only did he know the horse was there, but he, himself, had helped put it there, and the gentleman who owned it was at the table, if Tristan would only look.

Tristan did, round-eyed. His face was the same shape as Gwen's and he'd black hair, but he had great, melting brown eyes. Very soon, a good many girls would lose their hearts to those eyes. Just then, Warrick did. "The gingerbread is excellent," he said to Tristan when the little boy turned bashful. It was the right thing to say. Tristan had an avid interest in gingerbread.

He slid into the seat by Warrick, took a bite of gingerbread, and with it safely in his mouth said, "May I ride him?"

"You are speaking with your mouth full, Tris!" Arthur scolded as was an older brother's prerogative. "It isn't good manners. And it isn't good manners to ask to ride another person's horse, either."

"Your brother is quite right," Warrick affirmed, helping himself to another piece of the gingerbread. "You must wait to be invited to ride another person's horse. But you needn't wait long. Would you, and you, Arthur, care to go for a ride tomorrow?"

"Cor!" was Tristan's response, for he was just learning cant from a boy down the street.

Arthur was more formal. "Very much, sir."

Miss Trevelyan, bringing jam and tea to go with the gingerbread, asked Warrick where he lived. He admitted then that he was Lady Chumleigh's nephew. Though she still did not know she'd a marquess in her kitchen, Miss Trevelyan turned pink at the thought that she'd put Lady Chumleigh's nephew at her kitchen table, but Warrick soon put her at ease, insisting he was delighted to be there and would not be moved farther from the source of such delicious gingerbread.

And that was how Gwen found him, eating gingerbread with her brothers, a dab of jam on his cheek. She had not come through the mews and so had no warning whom she'd see when, her sisters chattering like magpies, her arms laden with parcels her cousin Esther had wanted, she stepped through the kitchen doorway and glanced to the group about the table.

Her jaw dropped.

It was the most inelegant and unsatisfying of responses, but she wasn't in a position to control herself. He had haunted her thoughts since she had left Wensley. She knew she had done the right thing by going, and yet the loss of him had been an ache that never receded. Even Tristan had remarked how subdued she was, and Esther had given her several searching looks. Now, when she had been so certain he could never trace her to Esther, there he sat, a bit of jam on his face, Tristan all but in his lap, and looking so unbearably handsome she almost couldn't look at him.

She heard a ringing in her ears, then realized it was only the sound of Warrick pushing his chair back from the table. "I think it would be best if I spoke with Mrs. Tarrant alone," he said to Miss Trevelyan.

"Of course, of course, Mr. Montfort. Gwen will show you the parlor. Gwen?"

Mr. Montfort? Warrick was smiling at Esther, who was, of course, beaming back at him. Gwen turned toward the hall and thought she heard, unbelievably, Arthur call out, "Good luck, sir," before she heard Warrick following her.

Opening the door to the parlor, Gwen led the way inside, then closing the door behind them, leaned back against it. Her pose was the one Warrick normally took, but she needed something to hold her upright.

He turned in the middle of the room, her place, to regard her steadily. His eyes were not gold green, but neither were they dark jade.

"You did not tell me you were a baron's daughter."

How had he learned that? Why was he there? How had he learned of Esther? Was he angry? He didn't sound angry.

She shrugged, the merest lifting of her slender shoulders. "The night you encountered my father did not seem quite the time for introductions."

"Damn! This is no time for joking."

Perhaps he was angry. She couldn't tell. She could only think how handsome he was; how she'd forgotten the precise shade of his dark blond hair, the way the lines of his mouth curved up at the corners, that he could dominate a room like her cousin's parlor with his size and sheer virility. She was glad to see him, so glad her heart was pumping too loudly.

Gwen tried to disregard her deafening heartbeats and collect her thoughts. If he was not angry, he was serious. He looked as if he were trying to see into her mind, in fact. "My father is not someone of whom I am proud. Even before he attempted to steal Lady Chumleigh's rubies, he was hiding from his creditors."

Lucian began to pace the little room. He felt nervous as a cat. Why did she just stand there by the door, as if she were prepared to fly out of the room at any minute? Did she hate him? Immediately every reason she should hate him occurred to him. He redoubled his pace and reminded himself he had not forced her to anything. She had lifted her lips to his. Nor could she have counterfeited her passion that night. He was too experienced to be fooled on that point. She had been willing. Nay she'd been more than willing; she'd been wildly eager, as eager as he.

What did that mean, though? Perhaps she had not been so innocent as he thought. Perhaps she had only refused to be his mistress because she believed her position as his aunt's companion to be more secure.

Perhaps she had no feeling for him at all. Perhaps she would prefer to work in a hat shop than to be his marchioness—eventually his duchess.

Warrick continued to pace. She was not mad. Proud, yes, but not mad. Yet, he didn't want her to come to him only to save herself from work. He wanted her to come to him freely, because she wanted to come, as she had come that night.

He was mad. He had never expected his wife would want him for himself. For the love of God, he was Warrick and would be Grafton. No woman could be immune to all that came with him.

"My lord."

He whirled at the sound of her voice. "Yes?" he said far more harshly than he had ever intended.

"You will wear a hole in my cousin's carpet if you continue to pace like that. Why have you come? How did you find me?"

He considering blurting that he had never felt so uncertain of himself in his life—that he wanted her more than life. God knew, but she looked unbearably beautiful, though all her silky hair was confined in that prim knot. But she didn't need her hair or any ornament to make her beautiful. A blind man, feeling the fine bones of her face would have said she was beautiful. Would he have known how desirable she was? Perhaps, if he touched her mouth.

Poor blind man, though. He'd never see the luminous blue of her eyes, nor hold her wide, clear, direct gaze. She could hold her own, his Gwen.

"My lord?"

Lucian blinked. And felt himself flush. Dear God, he had been staring like a boy.

"How did I find you? Your father came to Wensley." Gwen stared, unable to credit what he said, and Warrick's expression softened. "He's a rogue and a scoundrel, but he does care for you in his way. He had heard rumors of your sudden departure from the Hall and came because he thought I'd had you transported."

Her father had put himself out, nay in the way of harm, for her? Gwen could not believe it, but then she could feel tears pricking at the back of her eyes.

They were not merely pricking. Warrick saw them, and suddenly he was across the room, pulling her into his arms. "Please don't cry, Gwen. I could not bear the sound of you crying before when I thought I hated you. Now, I think I . . . dear God, don't cry."

He'd made her cry in earnest. But Gwen was not sobbing from sadness as she had before. Her father had not, quite, abandoned her. And Warrick was there, holding her. He felt so warm and vital and alive and smelled so good, she wanted to keep her head buried in his chest forever.

"My brave, brave girl. Don't cry. Please, don't cry." He pulled back to look down at her, and saw that though there were tears in her eyes, she was smiling unsteadily. "Thank God, you are not crying as you did that night." Carefully, he dried her cheek with the back of his hand. He was achingly aware of her arms around his waist and was afraid the slightest odd move might cause her to release him. He smiled back at her. "Even could I bear to listen to you cry like that again, I fear Miss Trevelyan would not approve the aftermath taking place in her parlor."

Gwen went red and buried her face in his chest again.

He laughed, as he had not laughed in what seemed to have been an eternity, and he held her tightly to him.

She wanted to die then, with him holding her, hearing his laugh rumble in his chest. Why had he come? It would be so much harder now to make him go.

The thought made her look up at him. She had to tip her head uncomfortably because she couldn't quite let go of him.

"Lucian, I cannot be your mistress."

"Lucian!" His eyes lit, and he squeezed her tightly to him as he brushed his cheek across the smooth, silky top of her head. "Do you have any idea how much I have wanted to hear you say my name, Gwen? It's frightening almost. My God, I have been so worried about you. I thought of all the men who might hurt you . . . I went all the way to St. Ives after you, Gwen!"

"St. Ives?" She looked astonished. "You went to St. Ives?"

"I didn't know where else to look for you. You didn't leave a forwarding address." There was a touch of anger, or perhaps it was the worry he'd felt, in his voice. "I chased the length of Cornwall and found only Mrs. Trask at the end of my journey."

"Mrs. Trask? Of course! You went to the Sailor's Rest. My grandfather was very fond of her ale."

"He liked his ale stout, then." Lucian grinned. "And his landladies."

Gwen giggled. "She is a broad thing, but she's also a dear. She brought more than one meal to me when my grandfather and mother were sick."

"She admires you as well. She not only told me you are Baron Llanover's daughter, but that you remind the folk in St. Ives of your proud great-grandmother."

Gwen smiled a little wistfully. "I just remember old Lady Llanover as she was always called. She died when I was six or so, having hung on to raise my father. His parents, you see, were killed in a boating accident when he was quite young. Perhaps he turned out so poorly because he hadn't a father to raise him. His grandmama would have been strict, but I doubt she'd had the energy to keep the sharp eye on him that he'd needed." Rubbing her forehead on Warrick's starched shirt, Gwen heaved a sigh. "I am prosing on. All this history is of little relevance, really. Have you charged him with his crime?"

She waited, head bowed to hear that Lucian meant to pillory her father. The baron deserved it, but he was her father.

"No. I have some sense of the difficulty old Lady Llanover must have experienced raising him. Your father is a canny rogue. And he is your father. I left him playing cards with Aunt Vi."

For a moment utter disbelief dominated Gwen's expression,

and then she laughed. "I shan't worry over Lady Chumleigh. She cheats, too."

Lucian grinned, his eyes lighting with that gleam she'd never thought to see again. "I think they make a good pair, actually. Just as we do."

The glow went out of her face. "Lucian, I meant it. I cannot be your mistress. I simply cannot."

"I haven't asked you to be my mistress, Gwen, at least not today." He was suddenly looking as grave as she. "I am asking you to be my wife."

He was holding her close enough; their hearts seemed to beat together. She stared up at him, lost in his green-gold eyes, and lost for any coherent reply. "Oh, Lucian," she whispered, her heart seeming to swell to fill her chest.

"Oh, Lucian, yes," he prompted, whispering, but not allowing her time to reply, for her lips were so close and inviting. A little later he lifted his mouth from hers. "Say it," he commanded, his eyes almost as dark a jade as when he was angry. "Say you will marry me."

"Lucian, I am so ineligible." She loved him. She'd not have him regret marrying her.

He held her face between his hands. "You are a baron's daughter. You're rank is higher than half a dozen girls my mother has thrown at me. Think of Jane Godolphin. Her father's only a baronet. And if you believe you are ineligible because you would bring me no property, allow me to assure you I am wealthy enough for us both. Years ago I inherited from my mother's father; in the future, I shall inherit from my father, who is one of the wealthiest men in England; and I am Aunt Vi's heir as well. Can you think of anyone she would rather greet as her niece by marriage than you? No, of course not. Now, my darling, can you forgive me for all the horrid things I thought of you, said to you, did to you? Thinking of facing you, I've been nervous as a boy."

He had been uncertain. The thought made Gwen smile. Lucian without assurance was like a cat without balance.

"Marry me, Gwen?"

"Oh, yes, Lucian. Oh, yes."

And going up on her tiptoes, she licked the jam off his cheek.